ASSASSIN

In Afghanistan, elite operative John Stratton leads a raid on a remote compound, leaving no survivors. Days later, in London, Stratton is contacted by an old friend in military intelligence with a curious message about being hunted by an assassin. When the officer vanishes, Stratton is drawn into a desperate race to secure a missing nuclear warhead that has been stolen from the Pakistan military. Against an unknown enemy, he begins a heart-stopping search for the bomb that will take him from a Taliban hideout, just a few miles outside Bagram Air Base, to the crowded streets of Manhattan.

Books by Duncan Falconer
Published by The House of Ulverscroft:

THE OPERATIVE
THE PROTECTOR
UNDERSEA PRISON
MERCENARY

DUNCAN FALCONER

◆

ASSASSIN

Complete and Unabridged

CHARNWOOD
Leicester

First published in Great Britain in 2012 by
Sphere
An imprint of
Little, Brown Book Group
London

First Charnwood Edition
published 2013
by arrangement with
Little, Brown Book Group
An Hachette UK Company
London

A catalogue record for this book is available
from the British Library.

ISBN 978–1–4448–1514–6

Published by
F. A. Thorpe (Publishing)
Anstey, Leicestershire

Set by Words & Graphics Ltd.
Anstey, Leicestershire
Printed and bound in Great Britain by
T. J. International Ltd., Padstow, Cornwall

This book is printed on acid-free paper

To my dearest Francesca

1

Stratton lay on a sleeping bag on a bunk bed in full desert combat fatigues. A windproof jacket covered him like a blanket, with only his boots sticking out at the bottom.

It was dark. Cold. His breath was turning to vapour as he exhaled easily before the dry and flaking mud walls of the hut.

His face was coated in broad dark-green, brown and black stripes. He held his grubby hands intertwined across his abdomen, inside soiled, thin black leather gloves from which he had removed the fingertips. His bright-green eyes stared at the stars through the gaps in the mud and straw roof.

A camouflaged Colt assault rifle was leaning against the wall by Stratton's head. It had a sophisticated scope attached to the top. A full magazine loaded into it and bits of dark, frayed cloth tied on in places to break up its shape. Beside it lay a bulky, nylon harness system with pouches full of munitions and combat equipment.

A low, hissing noise filled the small room, slightly louder than the sound of the chilly air whistling through the cracks in the walls. It was the carrier wave from a military radio sitting upright on the floor within arm's reach. A distant voice occasionally broke through, speaking English. Soldiers somewhere, passing information. Questions and replies. Nothing frantic. All was calm and controlled in his world at that point.

Stratton was taking a moment to relax before heading out into the night. The task was scheduled to last into the morning, depending on how successful it was. Rest when you can. The SF soldier's mantra.

He closed his eyes and tried to switch off. He hadn't heard from London in almost ten months. Military intelligence could usually be depended on for rescuing him from the mundane, repetitive tasks on offer in special forces. He hoped something would come along soon that had some real meat to it, and not in Afghanistan like his present operation.

He exhaled slowly and focused on letting his limbs grow heavy, reducing his heart rate and blood pressure. He was usually good at relaxing in hostile environments. Soon his breathing grew deeper and his mind emptied. And then, as if in a dream, he heard his name. Someone calling him faintly. Summoning him from a faraway place.

He crawled back to consciousness as he realised it was coming from the radio.

'Stratton, this is Ops,' a voice repeated.

He reached for the device and brought it to his mouth. 'Stratton.'

'Can you come to Ops?' the voice said.

'On my way.'

He sat up and stretched his back. Typical, he thought. Just as he was nodding off. They call.

He got to his feet. Lifted his heavy webbing onto a shoulder, picked up the assault rifle and went to the hut entrance. The door had long lost its hinges and leaned against the opening. He moved it to one side and walked outside.

The mud hut was one of a dozen in a dark, abandoned village. Situated on the side of a steep hill, it was surrounded by a thick, high wall that the rain and wind had attacked over the years until it was crumbling away in places. The village had been evacuated during the Russian invasion some twenty-five years earlier. It hadn't been repopulated, for whatever reason, after the Soviets had been ousted, and Stratton's squadron had made it their temporary HQ, once it had been declared free of booby-traps or mines by the advance reconnaissance team. Thirty SBS operatives, along with an HQ element, had moved in a couple of days ago. They would be gone soon.

Stratton walked between the ugly mud structures that housed the other teams. There were no lights anywhere. Everything was shades of grey to black. The enemy was miles away, but it was possible they might conduct a night patrol in the area. Although the village was on a route to nowhere in particular, military target-wise, as far as the Taliban were concerned. But there was no point in taking the risk. The lads could manage without lights anyway. They could warm their food in the huts. The smell would dissipate in the mountain winds long before any enemy would notice it.

Stratton stepped through a gap in the perimeter wall and headed towards the operations HQ tent, wondering why he'd been summoned. Perhaps there'd been a change in plan.

3

As he neared the camouflaged tent, which was specially designed to prevent any light escaping from within it, he could hear the barely perceptible hum from an otherwise silent generator tucked among the rocks metres away.

He saw three men standing outside the tent's airlock entrance. One was Captain Burns, the squadron commander and leader of the operation. Stratton had never seen the other two before. They were dressed in American-style combat fatigues. On the ground beside them sat a couple of small packs, with an assault rifle leaning against each. The strangers hadn't been at the site earlier in the day and had evidently just arrived. Even though it was so remote, no helicopters were permitted at the forward location and only a couple of vehicles had been allowed up to bring the heavier equipment and they would remain in situ until the camp was dismantled the following day. That meant the two men had yomped in on the rocky track. It was seven miles to the last permitted point for operational vehicles, at least in the past twenty-four hours. And they'd done it in darkness. They must be keen, he thought.

'That you, Stratton?' Burns called out.

'Yes, sir,' he replied as he closed in on the group.

'Sorry to disturb your slumber,' Burns said in his usual verging-on-sarcastic manner.

Stratton was used to it. He'd known Burns for several years and liked and respected him. He eyed the two other men, who were looking at him. Or more like examining him.

'I want to introduce you to a couple of visitors who'll be joining us on the operation,' Burns said. 'Jeff Wheeland and Mike Spinter.'

'How's it going?' Wheeland said, holding out a hand, a smile on his wide face.

Stratton kept his glove on as he took Wheeland's hand. The man had a strong grip that matched his square jaw. He was American, no doubt about it. Stratton thought he sounded Midwestern. Both men were dressed like soldiers but Burns hadn't given them ranks. That would have been unusual for military personnel. Which suggested they weren't. And if they weren't military and they were attending a special ops task, and they were American, then he figured they had to be Central Intelligence-type animals or spooks of some kind. Any one of a myriad of agencies under the US Homeland Security umbrella.

'Pleasure,' Spinter said. He sounded West Coast American and looked far more serious than his partner. Neither was he as solidly built, though he looked athletic. Stratton put both men in their early thirties. There was a similar intensity in the way they were looking at him.

'It wasn't mentioned in the briefing,' Burns said. 'But these guys are sponsoring this operation. You'll personally be babysitting these gentlemen, Stratton. Their focus will be the ops section of the main building. I've got a few things to do before we head out so why don't you get acquainted? We've got a little over an hour before we form up. I'll see you then.'

'Thanks for everything, Captain Burns,' Wheeland said.

5

'No problem,' Burns said, and went inside the tent, leaving them to stand out in the cold.

Stratton didn't have much small talk at the best of times, but he felt he ought to say something. 'If you'd like a cup of tea or coffee I could knock up some inside my hut,' he said. 'We're all on self-catering up here. No mess tent, I'm afraid.'

'We're good, thanks,' Wheeland said. 'We just had a cup of coffee in the HQ tent with your squadron commander.'

· Stratton got the feeling that Wheeland was the boss of the two.

'Winter seems to be early this year,' the American said as he took a cigar wallet from a pocket.

'You spend a lot of time in Afghanistan?' Stratton asked.

'On and off over the years,' Wheeland replied, offering a cigar to Stratton, who declined. The American took one out for himself. 'You a health nut too?' he said. 'Spinter here is purer than mountain water.'

'Not exactly. I've not matured enough for cigars,' Stratton said.

Wheeler took a lighter from his pocket and opened his coat to light the cigar. Spinter opened his own coat and added to the protection against the wind. It was an immediate and well-practised act.

'Been looking forward to meeting you, Stratton,' Wheeland said as he puffed on the cheroot to get it going. 'I've heard a little about you. Quite the tough guy.'

'Must be another Stratton.'

'So you're not the Stratton who broke into Styx. The underwater prison. And broke out of it as well. That was quite a feat.'

Stratton wasn't the boastful type. And since Wheeland apparently knew all about it there was nothing for him to say anyway.

'Your parent unit's the Special Boat Service but you do a lot of work for the Brit SIS,' Wheeland said. 'You could say you're my opposite number. I started life in the Navy SEALs. Then one day I got the call and went over to the dark side.'

Stratton wondered if Spinter was going to say anything.

'I said to Burns, 'I wanna be in the frontline of the assault,'' Wheeland said. ''Then you wanna be with Stratton,' Burns said. 'Would that be John Stratton?' I asked. 'That's the one,' he said.'

Stratton wanted to impress upon Wheeland how important it was not to get in the way of his team when they moved on the target. But he decided against it. The American would probably resent it. Stratton would leave it until they got on the ground. Maybe Wheeland wouldn't interfere anyway. Maybe he was all talk and would stay back when the action kicked in. Stratton couldn't quite make him out.

He decided he'd served protocol enough by talking as long as he had to them. 'I'm going to sort out my kit for the task,' he said, lying. His kit had long since been organised and ready to go. 'I'll meet you back here in an hour. You can keep warm in the HQ tent. It's the only place around here with heating.'

7

Stratton walked off. He thought he could hear a chuckle as he climbed through the gap in the mud wall perimeter. Typical spook arrogance, he thought. He had to wonder what they were doing here and why they wanted to join the operation. It wasn't entirely unusual. He had carried out entries for intelligence operatives in the past, both Brit and US, usually some boffin, some whiz-kid who needed hand-holding through the most hazardous phase of the mission, or delivering to their objective and sometimes bringing back on completion. But this particular job had been briefed simply as a hit on a Taliban commander and his men who'd been causing a lot of grief in the region, planting roadside bombs, building suicide vehicles and terrorising any local towns and villages whose people showed signs of tolerating coalition forces. That had been the essence of the brief at least. It was not a strange target by far and Stratton and the boys had done several like it on their current tour. Why this bunch of Taliban was of greater priority than any other was not obvious. Not that any of them gave much of a damn. One target was as good as another.

From experience, Stratton knew the only reason spooks would get personally involved in the actual fight was if they needed immediate access to someone or something on target and didn't want it delayed or contaminated by post-operational procedures. Or if perhaps there was something they didn't want to be seen by other personnel or agencies.

All he cared about was that there be no

surprises to put his men at risk.

He made his way back to his hut and lay down on his bunk. An hour later, after an unsuccessful attempt to sleep, he walked back through the village with his rifle, webbing and backpack, leaving nothing behind. The teams wouldn't be returning to the village on completion of the assault. They were to be picked up by helicopter on target, after it had been secured, and taken back to Camp Bastion. The HQ tent and everything else would be dismantled and the place evacuated as soon as they moved out.

Other squadron members were vacating their huts at the same time and making their way towards the ops HQ. There was little banter. The men had been active since the early hours of that morning and, other than any sleep they might have managed to grab in the previous few hours, they would be looking forward to thirty hours straight by the time they got back to base. They were all used to long hours and short naps. They'd spark up once they were walking with their heavy packs and weapons towards the objective.

Stratton saw Captain Burns in a clearing beyond the HQ tent, tooled up and camouflaged and ready to go. He put his pack down on the spot where he wanted to form up his own team and within a few minutes his men were with him.

'You get some rest?' he asked Jones, his second in command, a Welsh lad he had known for several years. Jones was a sound operator who he liked working with.

'A bit,' Jones said, in a lilting Snowdonian accent. He dumped his pack down on the floor. 'Not quite enough, mind you. But barely enough, if you know what I mean.'

To those who didn't know Jones he might sound as if he were a habitual complainer. But that was not the case by far. Like every other badged member of the Service, Jones could put up with an ungodly amount of discomfort. He merely liked to point out the detailed facts as and when he saw them. That included the negative as well as the positive. And he often repeated himself — not necessarily because he thought he'd not been heard. He liked to ensure those he was talking to were fully informed and had not missed anything. What's more, he couldn't care less what anyone else thought about his ways.

The rest of Stratton's lads arrived, four operators in their early twenties and keen as you like.

'We've got a couple of cling-ons,' Stratton said to Jones.

'Is that right? Who would that be, then?'

'Yank spooks.'

'Spooks?' Jones said, looking around for them.

'They never said as much but they bear all the hallmarks.'

'Interesting. What are they doing here then?'

'They want first look at the intellectual spoils.'

'Intellectual spoils. Of course. Have you told 'em they're required to walk ten metres in front of us and look for mines?'

'I don't think they're the type,' Stratton said. 'Here they are.'

Wheeland and Spinter made their way through

10

the growing muster point towards Stratton and his team. Both men carried small, light packs on their backs, which clearly indicated they were not equipped for any extended time in the field beyond the operation's expected termination time early that morning. Stratton wondered what they would do if for some reason the op was postponed and the teams had to wait it out in the hills for a day or so longer. Or if a weather front were to close in unexpectedly, which was not an unusual event in that part of the world. A storm. A torrential downpour. A sudden blizzard even. It was getting cold enough. Anything like that could prevent a helicopter extraction. They would be forced to share the lads' kit. They were either supremely confident no such event would occur or they were seriously inexperienced field operators. But then Wheeland claimed to have been Stratton's opposite number. Clearly it was confidence that drove them.

'Hey, guys,' Wheeland said as he arrived, looking about the whole team. 'How ya'll doin'?'

The younger members of Stratton's squad, who generally preferred to remain low profile and tight-lipped among superiors, simply nodded a hello and otherwise ignored him.

Jones was far less shy, having been more exposed to the social side of the business. And he was never intimidated by the variety of mysterious personalities that populated the world he operated in. 'We're fine, lads,' he said. 'Thanks for asking. Welcome aboard.'

'You guys enjoying everything so far?' Wheeland asked.

'We are indeed,' Jones said. 'I see you're travelling light. I hope that blizzard warning for later this morning doesn't happen. Otherwise you'll be sharing sleeping bags with one of us.' Then *sotto vocce*, 'I'd avoid Tim here if that's the case. He has a terrible case of bottom-bugle, if you get my meaning.'

Wheeland forced a grin.

Stratton noticed a general increase in activity in the centre of the rendezvous point, around Captain Burns. Men were pulling on their heavy backpacks and preparing to move out. He checked his watch. It was time to go.

'Mount up!' the squadron sergeant major called out.

Jones pulled on his heavy pack. 'You happy for Charlie to do point for this stretch?' he asked Stratton.

'All the way?'

'Why not? He's keen as mustard. And you love it out in front, don't you, Charlie? First in the contact and first to find those mines.'

Charlie, a squat, fresh-faced redhead, smiled as he pulled his pack onto his shoulders, then picked up his rifle, cradling it in his arms.

'OK,' Stratton said. 'You happy with the route?'

'Basic,' Charlie said as he checked the compass that was attached by a line to his jacket breast pocket. 'I thought I'd take an angle downhill. That way.' He pointed. 'Reduce the steepness a bit. Then at the bottom head along the river.'

'We like a point who cares about those who follow,' Stratton said. He looked over at Wheeland and Spinter. 'We're going to take the

12

lead,' he said to them. 'If you don't mind being in front of Jones. Team Bravo will be behind us. The other two teams will fall in behind them. No gaps.'

'Whatever you say, big guy,' Wheeland said.

Charlie made his way to the departure point at the edge of the village, three quarters up the side of the mountain. He looked out over the dark expanse that was all his to lead through and took a moment to check the GPS as well as his compass and tightly folded map inside its waterproof sheath. Technology was great but one always had to back it up with the fundamentals. Leading the squadron on an op was a hefty responsibility and he couldn't afford for anything to go wrong. He was young and this task was very much a part of building his reputation.

'Space it out, Charlie,' Stratton said.

Charlie acknowledged the command by setting off down the hill. He paused after thirty or so metres to wait for the rest of the squadron to form up behind him. They were going to move in single file, the safest and easiest way to move through the terrain, especially at night.

Stratton stepped in directly behind Charlie. He liked to hand down responsibility, but he preferred not to stray far from the sharp end either.

Jones took up the rear of Stratton's team. Wheeland and Spinter did as they were asked and lined up in front of him.

'Move when ready,' Stratton said to Charlie, who set off at an easy walk down the rocky incline.

2

In the dark the grey landscape resembled the moon. The jagged mountain the SBS squadron was traversing was part of a range that curved away and around their front. It was like walking on the edge of a massive asteroid crater. Stars were packed into the sky. The men snaked down the slope towards a vast, colourless plain and the parched riverbed that ran through it like an ugly scar. They walked among rocks of every dimension covering the mountainside, from pebbles to boulders the size of cars. Here and there tufts of brittle grass clung to dark crevices, blowing in the light wind.

Charlie took a meandering path, his aim, other than to get the squadron to its destination, to find a route that reduced the noise of the thirty men — as well as the chances of any of the more heavily loaded of them losing their footing. Among the teams they had four medium-sized machine guns and four thousand rounds of ammunition. Each man carried a couple of HEAT rockets plus his own weapon, ammunition, grenades and field equipment. Two sniper teams carried their complete weapons systems including a heavy half-inch gun, a metre-long silencer, a large scope and wind and distance calibrating accessories. From a long way off they would resemble a heavily laden foot caravan of nomads.

A couple of hours after leaving the camp

Charlie stepped off the foot of the mountain and onto the valley floor. The plain spread out in front of him. In the furthest distance the snow-capped peaks looked like shark's teeth. As they walked into the plain they left the hard terrain behind. There were fewer obstacles, the larger rocks disappeared and the ground beneath their feet turned powdery.

A kilometre out from the bottom of the slope Charlie reached the edge of the broad, dry riverbed they had seen from the village. He paused the snaking patrol once again, as he had done several times along the route. It was always wise to stop and listen, even when there was no sign of an enemy. It kept the snake organised and allowed gaps, caused for whatever reason, to close up.

But this stop was slightly different.

Charlie knelt and gave a signal to Stratton, who dropped down onto a knee several metres behind him. Stratton passed the signal back to the man behind him, a twirling motion with his hand above his head, before getting up and moving to the riverbank a few metres from his point man. The next man came to the opposite side to Charlie, the next to Stratton's side, but a few metres back from the edge of the bank. Jones guided Wheeland and Spinter in. The rest of the men continued the process until the squadron had formed a large circle, their backs to its centre. Some chose to remain on one knee while others lay down.

The tail-end operative reached the circle and turned around to face the way he'd come before lowering himself onto a knee. In the centre of the circle, with the sergeant major and signaller, Captain Burns crouched on a single knee, quietly looking over the riverbed.

The radio operator leaned close to him. 'Ops is acknowledging our location, sir.'

The operations HQ in Bastion had seen the satellite transponder markers carried by the team leaders come to a halt on their map monitors.

'Tell them all's good here and we're moving out in fifteen,' Burns said.

They were entering enemy territory. From this point on, the chances of running into the enemy was greater. So it was always wise to pause. Have a long listen. Get into the right frame of mind. Make any adjustments to weapons and equipment that were needed before pressing on.

The men remained like statues. The wind blew gently between them. A fine dust was constantly in the air and most had their scarves over their mouths. Afghanistan's dust was infamous. It got everywhere. A gentle cough broke the silence, followed by another.

The minutes clicked by. It seemed like they had been there an age. Several times Wheeland fidgeted with something in his pocket or adjusted his position. Stratton looked around at him. The spook looked over his shoulder towards Burns. Stratton had no doubt that if things were up to Wheeland they'd all be on their way by now. He wondered how long ago it was since he'd been in the SEALs. He'd certainly lost his field edge. Being a spook would do that to a person.

Burns got to his feet alone and made his way to the riverbank between Charlie and Stratton. 'All good, Stratton?' he said softly.

'All good, sir,' Stratton replied.

'Move off when you're ready then,' Burns said before stepping back to his radio operator.

Stratton figured they'd waited long enough. He gave Charlie a nod.

The soldier got to his feet and headed down a gentle slope onto the riverbed. When he reached the middle he turned upstream and headed along at an easy pace.

The river was bone dry as per usual for the time of year. On one side, to the left of the squadron as they walked, in the direction they had come from, the ground seemed to rise more steeply than it had felt while they walked down it. The peaks were ice-covered. On their right stretched the vast expanse of open land. Low, smooth rolling hills occupied the middle ground before the distant mountains. Clouds had begun to move in from the south, threatening to cover the night sky. Stratton hoped so. They would block out the moon and stars and reduce the light. Complete dark was good.

The going was rocky and treacherous underfoot. It would have been a smoother walk on either of the banks. But the riverbed was several metres lower. Anyone in the distance on either side would not see the silhouettes of the line of men.

The concealed approach was also important because that night's target was a hamlet on the open plain just a couple of hundred metres from the right side of the river. The attack was planned for an hour before dawn. That gave the teams ample time to move into position.

After another two hours of easy marching, Charlie went down on one knee and gave a signal. The entire squadron halted in its line and most of the operators went to ground. Everyone knew precisely where they were. They all had the coordinates on their GPS. After a minute of watching and listening, Stratton and Jones got up and broke from the line towards the right bank. Another pair left the snake and went to the opposite bank, where they would remain and observe the approaches to what would soon become the rear of the fighting patrol.

Stratton and Jones eased their way up the bank just enough to look onto the plain. In front of them, a few hundred metres away, they saw a line of buildings. The two of them observed the area carefully using thermal imagers. They saw no movement around the buildings. But some figures had gathered near a vehicle, one that had recently arrived or had been running for some reason. Most importantly, the movement they saw was concentrated around the hamlet and not anywhere near the river.

'This is Stratton,' he said into his throat mike. 'You're good to move in.'

Burns acknowledged receipt of the message. A signal went down the line in both directions to move into position. Every man turned to his right as he got to his feet and the extended line moved slowly out of the bottom of the riverbed to the bank where Stratton and Jones lay. The men didn't look above the sides and made themselves comfortable below the bank, while the team leaders climbed up to take a look at the target.

Stratton noted most of the lighting was electrical, coming from inside the houses. They obviously had a generator since the buildings were a few hundred kilometres from the nearest power lines. It would account for the distant droning they could all hear. But the wind was moving across his front, following the river, making it difficult to interpret the sounds coming from the hamlet.

The houses appeared to be joined together to form one long complex. There were no lights outside that he could see. The figures continued to move around the vehicle. A pick-up truck, Stratton decided. The thermal patterns around the wheels and engine compartment remained almost white in their intensity. The men appeared to be unloading something from the back. They carried the items around the other side of the building and out of sight. It seemed the side of the complex they couldn't see was the front.

'A couple more hours and these buggers are going to get well and truly battered,' Jones said.

Stratton checked the ground to the left and right beyond the ends of the complex. It looked to be clear of life. Nothing seemed to live out in the huge open spaces. He guessed the hamlet had originally been a farm. Perhaps it still was. But it was no longer occupied by the farmer and his family. They must have been booted out by the Taliban.

'The eye would pick up anything that was out there,' Jones said.

He was referring to the eye in the sky running surveillance for the operation. There were in fact two 'eyes' covering the task, although the British were aware of only one of them. That was a Royal Air Force Raptor, an unmanned aircraft circling 4500 metres or so above them. The other surveillance unit was operated by the CIA, a manned craft flying at twelve thousand metres. It was employed to observe many other aspects of the regional conflict. But it had been assigned to the task at the hamlet.

'The eyes don't see everything,' Stratton said. He'd had one experience in particular in Iraq that had served to remind him of the shortfalls of hi-tech surveillance. It was in the desert north of Ramadi, inside the Sunni Triangle. He'd been preparing to move to the edge of the town across country with three other members of his team and had been waiting for the all-clear from a Raptor. When it finally came the team moved off, across a stretch of parched farmland. They were exposed. Out in the open. But because the eye had given the all-clear to move, their confidence was high that they would not be seen.

They got halfway across the field when a dozen men appeared in front. It turned out they were insurgents living in a series of tunnels and underground habitats that they used primarily for ammunition storage. The meeting was purely coincidental. The insurgents had been waiting for nightfall before moving out on a mission of their own. The eye in the sky hadn't picked up any clues to their existence.

Stratton's men went to ground. But not quickly enough. The insurgents saw them in the darkness and opened fire immediately. Stratton and his team scattered. Two of them were quickly wounded, one seriously, but they managed to get to cover and defend their position until support arrived. The task wasn't the only thing aborted because of the incident. One of the men's careers was ended that night due to his injuries. Another was off ops for several months.

Needless to say, from that day on, whenever Stratton heard the 'all-clear to proceed' from an eye-in-the-sky operator, he proceeded, but with great caution.

'Have you been given a time to hit these guys?' Wheeland asked Stratton from below.

Stratton looked down the side of the bank to see the American standing there, cool as you like, smoking a cigar.

'That's going to be up to your Spooky' Stratton replied, going back to searching the horizon. 'They're calling the shots on this operation. They want daylight visibility.'

'That's because I asked for a daylight hit,' Wheeland said. 'We've got night eyes. But I don't want anyone getting away for whatever reason.'

Stratton could see the point. Things could get lost in the dark despite the use of sophisticated night optics.

'You ever seen Spooky in all its glory, Stratton?'

'A few times.'

'Beautiful sight, ain't it?'

Stratton had to agree. The Spooky the American referred to was not dedicated to the CIA, despite its name.

'Are you joining the primary move or will you be follow-up?' Stratton asked him, hoping for the latter.

'You've got to be kidding me,' Wheeland said, laughing. 'We're on the primary move, my man. Hell, we may even be out in front of you.'

Stratton got the intended bravado but he was bothered by it nonetheless. 'Do you have something specific you need to find?'

'Yep,' Wheeland said. And he left it at that.

Stratton got the feeling he wanted him to mind his own business. He wasn't offended. He respected the man's secrecy. He would have preferred to know more precise boundaries, though. Where not to go, for instance, or when to leave Wheeland and his buddy to themselves. He resented the lack of detail. 'Would you like us to clean any particular structure before you go in or will you clean them yourselves?' he said.

'I tell you how we're gonna play it, Stratton,' Wheeland said, as he thought it through. 'We'll take it one step at a time. One building at a time. One room at a time. You go ahead and do your thing. And when I say back off and leave it to me and Spinter, that's exactly what you'll do. How about that for a plan?'

Stratton made his way down the bank. 'OK,' he said. 'Let's see how that works out.' Wheeland's attitude was beginning to annoy him but he kept it to himself. He expected the

American was feeling the same way about him. He walked past the spook towards Burns and the ops HQ team.

Spinter came up to his boss as he watched Stratton walk away, ensuring they were out of earshot of anyone. 'That guy's trouble,' he said. 'He's too inquisitive.'

'Relax,' Wheeland said. 'He's got his own concerns. He won't be a problem.'

The teams settled in and waited for the first sign of light to edge its way over the eastern mountains. Stratton had a brief confab with Burns and settled himself just below the edge of the riverbank. Sunrise was the best time of day for him, in most parts of the world, but definitely in Afghanistan. Out in the wastelands there was no movement anywhere. No animals. Practically no life, just scrub. There was the constant chirp of unseen crickets. The wind when it changed pace. But sound was not a great part of the landscape. It wasn't missed. The drama of the plains and surrounding peaks was enough to keep the senses occupied.

Stratton raised his head a little above the bank to take another look through the thermal imager. The lights remained on in the windows of the complex. He saw no one moving around. The men had gone and the vehicle engines had grown cold.

As the daylight gradually increased, he identified several other Hilux pick-ups in the shadows.

Burns came along the line of men, pausing to have a brief chat with each team leader.

'All good?' he asked when he got to Stratton.

'We're all set.'

'Spooky's on his way in.' Burns looked around for Wheeland and saw him sitting a few metres away. 'You all set, Wheeland?'

'Hunky-dory,' the American said.

'It looks like we have a full house,' Burns said. 'Eye in the sky estimates a couple of hundred Taliban all told inside the various structures. Fifty or so arrived during the night before we got eyes on. We can't see their vehicles from this side.'

'The more the merrier.'

Burns checked his watch, looked to the skies and walked back to his position.

Fifteen minutes later the light had grown significantly. It seemed like the sun was going to break over the mountains at any second. They heard a muffled crack from nearby and a flare fired by the sergeant major shot into the air from the riverbank. It gave an audible whoosh, then burst into a bright white light. After a few seconds it went out. It was nothing more than a signal.

The silence did not return. Before the flare disappeared all of the squadron's men began to fire short bursts of machine-gun fire at the buildings. The powerful rounds ate through the weak mud brickwork easily. The hand-helds added to the battering. A thundering blast came from the line of men along the bank as a rocket shot from its housing on the shoulder of one of them and tore along a few feet from the ground. It struck one of the pick-ups, which burst into flames instantly. Several more rockets followed in quick succession, exploding holes in the buildings where they struck.

The attack was a moderate one due to the limited ammunition. It was only a persuader. Sufficient for the squadron's purpose, which was twofold. The first aim was to give the Taliban the impression that a large and invasive attack from the river was commencing on their position. The second was to drive them out of the front of the buildings onto the plain the other side. The teams weren't carrying enough ammunition to engage the Taliban, whose numbers were greater than their own, in an extended gunfight. They left that specific task to a huge American gunship. An AC-130 ground-attack aircraft.

Spooky.

Stratton didn't fire his weapon, content to observe. There were enough guns thumping away at the complex. He saw a dark object in the sky, six or seven hundred metres above ground and on a heading that paralleled the river towards them. It took shape quickly. He couldn't hear its turboprops above the cacophony of guns and rocket fire.

Spooky came in at around 300 mph, dropping all the time as it approached the impact zone. Spooky's sensors combined televisual, radar and infrared inputs to provide a broad, high-intensity visual capability at any time of day or night and virtually any poor weather conditions. Its main armaments were on the left side of the fuselage, to allow for a concentration of firepower.

Flying on a line that would take it across the

squadron's front and beyond the complex, the gunship could suddenly be heard. Its 40mm Bofors cannon opened up. The distinct staccato-like sound dominated the contact as the devastating rounds the size of salt cellars spat into targets at the front of the buildings out of view from the river. Stratton couldn't distinguish the explosions above everything else but before long he saw thick plumes of smoke begin to rise into the sky, coming from, he assumed, the pick-up car park on the other side of the complex.

Spooky's 105mm howitzer cannon opened up next, the first salvo striking the generator housing. Every light in the complex went out. Stratton knew the plan called for the destruction of all the buildings except the largest one on the east side. The Taliban radio, phone and micro-wave transmissions had all been concentrated in that structure, identifying it as the operations room. They had been clearly instructed not to touch it with anything other than small arms gunfire. Only targets fleeing the operations room could be targeted, not the structure itself.

Spooky gained height as it made a long turn out across the river and down the side of the mountain, keeping the complex on its left. The pilot was sticking to the same briefing as Stratton. Like the concentration of fire from the riverbank, it was intended to drive the Taliban to break from the buildings in the opposite direction to the river. No one wanted a head-on fight. Spooky was doing its job.

The RAF Raptor reported dozens of men fleeing from the buildings and heading into the valley. From its vantage point, it must have looked like rats deserting a burning barn.

Wheeland watched it all with great interest. 'When do you want to advance, Stratton?' he shouted above a rattling machine gun a few metres from him.

Stratton sighed to himself. With a task like this the bottom line was, for Stratton at least, zero casualties. In fact, zero injuries. Nothing about Afghanistan was worth getting hurt for, let alone dying for. In the early days it had been fun. Fresh. A new enemy. New kit to try out. New toys to play with. New terrain. The reasons he, and people like him, joined the military. Now the conflict was old. The equipment was getting old. It was mundane. Bombs and ambushes. That's all it was now. He wasn't about to let Wheeland put any of his men at risk.

'Captain Burns will give the advance,' he said.

'The way I understand it, he'll pretty much do whatever you say,' Wheeland countered.

Stratton knew the more passes Spooky made the more damage it was doing, the more Taliban it killed and the safer the assault would be for the men. Time was comfortably on their side. He suspected the American was worried that the longer they took to get going, the more time the enemy had to alter or destroy whatever it was he wanted. If that was so, it was the price Wheeland was paying for keeping everything to himself. Another minute wasn't going to hurt.

'Here she comes again,' Jones said.

They all looked towards the gunship as it came in for another run. Its 40mm opened up again and the complex appeared to shudder as dozens of rounds hit it. The howitzer blew something else to bits, out of sight to the teams on the riverbank.

Burns walked over to Stratton at a brisk pace. 'Raptor reports approximately a hundred and fifty Taliban running into the valley.'

'This is the bit I like best,' Jones said. 'You can see some of the Talibuts on the right there.'

He was right. They looked behind the buildings at a dozen or so men running as fast as they could into the plain.

'Why don't we get going and get a better seat?' Wheeland said.

His comment landed on deaf ears.

'Spooky's turning in on them now,' Burns said.

They all watched as the lumbering whale of an aircraft turned at the bottom of its run, this time further into the valley to come back at the target from the opposite direction. Like an eagle that had spotted its prey caught out in the open, it came in for the kill. Its talons flared, demonstrating for the watching soldiers the other special weapon that it carried. One that until now had remained silent. A weapon designed specifically for engaging widespread targets like this. A 25mm, five-barrelled, electrically powered Gatling gun affectionately known as the Equaliser. Although why it was called that was unclear to most. There was nothing equal about the weapon. On the contrary. It was a very one-sided piece of ordnance.

The gunship appeared to jostle a little as the

pilot fought to lose height as quickly as he could while at the same time lining up on the target for optimum efficiency of the weapon. As Spooky passed over the fleeing fighters, Stratton thought he could hear the electric motors of the Gatling gun wind up before the bullets spat from the cannon at a rate of thirty thousand a minute. They all heard the terrifying scream of the weapon's electric motors when they got up to full speed. It was claimed that on a single pass the Equaliser could place a bullet in every square foot of a piece of ground the width of a football pitch. Each of those rounds was over an inch thick. Just one alone made a terrible mess of anything it struck.

The combination of the roaring engines low in the sky and the screaming electric cannon must have terrified the men on the ground directly beneath it. The Afghans knew of such weapons. Those who hadn't seen the devastation it caused first-hand had heard the stories. For the men running as hard as they could across the plain, the sight of the soil literally exploding as the rounds struck it in a broad swath a hundred metres wide, and tearing towards them like a steel curtain, would have been simply terrifying. To run, lie down or stand still, the odds of surviving within the storm remained low to none.

When the gunfire ceased, the killing ground was obscured by a huge dust cloud. It quickly settled. When visibility returned, dead bodies lay everywhere.

Spooky rose up a little and banked heavily to

one side, its turboprops whining, and then sharply over onto the other side, turning tightly round as it dropped its nose to come in for yet another run. Raptor reported that it had obliterated all the Taliban furthest from the house but there were more. Spooky was hungry to eat up the rest of them. It provided the ultimate illustration of time standing still for some while racing on ahead for others. The Afghans' only advances in weaponry over the past two hundred years had been gifts from the West. But the West had kept the best for itself.

From the squadron's perspective in the river, as the aircraft reached the line of houses the thunderous Gatling gun opened up again. The firing lasted barely seconds. In that brief time the gunship had cleaned up the rest of the fighters. It was a massacre.

Raptor reported some minor movement among the prone bodies in the open ground but it was clear enough for the teams to move in.

'Now can we go?' Wheeland asked, trying not to sound exasperated and coming off a little childish.

Stratton looked at Burns for his response.

'Right,' Burns said. 'Let's go and clean up. Stratton, lead off if you would be so kind.'

Wheeland rolled his eyes at the Britishness of the squadron officer.

'Cease fire!' the squadron sergeant major called out. The order went down the line and the machine guns that had been maintaining a minimum strike rate to encourage any lurking Taliban to run from the river went still.

Stratton looked over at Jones, Charlie and the others in his team. They were ready and waiting to go. He looked at Wheeland and Spinter, who had their small packs on and weapons in hand.

'Do you mind staying in the rear?' Stratton asked. 'We work as a team to clear the ground and then the buildings.'

'Sure,' Wheeland said. 'I wouldn't want to interfere with your routines.' Stratton wasn't sure if the man was being sarcastic. Not that he minded. He suddenly realised he was envious of the American's enthusiasm. He suddenly felt like he was being the dick himself and that he ought to thank Wheeland, if anything.

Stratton stepped up onto the bank to look at the complex. Spooky roared overhead, so close to the ground he could see every detail. One of the howitzer gun crew standing by it on the open tailgate waved. When it had passed, and with it the diminishing roar of its engines, they could hear the sound of sporadic gunfire from beyond the buildings. Perhaps some Taliban had survived the Gatling gun and were taking pot shots at Spooky. If they were, it was of little consequence. The squadron had been outnumbered six or seven to one when they arrived. That had surely been reversed by now.

Stratton, Jones and the others in his team spread out in an extended line and advanced on the complex. The rest of the squadron made its way out of the riverbed and, in another extended line, advanced a dozen or so metres behind them.

The gunfire continued. Raptor reported no sign of life immediately around any of the buildings. A handful of stragglers were making a late dash into the valley but showed no interest in the buildings — as if they knew the enemy was closing in. There were a lot of bodies lying on the plain. Their thermal images would remain warm for several hours. Light bundles on a dark background. A couple of them appeared to move, suggesting they were wounded. All of this information got passed through the communications system to the team commanders. But not even the Raptor could see inside the buildings, where the main caution was required.

The approach to the complex was stony. Stratton did wonder if the ground might be mined — always the biggest concern anywhere in Afghanistan. The concept had been discussed in the operation's planning stage but had been discounted. The Taliban were not beyond booby-trapping their own facilities. On the contrary, several special forces operatives had died in recent times and many more had been severely injured by such devices in encampments that were detonated while in the middle of an attack. From the information they had received about the complex, Stratton had accepted it would not be the case here. Communications and eye-in-the-sky monitoring had revealed a laxness in the Taliban's security procedures, suggesting a confidence in the remoteness of the place. It was never something you could predict for sure, so it remained at the back of his mind.

As he walked across the open ground he felt

for his pistol in its holster at his hip. Then he checked his chest harness, by feel, making sure the grenades he carried were where they needed to be. Conventional ops usually required a standard shrag grenade. But due to the need to preserve the interiors, Stratton's entry team also carried stun grenades. It was useful not to get them mixed up. Wheeland for one would be most displeased if Stratton destroyed the Taliban operations room.

Stratton led the approach to the corner of the first building. His team spread further to his flank so that they didn't bunch at the corner. Wheeland and Spinter were only metres behind.

He turned the corner as Spooky flew past a few hundred metres away and let rip another long burst onto the valley floor to clean up the few individuals crazy enough to be taking pot shots at it.

Smoke drifted along the front of the complex towards Stratton, mostly from the burning trucks destroyed by Spooky He could see half a dozen Hilux pick-ups among the wreckage, all totalled. Dead bodies lay around. All wore Afghan clothes: long shirts, cotton trousers, heavy wool scarves and shawls. Turbans. Pakuls. Sandals. Boots. AK-47 assault rifles lay scattered among them. He saw charred and burning bodies inside several of the vehicles.

Outside the main building the Taliban had erected a tall pole, topped with an array of antennas. A thick coaxial cable led from its base, along the ground and into the end house through a window. Stratton moved slowly along the front of the building under the windows, which were so high he barely had to duck to pass beneath them without exposing himself to anyone who might be inside.

The large front door was ajar. Jones moved in closer in support and Stratton let his assault rifle hang from its harness as he took hold of his pistol. It didn't have the same penetration power as the rifle, but in room-clearing, he preferred the speed of engagement a pistol gave him. Jones preferred the rifle for its stopping power.

Charlie and the others came in tightly behind them.

Stratton took a moment to listen. It was hard to hear anything above the sound of the fires burning all around. Nothing was coming from inside. He stepped in through the doorway and moved away from the opening so as not to be silhouetted. Jones did the same a second behind him.

The two of them found themselves standing in a lobby. They saw several toppled chairs. A couple of AK-47 assault rifles on the floor, along with discarded magazines and several bullets. Two doors either side of the lobby led into opposite rooms. A soft noise came from one of them. A hissing sound. Like an out-of-tune television set.

Stratton stepped to the doorway and Jones followed. Charlie and the other operators moved quietly into the lobby. Two of them went to the opposite doorway. Stratton stepped through the half-open door, closely followed by Jones, their guns at the ready while they scanned every inch of the room. It was a mess. All the signs of a hasty evacuation. Totally void of man, dead or alive. Against a wall a long bench covered with communications equipment, several laptop computers, a printer and scanner, and bits and pieces of things Stratton didn't readily recognise.

On a shelf above, DVD players, CD copiers and a couple of digital video cameras.

There was a safe on the floor directly in front of him, its door open. Money spilled out in front of it. A few thousand US dollars and euros. There were some papers inside. Boxes of spilled paperwork were everywhere. A radio scanner was on. The static noise they'd heard from outside was coming from a speaker beside the scanner.

Spooky flew low past the building and the single remaining unbroken window rattled. A moment later the sound of its 40mm cannon stuttered in the distance, followed by explosions. Communications over the network revealed it was still chasing fleeing Taliban.

'We'll take it from here,' Wheeland said, putting his gun down onto the bench. 'You can leave. Now. If you don't mind.' His tone was suddenly far harsher than it had been.

Spinter stepped in behind him. 'The other room's clean,' he said.

'This is the operations room,' Wheeland said.

Jones looked at Stratton, waiting for the word from *his* boss.

Stratton headed for the door, and Jones followed. Spinter moved aside to let them pass.

Stratton paused to look back at the spooks. They were already focused on the room. Spinter glanced back to see Stratton watching him and

35

closed the door in his face.

Stratton stood in the lobby, annoyed with Wheeland's sudden aggressive attitude, not really listening. But they weren't trying to hide what they were saying.

'It has to be in here,' he heard Spinter say.

'We know it's here,' Wheeland said, correcting. 'Rohami made a call from this room yesterday. He told the general that he had the codes and would deliver them to Bagram.'

Stratton felt a tad guilty for eavesdropping — Wheeland would be justifiably pissed off if he knew. Stratton walked outside.

Jones and the others were waiting for him. The rest of the squadron were clearing the other buildings. It would appear that none of the Taliban had remained inside the complex. They all knew the consequences of not fleeing. The Taliban showed no pity to Western forces whenever they captured any alive. And they had learned over the years that as a result of their own ruthlessness, some Westerners had grown less inclined to take prisoners themselves, unless they specifically wanted to.

Spooky remained in the far distance. Flying low, following the inside curve of the mountains. It had only one thing left to do and was waiting for the ground forces to move out before completing its mission.

'That was short and sweet,' Jones said. 'Hardly worth it, if you ask me. I thought it was all about wasting a Taliban command structure, but now I reckon that was secondary. These spooks are the real reason we're here. Isn't that right?'

'Doesn't matter,' Charlie piped up. He never spoke much. Not just because he was junior to Jones and Stratton. He wasn't much of a talker at the best of times. But when he did talk, he usually had something useful to say. 'We never lost anyone. Not even a twisted ankle. And we wasted a lot of Talibuts.'

It was a valid enough point that no one could argue with.

'Aye,' Jones said. 'It was a good couple of days out. A nice walk. A bit of fresh air. And a little bit of horse play at the end of it.'

Stratton walked away from the building into the open ground and looked out over the plain. The sun was easing its way over the jagged mountains to his left, the light bathing the valley floor and the dozens of dead bodies spread out in front of him. The hard ground had been chewed up by the gunship.

A gentle wind blew, toying with Stratton's clothes and those of the dead men around him. Most of them looked like they'd been hit by at least a couple of the rounds from Spooky's Gatling gun. A bloody mess.

He noticed a metal box lying beside one of the dead Afghans, his eyes attracted to the flapping paper sticking from it. He took a few steps closer. The box looked robust, the size of a shoebox, with large brass hinges. It had been hit and the lid was partly open.

Stratton crouched to get a better look. He picked it up. Inside the box was a booklet. The pages fluttered in the breeze. It was a typeset document written in Urdu. He couldn't read the text but he'd seen it often enough to be able to tell the difference. He began flicking through the booklet, seeing in the middle a page of letters and numbers in bolder, larger font than the rest. It looked like a code of some kind.

As he examined the document he was aware of footsteps approaching. He looked round as a hand shoved him forcefully away while another grabbed the box and booklet at the same time.

'Where the hell did you get that?' growled Wheeland. 'Did you take it from the operations room?'

'You know I didn't,' he said, squaring up to the spook. Spinter appeared and raised his weapon, aiming it at Stratton's face.

Stratton's blood came up at Spinter's audacity. 'Lower your weapon or I'll shove it up your arse,' he said.

'You stick your nose in places you shouldn't, Stratton,' Wheeland said as he examined the papers. 'You should know better than most that's not a wise thing to do.'

Jones placed the end of his assault rifle inside Spinter's ear. 'If you don't lower your weapon away from my friend, there's going to be a sudden case of death by friendly fire.'

Spinter didn't move, giving Jones only the slightest of glances. Stratton thought he could sense hesitation in the American, but couldn't be sure.

'Put your gun down, Spinter,' Wheeland said.

Spinter lowered the weapon, as Burns saw the kerfuffle and came over. 'What the bloody hell's going on here?'

'Hey, look, I'm sorry,' Wheeland said, looking from Burns to Stratton. 'You have no idea how important this operation is. When I saw you with this' — he held up the booklet — 'I lost it. I apologise.'

Burns glanced at the box and papers, none the wiser.

Wheeland put the booklet back inside the box and closed it. 'I appreciate all you've done. I'm sorry. No hard feelings.' He held out a hand to Stratton.

Stratton's blood was still up. As he fought against his instincts and leaned forward to shake Wheeland's hand, the sound of an approaching jet helicopter interrupted them. All eyes went skywards.

A sleek, white, civilianised Bell hovered to land fifty metres away.

'That's my ride. You guys enjoy the rest of the day,' Wheeland said. 'Hope to see you again somewhere soon.' He seemed to be directing this last at Stratton. Wheeland winked at him before departing.

The two Americans made their way over to the helicopter, which had not reduced its power as it sat lightly on the dusty ground. A side door opened and the spooks climbed inside. As the door closed the helicopter rose up and powered away, a couple of hundred metres below another helicopter on its way into the hamlet. This one was a Chinook, huge in comparison to the Bell. It came in slowly, its dual rotors thudding out a percussive tattoo as it manoeuvred overhead before descending.

'What was all that about?' Burns asked Stratton.

Stratton shook his head. 'I don't know.'

The Chinook landed close to the complex and within a few minutes the squadron was piling aboard.

As the helicopter left the ground, Spooky turned away from the mountains, on its last task of the day, heading back towards the buildings, keeping them to one side of its flightpath. When it went over it unleashed pure hellfire.

It was like the crew had decided to fire everything they had left at the complex, which burst into flames. Walls collapsed. Roofs caved in. Entire structures shattered outwards as bombs exploded inside.

Spooky and the squadron exited the valley, leaving behind a billowing black plume reaching into the skies.

3

General Javas Mahuba stood on the edge of a
winding dirt road halfway up Sheraghund
Mountain, looking in the direction of the
highway between Islamabad and Peshawar. He
couldn't see the road from where he was but it
was visible in his mind's eye. It crossed east-west
seventy kilometres to the south. He was thinking
how he would soon be driving along it on his
way into Afghanistan.

It was almost midnight. Lights from the small
town named after the mountain sparkled in
the distance, way below where Mahuba was
standing. Winter was still a good month or so
away. But the air was already bitterly cold. He
recollected the unusually heavy rainy season that
year, which often meant a hard winter would
follow. He put his hands inside the deep pockets
of his black, woollen Savile Row overcoat and
buried his grey, bearded chin in the delicately
woven pashmina wrapped around his neck.

He felt calm, though his nerves were tingling a
little. He was quite used to nervous tension. He
was usually good at bringing it under control.
Over twenty years in the military had seen to
that. But nothing in the past could begin to com-
pare with his present. Not the long and rocky
road that had brought him to the side of this
mountain, to his current position.

A pair of lights appeared, slowly strobing

through the trees as they climbed the road. He heard the sound of the heavy diesel engine labouring to drive the truck up the steep incline. Mahuba looked over his shoulder to a white Hilux Toyota pick-up truck parked off the road and a man with a black book-shaped beard sprinkled with grey. The Afghan climbed out of the Toyota. He wore a brown pakul and a thick chapan over a long woollen shirt that was tucked into a pair of baggy, woollen trousers. His dark eyes looked between his boss of many years and the approaching truck. Mahuba took a small flashlight from his pocket and turned it on. The end was covered in red tape. As the truck rounded the corner and came out from behind the trees, he went to the edge of the road, waving the torch from side to side.

The brakes of the aged Bedford four-ton truck squealed as the driver applied them. The heavy vehicle rolled to a halt about ten metres from Mahuba. As he walked over to the driver's side of the cab, the door opened and the driver leaned out to look down at him.

He didn't recognise Mahuba. He'd never seen the face before. His instructions had been simple enough: drive up the Sheraghund Mountain road until you are stopped by a red light. If the man you meet bears a letter of authorisation signed by the head of the Pakistani Army, obey every order he gives you from that moment forward. Defy these orders on pain of death.

Mahuba took a letter from inside his breast pocket and reached it up to the driver. The man opened it, turned on his cab light and read it slowly and carefully. When he got to the end he nodded, more to himself, before handing it back. He seemed satisfied with the credentials.

'Turn off the engine,' Mahuba ordered. He delivered his orders without effort, as though accustomed to total obedience.

The heavy diesel engine stuttered before reluctantly shutting down with a throaty rumble. The air was still once again.

'Get out,' Mahuba said. He walked to the back of the canvas-covered bed. The canvas flap had been tossed up onto the roof. Inside the truck he saw a dozen armed soldiers seated on the two benches that ran down both sides. They looked half-frozen. But on seeing the immaculately dressed man outside who was clearly of some importance, they stiffened a little.

'Get out,' Mahuba said.

The driver unpinned one side of the tailboard, while one of the soldiers unpinned the other. They gave it a shove and the tailgate came down with a loud slam. The men quickly jumped down onto the road. They all wore fatigues and carried rifles. They had pouches attached to their belts, filled with ammunition. None of them seemed to know where they were.

Mahuba's eyes were fixed on a crate at the back of the truck. It was everything to him now. 'Put it on the back of the pick-up,' he said.

The driver barked an order and several of the men scrambled back into the truck to the box. They gave it a heave and slid it along the floor of the bed to the rear.

Mahuba hadn't taken his eyes off it. He'd

never seen the thing it held before but he knew all of its mysteries.

'Easy with it, you idiots!' he shouted as they lifted the crate out of the truck, struggling to take its weight.

Whatever was inside was heavy, easily as much as two men. The soldiers took heed and steadied the weight between them, shuffling with it down the side of the truck towards the pick-up. The driver directed them to load it onto the bed and push it all the way to the back, up against the cab. When it was in place, Mahuba's servant covered the box in a canvas tarpaulin, securing it with a rope.

'Back inside the truck,' the general said.

The soldiers made their way back to the truck and piled inside but the driver stood where he was, as if waiting for his own instructions.

Mahuba looked at him. 'Join your men,' he said. 'In the back. Wait for me to tell you to leave. Do not move from the truck until you hear from me. Do you understand?'

'Yes, sir,' the driver said and he went to the back of the truck and climbed up and inside.

Mahuba gave his man a look that was a clear command.

The Afghan walked around the front of the pick-up to a trolley loaded with boxes. With a great effort, he managed to get the heavy load moving. He wheeled it along the road to the truck and manoeuvred it so that he could push it beneath the Bedford. It fitted snugly to one side, though not quite completely underneath. It didn't matter.

The Afghan returned to the cab of the pick-up. He brought out a large cloth bundle and carried it to the truck, inside which the soldiers were chatting. He opened the bundle and placed the charred fragments that had been in it around the road, before returning to Mahuba.

'Let's go,' the general said.

They climbed into the pick-up and the Afghan started it up and pulled onto the road, heading down the hill towards the Islamabad-Peshawar highway. After they had passed the stand of trees that shielded their view of the truck, Mahuba raised a hand. 'This will do,' he said.

The Afghan brought the pick-up to a stop but kept the engine running. Mahuba removed a mobile phone from his pocket. He punched in a number. Pressed the send button.

A tremendous explosion shattered the night beyond the trees. The sky lit up with a momentary flash. Miles away the sudden light might be mistaken for a lightning bolt, the sound of the explosion rolling thunder.

The ninety kilos of high explosives on the trolley had done their job. The soldiers could never have survived the blast, never mind the shrapnel that would have torn through them.

The Afghan released the brake and they drove on down the hill. Mahuba removed the back of the phone and took out the SIM card. He opened the window and tossed the phone into the wind. He chewed the SIM card until it was destroyed and tossed it out too.

The following day the bomb site would be roped off by the police and closely examined.

The investigators would find pieces of a weapon familiar to them, especially to those with experience of air attacks on Taliban commanders. The pieces Mahuba's servant had distributed were parts of a Hellfire laser-guided missile commonly launched from US military Predator drones. It was a simple way of getting rid of the witnesses and muddying the waters at the same time.

When the Toyota pick-up reached the Islamabad-Peshawar road forty-five minutes later, they turned right and headed west, towards the Afghan border. Mahuba's nervous tension had not subsided. But overall he felt pleased with the recent transition and was all the more confident he would complete the rest of the operation.

This was it. The mission that had taken all this time to plan was truly into its final stages. But one thing still bothered him greatly. And he wasn't sure how he was going to deal with it.

4

Stratton leaned against the old, polished wooden bar top in the St Stephens Inn across the road from the Houses of Parliament. It was precisely twelve forty-five in the afternoon as he sipped his first pint of the day. Big Ben took up the majority of the view through the large windows on that side of the bar. It was difficult to miss the time.

'Quarter to the hour,' the Polish bartender politely informed him in a strong accent as he poured a pint in front of Stratton for another customer. 'Beautiful soundings,' he added with a smile.

Stratton nodded politely. The man spoke in a manner that suggested he was practising his new language. That he was telling his customers the obvious seemed unimportant.

It was unusual for Stratton to partake in an alcoholic beverage at that time of day. His decision was based on the knowledge that the afternoon would more than likely degenerate into a lunchtime sesh, as per the Naval vernacular. He was there to meet someone. A former SBS commanding officer, to be precise. Berry Chandos. Who had a reputation for drinking heavily whenever he met any of his old lads from the SBS. Either in a pub or if they called on his cottage in the verdant hills east of Warminster. Be they officer or ranker. And he didn't care to drink heavily alone and took offence if he was left to do so.

As Stratton took a sip the saloon lounge door opened and a man in a three-quarter-length winter coat, scarf and crumpled tweed hat stepped into the bar. Stratton recognised the inscrutable figure of Chandos as he felt the blast of chilly wind that accompanied his arrival. The breeze ceased as the door closed behind Chandos on its spring return.

He paused in the room. His eyes went directly to Stratton. But he looked around the entire place without taking another step. His gaze finally returned to Stratton.

The operative thought he could detect a level of concern in his old boss's eyes. They looked tired. He'd been ready for the usual loud and gregarious salute. But there was no sign of it. Chandos walked over, making an effort at a smile but it lasted seconds. 'Good to see you, Stratton,' he said.

'You too,' Stratton said. 'Pint?'

Chandos paused as if to consider his answer. This was another uncharacteristic response to the offer of an alcoholic beverage. It was to get worse still. 'I might just have a soda water for now,' he said.

'Are you not well?' It was all Stratton could think of that might explain this behaviour.

Chandos took off his hat and placed it on the bar. Ran a hand through his scruffy, greying, full head of hair. 'I wouldn't have ventured to meet anyone else,' he said. 'But I had to see you.'

Stratton scrutinised his former boss. There was something intense about him. It could

48

almost be described as fearful, although that had to be rubbish. Chandos was nearly sixty but he had been one of the more accomplished commanders of the SBS. A tireless worker. Determined and highly intelligent. He'd achieved one of the highest scores in staff college for his generation. In his heyday he was superbly fit. The kind of officer who expected every one of his men to be operationally ready at a moment's notice. Any time of the day or night. Weekends or holidays. He'd also been prepared to put that to the test. He became famous, or infamous, throughout special forces for doing just that, calling in the men on a priority alert when they least expected it and putting them through their paces.

Chandos glanced around quickly to ensure neither the bartender nor anyone else was listening. 'Do you know why you were selected for SIS operations?' he asked.

'I've always understood that every operative in the SAS and SBS was secretly reviewed for possible recruitment,' Stratton replied. 'I was lucky enough to be selected, I suppose.'

'Do you know of any other members of the SBS or SAS who've served in the SIS? I'm talking about long-term service employment like yours, not for the occasional task.'

Stratton paused to think. He shrugged. 'How would I? That role is essentially secret.'

'Most members of the SBS know you work for the SIS.'

'Some suspect you do too.'

'Just because you've seen me in the stables doesn't mean I'm one of the jockeys.'

49

Stratton knew what he was getting at. When Chandos retired from the Service he'd disappeared completely. No one seemed to know where he'd gone, not even the most senior officers. Some thought he'd retired to the Scottish highlands. Another rumour was he'd gone to Africa, Kenya perhaps, and was living a quiet and private life in the countryside. But then Stratton saw him at MI6. It was only the second time he'd been there himself since his own secret recruitment to operations, and there was Chandos talking to a mandarin in one of the corridors of 'Legoland', as the spooks called headquarters. Chandos saw Stratton too. They hadn't seen each other for five years and his only acknowledgement was a wink as he walked away. Stratton remembered how his morale had been lifted. He'd always felt that Chandos had left the Service prematurely. The man still had so much to offer. He remembered feeling suddenly encouraged by the organisation. If it employed the likes of Berry, then it had people who knew what they were doing.

'What's your point?' he asked. 'If you don't mind me pushing you to get to it?'

'There's never been a full-time dual SBS or SAS and SIS operative before you,' Chandos said. 'You're the first.'

'And how would you know that, if you weren't connected to the organisation?'

'Because I made you,' Chandos said.

It was an interesting comment. And Stratton believed him. But he didn't feel impressed by it. In fact he suddenly doubted his mentor. His character more than what he actually said. He wasn't himself.

'I'm sorry,' Chandos said, seeing the doubt in Stratton's eyes. 'I'll explain. In a minute.' He looked towards the end of the bar. 'Bartender?'

The bartender walked down the bar to stand opposite the men. 'Yes, sir,' he said, smiling. 'How can I be in service?'

'A bottle of that Mont Ventoux,' Chandos said, pointing to a line of bottles on a shelf behind the bar. 'That one. The red.'

'Two glasses, sir?'

'Yes.' While the bartender busied himself, Chandos turned back to Stratton. 'Bugger them,' he said in a lowered voice. 'Might as well enjoy it to the bitter end.'

The bartender brought the wine over and tipped a sample into a glass, waiting for them to taste it.

'If it's corked, I'll let you know,' Chandos said, not in the mood for such ceremony.

The bartender filled both glasses and left the pair alone.

Stratton had convinced himself Chandos was about to tell him he was terminally ill. Maybe he'd had some news from the doctor. He looked bad enough. Chandos was never dramatic. On the contrary. He was famously understated. No matter what the threat.

'Officers could never be dual SF and military intelligence,' Chandos said. 'Not full time. Their careers are too structured. It would have to be either one or the other. And few officers would elect to join MI6. There's little money in it. Little

51

chance of promotion. And much of the romance of the business is restricted to the pages of the novels that have been written about it. NCOs are a better choice to cross-deck. Theoretically. But the pickings are slim. There are many qualities required for an SIS operative. Few have most. You are rare, my boy. Don't get too cocky, though. You don't have 'em all. You've gained some over time. And you've lost some.'

Stratton could hardly guess what he was referring to. He did wonder what he'd lost, though. His enthusiasm perhaps. He never showed it in the early days. Nowadays he was more of a cynic. He'd lost his naivety too.

'That happens,' Chandos said, as if to soften the criticism. 'There are the inevitable pressures. We grow stronger in some ways. Weaker in others. Our scepticism weakens us. As does our paranoia. That's a strength too of course. We begin to think we want to quit. But we don't really. Not really.' He took a sip of wine. 'I was recruited into the SIS immediately after I left the SBS.'

Stratton was impressed. Not about the contents of the revelation, which he'd suspected for a long time, ever since he'd seen Chandos at headquarters. It was that he had chosen to tell him.

'I was too old to be a frontline mechanic like you. They used me for light footwork at first. Planning. Spy contacts. Ops organising. Crisis management. That sort of thing. I expect you're wondering why I'm suddenly telling you all of this.'

Stratton was. But he shrugged as he finished off his beer and put the empty glass to one side.

The door opened and Chandos turned quickly to look at the man who walked in on the cold breeze. It wasn't a subtle examination. The new arrival, dressed in a business suit, walked across the room and greeted two other well-dressed men. The way they immediately laughed suggested they were chums. None looked in Chandos's direction.

Chandos took a large gulp of wine from his glass and put it back down on the bar. 'I thought life would get less complicated when I joined military intelligence. Less responsibility at least. Instead of running the whole show as I did in the SBS. I expected, as a foot soldier, if you like, to be given orders and to follow them through. And after the job was done, kick back and relax while waiting for the next. Rather like you do now.

'But that wasn't to be the case. I became involved. I ran double lives. I became more than one person, to others as well as to myself. Life became more complicated than it had ever been before.'

Chandos reached for the wine again. 'I'm not making much sense but perhaps it'll come together in a minute. When I joined the SIS I was rather cavalier. No surprise there, I hear you thinking. When I pushed for your involvement it was mostly because I could. Of course, I believed you would be an asset, as you have been. But it was mostly arrogance on my part. I thought it was a game I was going to enjoy, on the sidelines as much as on the pitch. I knew you'd enjoy it too. Is that true?' Chandos suddenly looked unsure about something. 'Have you enjoyed it?'

Stratton shrugged. He wasn't entirely sure how to answer. 'For the most part, I suppose,' he said. As he thought about it some more he decided he'd enjoyed the early days immensely Mostly the freedom to operate alone. But over time he'd grown jaded. By the system. By the attitude of some of his employers. They seemed to be more interested in their own importance. Placing personal ambitions ahead of what was best for the country. And the operatives on the ground at times. It seemed to him that patriotism was not a driving force for the mandarins or politicians. But they expected it, or better still, demanded it, from the lower ranks.

'I've made enemies over time,' Chandos said. 'Not that that was ever a real concern. It's all a part of the job. You see, you make enemies on an operation, you can usually leave them there. But I made enemies too close to home. And they can't be avoided so easily.'

Chandos took another sip of wine. 'You know how you make a serious enemy in this business, don't you?'

Stratton expected it was a rhetorical question and waited for Chandos to answer.

'You don't do it by revealing their incompetence or lack of patriotism. You do it by letting them find out that you know they're not on our side at all.' Chandos finished the glass and refilled it and Stratton's own.

Stratton decided not to let his friend drink alone and took a sip. 'Are you talking about double agents?' he asked, unsure. Even saying the words felt odd. It seemed like an outdated phrase. From the Cold War.

'I'm talking about people who work only for themselves. And they have partners on other teams. In other countries. Among our friends as well as our foes. It's sickening. It makes a mockery of everything people like you and me live for. And of those friends who have died. And the real joke of it is, those bastards couldn't do it if we weren't patriots — they make sure we are. And we feel good about that and we ensure everyone else on the team is too. And they laugh at us even more for it.'

'I don't understand,' Stratton said, starting to feel a tad irritated with Chandos's increasing lack of clarity. Berry was usually a great talker. Particularly on the subject of geopolitics. But not like this. His favourite topic was normally the old days and the evolution of the Service.

The front door banged shut as a couple of people left and Chandos jerked around to look at it.

He turned back to the bar again, realising he was tense and that Stratton was aware of it.

'Can I give you some advice?' he said.

'Your advice has always been sound.'

'Quit the SIS.'

The advice didn't sit well with Stratton. He didn't want to quit and saw no reason to. 'What's bothering you?' he asked.

Chandos finished off the wine. 'I received a warning today from a friend. Someone I trust. And there are few of them these days.' He had his elbows on the bar, looking directly ahead. 'I'm being hunted.'

Stratton found himself thinking about Chandos's so-called retirement again. He had been a highly respected and much-loved SBS commander. He'd been one of the great leaders and operational planners of his day. He was highly decorated and had been mentioned in several military history books, not always by his real name. There was a photograph of him on the stairs in the Special Forces Club in Knightsbridge.

'What do you mean, 'hunted'?'

'It's a specialist. Not some rank amateur. A professional. It's a bit like being told you have an incurable disease and that you'll expire at any moment. Without warning. Pop!'

Stratton knew better than to ask if there was anything Chandos could do on an official level. Berry was no fool. He had recognised Stratton's own potential from the start. He'd been a mentor to him from the earliest days after Stratton's arrival at the SBS HQ in Poole.

'Maybe together we could do something,' Stratton said.

Chandos shook his head. 'Even if we succeeded, he'd be replaced by another. You'd become a target too.'

'Are you saying there's absolutely nothing you can do?'

'There is something. It's all I can think of. I need to get to the person who sent the assassin against me. But I don't know how much time I've got.' He turned to Stratton and looked at him as if he'd arrived at the crux of the meeting.

'I came here for a specific reason, Stratton. But you have to know that if you take it on, your life will also be in danger.'

This was beginning to sound as if it would be unsupported. Independent of assistance from government or allies. Stratton wouldn't be getting a briefing in a pub otherwise.

'What do you want me to do?' he asked.

'Finish what I started.' Chandos was looking at him with great sincerity. It was as close to pleading as Stratton had ever seen from him. 'I wouldn't ask if there wasn't so much at stake. In the short term, it could involve several thousands of lives. But it could ultimately lead to the loss of many more.'

Stratton was reminded of why he'd agreed to come here after Chandos's call out of the blue. Chandos certainly believed what he was saying. But the talk of an assassin had made Stratton a little suspicious of Chandos's mental state. Just enough to sow a seed of doubt. On the other hand, he owed Chandos the right to be believed. After all those years, and after so much that Chandos had meant to him, he had to give the man the benefit of the doubt.

'What do you want me to do?' he asked.

'Nothing yet. Only if I fail. If anything happens to me, you'll be contacted by a close and special friend. Someone I trust implicitly. Remember the name Bullfrog. They'll tell you the objective. The rest will be up to you. You can take it or walk away.'

Chandos took some money from his pocket and dropped it on the bar. 'Forget about the assassin,' he said. 'At the risk of damaging your pride, you'd not be anywhere near good enough to take him on.' Chandos paused a moment as if to examine his thoughts. 'If I fail, if I die and you decide not to take it on, then do what I said, leave the business. Quit it all and walk away. Go to the mountains and raise sheep or something. There's no point if we're not going to take on the big tasks. We can't let these people take over. Although sometimes I fear they may have already.'

He put a hand in his pocket and removed something from it. A large silver coin with a small chain attached. He put it on the bar in front of Stratton.

Stratton picked it up to look at both sides. It was an SBS stone. A coin every retired member could ask for on leaving the Service. It had the SBS badge on one side: a frog with crossed canoe paddles, a parachute and inscribed with the SBS motto, 'By Strength By Guile'. On the other side was Chandos's name. The coin didn't come with a small chain, something Chandos had added himself.

'It's your stone,' Stratton said.

'I want you to keep it,' Chandos said. 'Keep it with you. Will you do that?'

Stratton thought it was an odd request. He would, unless it threatened to compromise him in any way. 'Sure,' he said.

'I mean to have it back one day. Least that's the plan.'

'I'm sure you will,' Stratton said. It was all he could think of saying by way of encouragement.

58

Chandos held out a hand. 'All the best,' he said.

As Stratton took hold of his mentor's hand, he felt very odd. It seemed that more should have been said in terms of farewell, considering they might never see each other again. He was about to say something, but before he could form a word, Chandos released his hand and walked to the door. He opened it and left on the breeze he had swept in on, without a look back.

Stratton felt very strange about the meeting. Chandos had apparently gone to his death, or at least to try and save himself from it. Though he clearly doubted his chances of succeeding. And as for Stratton, if the worst was to happen, if Chandos was to die, he was supposed to pick up the pieces of some mysterious and world shattering plot and try and put them together.

He felt very strange indeed.

5

General Mahuba sat beside his servant as they drove the Toyota along a never-ending line of parked trucks. Old and new. Battered and shiny. An assortment of fuel transports and container trucks parked nose to tail along one side of the road. The vehicles' drivers slept in their cabs or congregated in small groups around their vehicles or on the verges. Some resting beneath them. Smoking, cooking, drinking tea. This was the habitually congested Torkham checkpoint on the Afghanistan and Pakistan border. It was a mass of convoy transportation waiting to move through the narrow customs, police and army checkpoint into Afghanistan. A snake of supply vehicles several miles long patiently waited to gain entry to feed and fuel the country, as well as the massive NATO and US war machines that occupied it. Full transports going into Afghanistan, empty ones coming out. Vehicle and aviation fuel. Fresh fruits and vegetables. Ice cream and hot dogs. Spare parts for vehicles and machinery. Sacks of corn. A line of flatbeds carried a dozen brand-new US military Humvees. All the vehicles waited for their paperwork to be verified and, in some cases, the loads checked.

Mahuba looked over his shoulder through the rear window as he had done a thousand times since leaving the Sheraghund Mountains the night before. He wasn't so much interested in what or who was behind him as in the contents of his small flatbed. The crate was still there. Tightly lashed down.

They drove past a group of burned-out fuel trucks. The result of a Taliban attack a few days before. Mahuba noted that the Taliban were finally listening to his advice. It wasn't always the case. The commanders were a stubborn lot and thought they knew everything. He'd become irritated with them of late. They'd pressed few successful attacks against US and NATO supply lines within Afghanistan and he'd been urging them to conduct more of that activity within Pakistan where there was far less security on the convoys. Sometimes none. And there were definitely no US or coalition military to chase them. He'd met stiff resistance from within Pakistan itself when he first suggested such a plan. But Mahuba had ignored it. The Pakistan military and government were full of the weak and the corrupt. And the Americans had too much control over enough of them to make things difficult.

The truth was he no longer cared about all of that. The Taliban were never going to wrest control from the Americans, the way they were going about the war. Their only chance lay in waiting until the Americans left. But that would mean the loss of their enemy and the loss of opportunity. It would be very difficult to hit the Americans once they ran home.

So things were about to change. Mahuba was going to tip the balance. But one subject always followed when he thought of his task. And that was, he would not live to see the results. He kept telling himself it didn't matter. The outcome would be in his favour. Wherever he was. But that's where his troubles lay. His faith was not as strong as it should be.

The Toyota reached the border and the Afghan servant presented their papers to the guard. As the soldier read them, he seemed unsure about something and looked over his shoulder towards an Army captain in command of the checkpoint. The captain registered the soldier's expression and beckoned him over. The guard hurried to him.

Mahuba watched the captain take a look at the paperwork and decide himself to inspect the man sitting in a Toyota pick-up truck with such important credentials. The general ignored the soldier, who looked at driver and passenger before withdrawing to examine the crate in the back. Mahuba watched him in the rear-view. The soldier came back to the cab and Mahuba sensed the man's curiosity. He turned his head to look at the captain, who saw the warning in Mahuba's eyes and thought better of it.

The captain handed the documents back to the guard, nodded to him and walked away. The guard handed the papers back to the servant and waved them through. When they arrived at the Afghan checkpoint fifty metres further on, the guards were dealing with a truck driver who seemed to be arguing because they were refusing him entry.

An officer broke away from the debate and

came over to the Toyota. The servant offered the guard a different set of papers. The soldier read the document, glanced at the crate in the back with little interest and back towards the angry truck driver, who'd begun screaming at the other guards. The officer handed the papers back to the servant and waved them through.

Mahuba and his servant headed into Afghanistan. The vast, undeveloped country lay before them. After half a mile they approached three Hilux pick-up trucks parked on the side of the road. Two of the pick-ups had mounted PKM machine guns. A dozen Afghan fighters were gathered near the vehicles and seated on the ground nearby, all armed with AK-47 rifles. Three had RPG-7 rocket launchers.

The servant pulled the Toyota over and stopped it behind the rear Hilux. The men watched without moving. One got up and walked to where he could see the new arrivals. When Mahuba climbed out, the fighter recognised him and came over to greet the general. After a brief exchange the fighter barked a command and his men climbed into their pick-ups, while Mahuba returned to his own. The fighter got into the first Hilux and it pulled away. Mahuba and his servant followed. The other two pick-ups dropped in behind Mahuba.

The road to Kabul was characterised by long, quiet stretches of barren terrain followed by sections packed with civilian fuel and supply convoys and the occasional line of military vehicles. Mahuba's little group spent much of the drive overtaking where they could to make headway.

When they reached Kabul they avoided the

main gate to the city and cut across to the Bagram road. Although it was a significant highway, it was not a great piece of engineering. And single lane for the most part, much of it potholed and lumpy. To add to that, it was hellish busy. Full, sluggish convoys headed to Bagram while empty trucks returned.

The road was significant because it was the only highway connecting a major military base with the capital. The military used it heavily. That made it relatively safe compared with many of the other roads in Afghanistan. And because it was safe, it was frequented by the Afghan police, who rarely travelled through dangerous locations if they could help it.

Mahuba grew more at ease with every mile they travelled towards Bagram. The hours to the attack were ticking away. And then, as per usual, he began to think of his own imminent death. One of the earliest questions they'd all asked in the planning stage was, who will press the button? At the time, he had been filled with the excitement of the venture. None of those involved would survive anyway. Not for long. So he'd volunteered to be the one to initiate. If the plot had been uncovered before they completed, their lives would have ended sooner, and at the hands of any one of a multitude of internal and external sources. And if they were successful, every one of them, and anyone remotely related to the operation, would be hunted down by every major intelligence organisation on the planet — except their own — until they were dead. But as time moved on he felt the urge to taste the complete meal of victory.

The suicide bomber could never be sure of his success. Mahuba wanted to know and experience the aftermath.

So he began to examine ways in which he could succeed in the mission while at the same time experiencing the full extent of the event and its subsequent effects. He wouldn't risk compromising the outcome. It had to succeed. And if the only way to achieve that was to die while ensuring its success, he would do that. Failure was not an option.

But if he could find a way to survive, if only for a short time, he would consider it. And that was the problem that constantly bugged him. He couldn't think of a way to do it.

6

Chandos walked into the loud, bustling hall of Waterloo Station, pausing to look up at the huge departures board above the platform entrances. The next train to Winchester was leaving from platform 12 in ten minutes.

He checked his pockets again to ensure he could feel his passport and the envelope of money he'd taken from the safe of his London apartment. It was all there, including his wallet. Once again his senses warned him that someone was looking directly at his back. He'd felt it a dozen times since leaving the pub where he'd met Stratton. The eyes had followed him to Trafalgar Square and watched him while he caught a taxi. Each time he tried to catch them out he saw no one obvious. There were hundreds of people milling along the pavements and now inside the train station. It was impossible. Unless they were rank amateurs, which he knew they would not be.

He'd hoped to make eye contact with whoever it was. He wanted to get some idea who to target should he find the opportunity. But also just to prove that the follower wasn't a figment of his own overactive imagination. He hadn't actually seen any evidence that he was being followed.

But he'd been in the surveillance game for too many years and knew that a talented and experienced follower would be difficult to detect.

Especially in such a crowded environment. His experience also reminded him that the crowds could be preventing the assassin from carrying out the hit just yet. If Chandos were to lead him to a quieter location where he might be able to identify the follower, it would also greatly increase his own vulnerability.

He set off across the crowded ticket hall. He contemplated carrying out some more anti-surveillance drills, manoeuvres intended to catch out a follower by surprising them. An abrupt halt and about-turn to see who was behind. Look for any reactions. A circular walk that might put the hare behind the hound. But the problem with such ploys was that once the hound knew he'd been discovered, he might act.

Which was why in most cases it was best for the hare not to do anything rash. Not let the follower know they were aware of them. It was the best course of action if the hare wanted to escape. And Chandos so desperately wanted to get away. If not, he was going to die. He was certain of that.

He passed through the ticket gate of platform 10 and headed along the busy platform. The train had just arrived, its doors were open and people were streaming out of the carriages, multiplying the throng of bodies on the platform. Chandos kept walking towards the far end of the train. He speeded up as he reached the last carriage, took off his hat, jumped down onto the track in front of the carriage and hurried across the rails. A whistle blew as a member of the railway staff saw him.

He clambered up onto the next platform. Past several people who stopped to look at him. Down onto the next set of rails. Whistles blew again. He ran to beyond the end carriage of another parked train. He climbed up onto the platform where the train was stopped, and strode along it, past several carriages that people were climbing aboard, and ducked inside one of them.

Chandos was fit for his age but he'd pushed himself hard in his brief steeplechase and breathed deeply. He stood in the carriage doorway, not wanting to take a seat just yet, resisting the urge to look outside to see if anyone was searching for him. A member of the railway staff ran past.

He stuffed his hat in his coat pocket and removed the coat entirely, folding it up and putting it on a shelf. A couple more railway staff walked by, looking in the windows and doors. Chandos picked a newspaper off the floor, took a seat and opened the pages.

One of the train guards entered the carriage and began walking along it. Chandos did his utmost to control his breathing. He took in a deep breath and held it as the man passed him. He didn't let it out until the guard had stepped back outside onto the platform. He watched him step into the next carriage.

Chandos exhaled slowly and lowered his paper to look at the people around him. No one was taking any notice. He checked his watch. If he'd timed it well enough, the doors would be closing any moment.

A whistle blew outside. If the railway staff

couldn't identify the man by the time the train was ready to leave, it would have to depart on time, Chandos figured. Seconds later he heard a loud hiss as all of the doors closed. A few seconds after that the carriage shunted hard and the train eased itself away from the platform, moving out from under the cover of the high station roof and into the city. The skies were growing dark as evening encroached. All he could think of was the follower: had he shaken them or not? It was impossible to know right then. But he wasn't relying solely on the leap between platforms. He had several moves yet to make. The next would be even more daring. And much more revealing, should his follower choose to try to keep up with him.

He put the paper down and got out of his seat. Retrieved his coat from the shelf and went to the door, where he looked through the window as far ahead as he could. A block of offices loomed. The area would do just fine. He was anxious to get going. If the assassin had got onto the train, he could be making his way along the carriages at that very moment. He could be in the next carriage. By running across the platforms Chandos had reliably informed the man that he was aware of him. The assassin might strike before he could try anything else.

He reached up for the emergency stop handle and yanked it out of its housing. A second later the train's brakes applied, the wheels screeching violently as the carriage jolted. Passengers braced for the sudden stop. All looking around. Questioning what was happening.

The train came to a hard stop. Chandos was already pressing the open button. There was a loud gush and the doors slid open slowly. People nearby looked in his direction. He jumped before the door was fully open. He landed hard on the stones between the tracks and fell onto his knees, his first thought that another train might be passing.

It was clear.

He gathered himself and leaped forward, scanning left and right as he ran, looking for anyone jumping out after him. He skipped across several tracks before reaching a low wall that marked the track boundary. He paused, breathing heavily, as he looked back along the length of the train, which curved away in both directions. No one appeared to have followed. A man stood in the open doorway that he'd leaped from. But he only watched Chandos. He wondered if it was the assassin. And if so, why wasn't he following?

Chandos didn't fancy waiting for an answer to the question. He scrambled over the low wall. The ground the other side was lower and on a steep incline. He dropped onto it, lost his footing and rolled most of the way down, winded and somewhat dizzy when he hit bottom. But within seconds he was up on his feet and pulling on his coat while hurrying down a tarmac path towards a main road.

He looked back up the incline as he passed a row of trees that blocked much of his view of the boundary to the track. There was still no sign of a follower. At the main road he stopped briefly to decide on a direction. Office buildings ran the length of the other side of the road. There was a lot of traffic. He charged out into the road. Hurried through the crawling traffic. Mounted the pavement the other side. Ran through a gap between some buildings, across a car park the other side and onto another road lined with parked cars nose to tail. He kept going up it. When he reached the next junction, he paused to look back and catch his breath.

A man came out of one of the buildings. He was wearing a business suit and headed away from Chandos. There was no one else.

Chandos felt encouraged but forced himself not to be complacent and to seek complete success for that stage of the plan. There was a long way yet to go.

He saw a taxi dropping someone off and ran across the road towards it. As the passenger walked away, Chandos pulled open the door and climbed into the back of the cab.

'Heathrow Airport, please,' he said, out of breath, as he looked back in the direction he'd come.

'That'll be around fifty quid from 'ere, mate?' the driver said.

'That's fine. I'm in a hurry, if you don't mind.'

The driver pulled the cab away from the kerb and they headed away from the junction. Chandos kept his eyes out of the rear window. No one appeared.

As the cab took another turn, Chandos relaxed just a little. He looked ahead, confident he'd shaken the assassin, for the time being at least.

He was under no illusion of escaping the killer completely. That would be impossible. He knew that. All he'd done was buy some time.

His next move was even dicier. It would throw up a flag that would signal his location. But it was essential to his overall plan. He only hoped he'd have enough time to do it.

7

Mahuba felt tired as they drove along the bumpy, busy road to Bagram. His backside ached on the lumpy seat and his shoulders felt stiff. But he'd allow nothing to slow him down or deter him from reaching the destination. A couple more hours and he'd be there.

The road began to climb and wind its way up into the hills. They passed several village compounds built on the treeless land either side of the highway, each a collection of mud houses surrounded by a single high wall. None were occupied and all had long since been abandoned.

The land in all directions was vast and open. A boundary of distant mountains paralleled the road on their left. Those on the right were out of view but Mahuba knew they were there. He could see small bands of nomads on the distant plains. Their handful of tents. Trucks and camels. Goats. The Pakistani general glanced in his rear-view mirror to see the crate still there.

Such an innocuous-looking object, he thought.

He shifted his focus to the Hilux behind, its driver and passenger in the front, three armed Afghans sitting on the flatbed. The other Hilux behind that. Another in front.

The Afghan escort had done its job well. Their presence alone was sufficient. They'd passed through two checkpoints without any problems.

The police showed no interest in them or the crate. They had paperwork listing spare parts for a generator, but it had not been needed. His escorts, all handpicked Taliban, had assumed the identity of security guards from a known convoy company that specialised in protecting vehicles along the Kabul-Bagram road. The Taliban commander was a well-known convoy commander from that company. The police didn't give his men a second look once they recognised him.

It was late afternoon when Mahuba's small convoy rolled into the town of Bagram along the central road leading to the main checkpoint into the vast US air base that sprawled less than a kilometre to the east.

Bagram Town was a tightly compact and busy place. Most of the buildings were single-storey and constructed from a combination of mud bricks and concrete blocks. The main thoroughfare was a focus of local industry, lined with filthy shacks and lean-tos providing all types of vehicle tuning, tyre repairs, welding and other sundry services. Market stalls sold sad-looking local produce, clothes and footwear. They passed stripped vehicle carcases, left where they'd broken down. Many were Russian, from the days when the Soviets dominated Afghanistan. The air was filled with the smoke from countless cooking fires, inside and outside of the dwellings.

The lead Hilux turned off the main thoroughfare and headed along a sandy road past several muddy, garbage-ridden backstreets. The US base's impenetrable perimeter could occasionally be seen from the road. A grey-brown wall of earth and razor wire. The houses each side of the road had been built close together, but as the convoy drove away from the centre they grew further apart. Half a kilometre from the town the lead vehicle came to a stop outside a large walled compound, around thirty metres wide at the front, with a set of rusting, wrought-iron gates in the middle.

The driver sounded his horn. A couple of armed Afghans sauntered into view through the gate. They unbolted it and pulled open both sides. The pick-ups drove in and the men closed and locked the gates behind them. They eased between a handful of dirty houses, scattering goats and chickens out of their way, to the back of the compound and the grandest building in comparison, about twice the size of the others. They stopped outside it and Mahuba climbed out, carrying a laptop bag and stretched his aching body while he looked around. A dozen bearded fighters were spread about, all carrying AK-47 assault rifles over their shoulders. They were a mixture of ages. Teenagers to men old enough to have seen the end of the Russian-Afghan war over two decades before. Clothes on washing lines outside the other smaller homes bore evidence of women and children living in them.

Mahuba wasn't pleased with the location. He'd asked for, and had been expecting, complete isolation. But he'd had little control over the execution of the planning in that respect. Particularly inside Afghanistan. It had been left up to third parties who weren't privy to all the details of the operation. There was no point in complaining. It would have to do. He wasn't about to start shopping around for a better house at this stage.

The guards watched him with mixed curiosity. They knew he was a Pakistani. They could tell he had breeding. Riches or rank. As to what he was doing in Bagram, they didn't have a clue. But then, they were never privy to information on anything of strategic value. Their lot in life was simply to obey. Without question. They had been ordered to protect the compound with their lives. And that is what they would do. None of them cared that they were eight hundred metres from one of the largest US military bases in Afghanistan. Ten thousand American troops. They believed the Americans would eventually be defeated and would leave their country, like every other invader had over the last few hundred years. The Afghans were in no hurry. Life was all about eating, resting, praying and fighting. That was their purpose, come rain or shine, shelter or hunger, apart for a break in the winter for some. There was no need to get excited about anything. They were energetic only when ordered to be. They measured each day by the number of prayers they made and the meals they ate. Life was simple. They would never be wealthy and none bothered as much as even to hope to be.

Mahuba walked into the main building, followed by his servant. A house boy bowed to him as he entered the lobby. He ignored the boy and walked along a short corridor and through a doorway into a spacious though nearly empty living room. It had a table and chairs, a couch and a couple of rugs, and empty walls. He went to the nearest window, its simple wooden frame locked on the inside. An iron grille had been built into the masonry outside. A glance around at the other windows revealed they were of a similar construction.

He decided it was probably perfect for what he needed. Austere felt right. All he required was solitude and security. And space to think.

He put his laptop bag on the table, then leaned heavily on the top. It felt strong. He was satisfied. It would do.

'Tea,' he said.

His servant relayed the order to the house boy who was standing in the doorway. He shoved the boy ahead of him as he led the way to the kitchen.

Mahuba went back into the hallway. An open door to one side led to a flight of stairs inside an alcove. The narrow staircase turned tightly in the small space as it led up to the next and only other level of the building. He climbed the steps and came out through an open hatch onto the flat, dusty roof. An Afghan was sitting against a semi-circle of sandbags in one corner. Leaning against the short wall of sand-filled nylon sacks was a PKM 7.62mm machine gun with an extra-long barrel. He had several boxes of ammunition close to hand.

The guard was smoking a cigarette. When he saw Mahuba he got to his feet and bowed slightly.

Mahuba walked to the edge of the roof and

looked about the town. And then he focused on the purpose of his visit.

The US air base. Its perimeter had been constructed of countless rows of grey-brown HESCO parcels — large cube-shaped wire and cloth containers filled with earth — stacked side by side and one on top of the other in a pyramid fashion to create height and depth. With razor wire spread about them like it was a WWI battlefield. Beyond them he could see rows of concrete blast walls five metres high. Watch towers had been placed at intervals along the boundary, which went off into the distance for miles. A modern makeshift fortress.

He could see only a portion of the base, it was so large. He watched a transport aircraft slowly fly out in the distance. A couple of jet fighters passed overhead. Helicopters hovered somewhere in the middle of the base. Waiting to land or having just taken off. The air seemed as busy as the ground.

The Americans didn't appear to be concerned about ground-to-air rocket attacks. Some of the aircraft were flying quite low. They had to be confident the area around the base was secure. Which it was.

That was all about to change. As the base stood, with the current weapons arrayed against it, it was largely impregnable. The security entrances would be difficult to pass through without the right credentials. Every vehicle got thoroughly searched. But none of that mattered to him and the solution he had to the problem.

Mahuba looked down at the vehicles in the

compound, in particular his pick-up. To his absolute and sudden horror several of the fighters were dragging the crate off the back of it.

'Stop!' he shouted. 'Do nothing! Leave it alone!'

He hurried back to the hatch and down the stairs. He ran out of the house and into the courtyard to find the men had obeyed him to the letter and were holding the crate half on and half off the flatbed while waiting to hear what he wanted them to do next.

Mahuba controlled himself. Realised he was overreacting. The men were doing just fine and what they believed they should be doing. There were four of them around the box, enough to carry it safely.

He took a calming breath. 'Bring it into the house,' he said. 'Carefully.'

The men eased it off the truck. It dipped a little in their hands, heavier than they had anticipated. They carried it in through the front door, along the short corridor and into the main room. Mahuba kept ahead of them and went to the sturdy table and removed his laptop.

'On here,' he said.

The men shuffled over with the crate and placed it clumsily onto the table, eager to be rid of the weight.

'Careful,' Mahuba said angrily.

They pushed it so that it was in the middle.

'Leave it alone,' he ordered. He didn't want them doing anything more to it. 'Go.'

The four men let go of the crate and left the room.

Mahuba's servant arrived with the tea and placed it on the table by the crate.

'Get me a large screwdriver or crowbar, or something to remove the wood,' Mahuba said, taking the small glass cup of tea. He sipped it. The tea was hot and sweet. It felt good. He put it down and drew the curtains across the window that directly overlooked the table.

The servant returned holding a steel pry bar.

'Go,' Mahuba said, and the servant handed him the bar and walked out, closing the door behind him.

Mahuba took a mobile phone from his pocket, selected a number from the contacts list and hit the SEND key. He waited patiently with the phone to his ear. It beeped, signalling his call had been answered.

'I have arrived,' he said.

A voice on the other end acknowledged him.

'Do the timings remain the same?'

'Yes,' the voice replied.

Mahuba disconnected the phone and put it back in his pocket. He picked up the tea and stared into space as he put the cup to his lips and drank the rest of it. After a time, he put down the empty cup and regarded the crate.

He picked up the pry bar and jammed the end into the side of the wood. Levered it. Wiggled it in further. Levered it again. The gap widened. He repeated the process around the top of the crate until the lid came up. He pushed it up, separating it from the rest of the crate.

He removed the lid and placed it on the floor. The sides came away a lot more easily with the top gone. Within a few minutes he'd exposed a black plastic moulded box. It had a hinged lid. He unclipped three latches along one side, gripped the lid and raised it up on its hinges. He let it down the other side. All of his actions had been conducted with a kind of reverence. Respect for what was inside the box.

He looked at the object. It was the shape and size of a keg of beer.

It was the first time he'd ever seen an atomic bomb. He'd studied a pamphlet on this particular kind and knew it well. It was an impact device, designed to fit into a ground-to-ground rocket, or it could be dropped from an aircraft. With a little modification, it could be detonated in a static location. To actually see it live for the first time. To be able to touch it. Such a weapon of destruction. That was remarkable.

A portion of the box was taken up by a power source. A battery. Leads connected it to the device. Essential power to keep the bomb primed. Without it the device would die in time and become inoperable.

Mahuba placed the flat of his hand on it, his fingers outstretched. He didn't need to enter the US base to destroy it. He could do that from where he was. The bomb would destroy everything within a radius of six kilometres. The radiation would reach much further. The fallout even further still, depending on the weather. Everyone in the base would die. And of course, those in Bagram Town and the outlying villages would also perish. A small price to pay.

He remembered once mentioning to one of his

ISI colleagues about his disappointment at not being able to see the outcome of the attack. He'd be able to see it from the other side of life, his colleague had replied. Mahuba had left the conversation at that point. In truth, his faith wasn't strong enough to accept advice of that nature. His planned attack on the Americans had nothing to do with Islam. It was about national pride. He believed they were plotting to destroy his people's way of life. In order to preserve that, sacrifices had to be made.

His main problem was that he couldn't put any distance between himself and the bomb between trigger and detonation. There was no timer. The bomb's current configuration allowed it to explode once the arming codes had been inserted. A delay had not been a component of the plan. He knew the rudiments of the device but certainly not enough to tamper with its con-figuration. Manual detonation was the common component in these matters. It meant the death of the operator, of course.

He unclipped a cover on the side of the bomb, as the manual had instructed, and raised the lid. Several LEDs twinkled inside. There was a keypad. All he needed to do was enter the arming codes and push a final key to align them. Then *boom*.

That's the bit he was having a problem with. He had estimated he needed half an hour at least to get out of range of the blast. That was travelling in his Toyota at top speed from the gates of the compound and not running into traffic. The prevailing winds of the day would tell him in which direction he should travel.

Buying himself that precious half-hour was the difficult part. The more he thought about it, the more he wanted to survive the explosion. It was beginning to eat away at him and become his only thought. If he truly wanted to achieve that, and he believed he did, he was going to have to come up with a plan, and soon. He didn't have a lot of time. The codes would soon arrive at the house. He needed to be able to push the button without being there. He couldn't trust anyone else to do it. They might have the same pang for survival he did. There had to be a solution. And he would spend every moment from then on thinking about it.

8

Chandos stepped out of the arrivals hall of Murtala Muhammed International airport carrying a small holdall. The air was warm. His white shirt and slacks were crumpled after the flight from London.

'You want a taxi?' a tall, young Nigerian asked him.

Another quickly came alongside him. 'Taxi?' the newcomer offered.

Two more men approached, in the hope of making a sale, all tidily dressed and presentable.

Chandos looked at their faces as they pushed their offers on him. There was always a risk factor attached to catching a taxi cold in Lagos. Kidnapping wasn't too commonplace in the port city compared with other parts of Nigeria, but that was mainly because Westerners had generally learned to organise things like transport from the airport prior to their arrival. And no pale-faced tourist in their right mind would fly to Nigeria simply to go sightseeing.

The opportunity for mishap was mostly due to crime. But there was a growing breed of Islamic sympathisers, as well as home-grown eco-terrorists, or patriots, as they preferred to be called. Either way, it was a dangerous place to turn up without prior security and transportation arrangements.

But the risks of being mugged were small potatoes to the threat he faced. Even in Nigeria, there were more locals trying to play it straight than there were those trying to be crooks. He figured the odds were in his favour. Chandos looked into the eyes of the first taxi driver who had offered his services and decided to trust him. 'Thank you,' he said. 'Lead the way.'

The man smiled appreciatively and reached for Chandos's bag. Chandos moved it to the other side of his body and raised a hand as he smiled. 'I can carry it,' he said.

The man didn't argue and they walked around the side of the terminal to a large car park surrounded by a dilapidated chain-link fence. It was full of vehicles and people. Everything had a dirty, greasy feel to it — except for the cars, most of which looked clean and shiny.

The driver opened the rear door of a sparkling sedan and Chandos climbed in, and within minutes they were heading out of the airport.

'Where to, sir?' the driver asked.

'The Sheraton,' Chandos said.

The man knew precisely where the hotel was. It was probably the most popular one for Westerners staying for short periods in the city. In the car, Chandos got to thinking about his situation. He was confident he'd lost his follower at Waterloo. But he had to assume the assassin would have picked up his departure within a few hours of him checking in at Heathrow. Maybe even sooner. He had purchased the ticket with the minimum amount of time he needed to catch the plane. That would have made it difficult for the follower to catch the same flight. Even if they had a Nigerian visa. That would take a few hours at least to acquire, even with connections. He hoped.

He happened to have a six month multi-entry visa from a previous operation that year. It was one of the reasons he'd chosen the location. He knew the city moderately well. The next commercial flight from the UK was the following day. His calculations included any combination of connecting flights from every other main hub in Europe. Short of the assassin taking a private flight, they wouldn't arrive in Lagos until tomorrow afternoon.

He had used a false name to book a room at the Sheraton, which was easy enough to get around. He had stayed at the hotel several times before. The Nigerians weren't exactly efficient when it came to bureaucracy. And if he encountered any problems, a bribe always worked.

The Sheraton might be an obvious hotel to start looking, but the assassin would still have to figure it out. Chandos hoped that by the time anyone found a trace of him it would all be over, his plan completed. He was confident of that. He had to be. It's what was keeping him going.

He sat back in the car and tried to relax. Nigeria was his best option. Because his death was going to be awkward for London to explain. That was also part of his reasoning. They might dig deeper if they were confused. Find more.

He suddenly felt unhappy, as well as doubtful. Unhappy that he was going to die. And doubtful the overall plan would succeed. He knew through his dear friend Bullfrog that Mahuba would collect and deliver the nuclear weapon. If the general had not done so already. Chandos knew the target was in Afghanistan and one of the larger US bases. Probably Bagram because it was the easiest and safest of the biggest targets to get to from Pakistan. But what had thrown the metaphorical emergency flares skywards was the discovery that someone else knew about the theft of the weapon before Mahuba did. Someone who was keeping the information secret to allow Mahuba to continue with his mission.

Chandos cursed his own stupidity. There was one other card of course. Stratton. But he had little hope for that one either. Stratton wasn't experienced enough for this kind of operation. This required manipulation and subtlety. Espionage. Investigation. Not a battering ram. He suddenly felt more hopeless than ever. The taxi drove through the security checkpoint at the entrance to the grounds of the hotel, wound its way around the front gardens and pulled up outside the main entrance.

He paid the driver and climbed out. An enthusiastic porter took his bag from the car before he could stop him and hurried into the busy hotel with it. Chandos followed at a good pace.

The lobby was spacious with a reception area and a bar on one side, and entrances to several restaurants. The place was busy. And smoky. A couple of ladies seated in the lounge area and dressed in evening wear eyed him predatorily as he walked in.

The porter had placed his bag at a reception desk around a corner. Several uniformed staff behind the counter attended to a line of guests checking in and out. He picked up the bag and joined one of the lines.

When he was through the booking process he took the elevator to the eighth floor. His room was tired and well overdue for a facelift. It smelled of cigarette smoke. He didn't particularly care. One always adjusted one's expectations to one's surroundings. The condition of the room was a low priority at that moment in time. He took his computer from his bag and set it up on a writing desk by the window. Plugged in the internet cable.

He opened his inbox and the emails streamed in. Most were standard intelligence reports from MI6. He was looking for one in particular. He found it with some relief, even though he'd been expecting it. A file was attached to the mail. He opened it. A window asked him to type in the password to the highly encrypted file. He wasn't worried about anyone stealing the file and breaking the code. No one could do that. The National Security Agency would take a hundred years or more to break the encryption.

He disconnected the internet cable. Then he clicked on the file icon and it opened in another window. It was a simple message:

BLUE CIVIC, IMPERIAL, SURULERE

He checked his watch. He'd four and a half hours to kill before picking up the car. It would take him half an hour to get to the location from the Sheraton. He scribbled the details on the hotel notepad and closed down the laptop.

Chandos was good at killing time.

He went into the bathroom and ran the bath. He poured a bottle of shampoo into it as a poor substitute for bubble bath. After an hour-long soak that included a shave, he got dressed into a clean pair of slacks and a shirt and went down to the lobby. He selected a restaurant and ate a simple meal washed down with fizzy water. He signed for the meal using his room number and then went back upstairs to get his coat and bag.

Ten minutes later he stepped outside the front of the hotel to find a taxi. The smiling doorman, in his purple uniform and gold braid epaulettes, assured him one would be along shortly.

The sun had set beyond the city. It was rapidly growing dark. Street lighting in Lagos was either poor or nonexistent. Apart from the occasional lighted building, no traffic meant darkness — but the traffic could be chaotic well into the small hours.

He watched a car drive into the hotel grounds through the well-lit main security gate. He could see it was a red sedan. He followed it not because he was particularly suspicious, it was out of habit. The car went around the circuitous route through the front gardens, but stopped fifty metres short of the hotel in the shadow of a large tree. He couldn't see inside it because whoever was driving hadn't turned off the headlights.

A taxi came through the security gate and the gardens. It passed the sedan and pulled to a stop outside the entrance. A couple of people climbed out and Chandos took their place inside the back.

'Imperial Restaurant, Surulere, please,' he said.

The driver nodded and the car pulled away. Once out of the hotel grounds, they joined the heavy traffic on the main road. Chandos turned in his seat and looked back through the rear window. The habit was getting hard to break. And also because the red sedan had niggled him a little.

His heart jumped a little at the sight of it driving out of the security gate. He stared at the car. His taxi was slowed by heavy traffic but the driver managed to edge across the three-lane highway to the far left side to make the next turn. The red sedan merged with the traffic and seemed borderline aggressive in its efforts to get into the same lane as his taxi.

Chandos couldn't believe the assassin had managed to get to Lagos so soon. Surely it wasn't possible? he asked himself. Unless they had access to a private jet. And how did they find his hotel so quickly? It was possible he was mistaken about the car. Maybe it wasn't following him and just a coincidence. He couldn't control his anxiety, though. He was so close to his goal. But if it was the assassin following him, he had every chance of failing.

The taxi took a left at the next set of lights and accelerated easily down the road. Chandos kept his eyes out the rear window the whole time. The sedan was four or five cars back. Several of the cars also took the turn. The majority of the traffic was going straight on. The lights changed.

But a car made the turn. It was the red sedan. He fought to keep calm.

He had evaded the assassin before and he could do it again. He needed less than an hour. He had to get to the restaurant and then to the car that was waiting for him. The taxi took another turn. Two of the cars behind followed, the rear one the red sedan. Chandos could no longer try and convince himself he wasn't being followed.

'How far to the restaurant?' he asked the driver.

'Ten minutes, sah,' the man replied cheerfully.

Chandos reached into his pocket, pulled out his wallet and held a note over the seat so that the driver could see it. 'Here's a hundred dollars. I'm being followed by a red car. If you lose him, I'll give you another hundred at the restaurant.'

The driver pocketed the note and looked into his rear-view to find the red sedan. He was up for it. His foot hit the floor and the car shot forward, throwing Chandos back into the seat. The taxi swerved out into oncoming traffic to overtake the car in front. Despite a van bearing down on them along the narrow road, the driver's ambitions extended to the next car and the one in front of that. He swerved the taxi back into lane, tightly between the cars as the oncoming van screeched and swerved to avoid a collision. Horns blared. The van driver had screamed something. Chandos looked at the taxi driver in the rear-view. Judging by his expression, he'd frightened himself. But he recovered quickly to take the car in front. It was still game on.

Chandos looked back for the sedan. After a few seconds, five cars back, he saw the nose of the vehicle pull out to overtake. But there were too many cars heading towards it and it cut back in.

The taxi driver had an eye in his rear-view and knew he had not yet succeeded in shaking the sedan. He suddenly swerved the car violently to the right and into a side street. His turn was a touch early and the rear nearside wheel bounced over the kerb, throwing Chandos across his seat. The driver accelerated the car hard down the road and in no time at all they were doing 80 mph along a short stretch of residential street with cars parked on both sides. As they approached the end of the road, the driver braked hard and turned left, the tyres screeching violently. Chandos saw a hubcap go flying off into a parked car and bouncing over it.

'Can you pay for the hubcap, sah?' the driver called out.

'Yes. Go!' Chandos shouted as he looked back in time to see a pair of headlights turn into the side road. He couldn't tell if it was the red sedan but it had to be.

There were several more hard accelerations through suburban streets followed by equally hard braking and violent turns. Another hubcap was sacrificed during that period. The driver conducted a series of perilous overtakes and one particularly nerve-wrenching journey the wrong way down a narrow one-way street, where he forced a cyclist off his bike.

The taxi driver abruptly pulled the car to a halt and turned in his seat with a broad grin. Chandos had been hanging onto the seat belts like a charioteer and was surprised by the sudden stop.

'We're here, sah.'

Chandos looked out of the window to see the Chinese restaurant and the entrance to its car park. He looked back through the rear window to see the street behind empty. He thrust the second hundred-dollar bill into the man's hand. 'Well done. Can you keep it up for a few more streets? Here's another hundred for that, and another for the hubcaps.'

'Yes, sah,' the driver said, taking the money and then gripping the wheel as he waited for Chandos to get out. Chandos grabbed his bag, quickly climbed out of the taxi and slammed the door shut. The vehicle's wheels screeched as the driver hit the gas and the car pulled off down the street.

Chandos hurried to the restaurant and went inside. He walked through the dining room, nodding hello to the hostess, and went out the other side and into the car park. He didn't want to wait and see if the red sedan passed the restaurant. If he could see it, someone inside might see him. It was best to press on to his next objective.

It was immediately obvious why the place had been chosen. The car park had armed security to protect its customers from being mugged as they walked to their vehicles. He spotted the blue Honda Civic easily enough and walked over to it and reached under the front nearside fender. The keys were on the wheel.

He opened the driver's door and climbed in, closing the door. There was no time to recover from the taxi ride. He reached into the passenger footwell and found a backpack. He pulled it out. Placed it on the seat. Opened it.

The first thing he saw was the barrel of a gun. He looked around outside. The security guard was thirty metres away, standing by the entrance. Another guard stood in the middle of the car park, looking towards the entrance. Neither was paying Chandos any attention.

He removed the weapon, a submachine gun. An old Sterling, in fact. He hadn't seen one of those in thirty-five years. It looked in good nick, with an extension he had not seen before. A suppressor. It wouldn't make the weapon completely silent but it would be much quieter than normal. There were three full magazines, each holding thirty rounds. He put them to one side.

He pulled out an envelope. Inside it were some instructions and directions to two places. One was in the city, the other at the docks. The latter included the name of a ship and its captain. The last item was a plastic bundle secured by tape. Firm. Heavy. A metre-long tail coming from it. A fuse. A lighter had been conveniently taped to the bag.

He took a closer look at the directions to the address, which included a diagram of a street. A house had been highlighted. Bullfrog had delivered everything he'd asked for. He felt a sudden pang of nerves at the prospect of what he was about to do. He hadn't done a job anywhere near as audacious as this in his career. But then again, he'd been an officer. The men did all that sort of stuff. Planning it was one thing. Doing it was something completely different. He believed he was up to the task, but he lacked the real experience. This was right up Stratton's street, he thought. He told himself just to think like him.

A knock on the window almost gave him a heart attack. Chandos snapped his head round to look through the glass, as he shoved the bundle back into the backpack.

It was one of the security guards. Grinning at him.

Chandos wound down the window.

'Are you OK, sah?' the man asked.

'Yes. Fine, thanks.'

'Are you having a trouble starting your car?' The guard was still smiling, his grin seemed to be a fixture.

'No. I'm just leaving. Thanks very much,' Chandos said, making an effort to smile broadly back at him.

'OK, sah. If you have trouble starting your car, just let me know and I will help you.'

'You're very kind. Thank you.'

Chandos wound up the window and shoved the key into the ignition. He turned it and the engine fired. It sounded in good condition. He looked for the guard, who was already behind the vehicle and waving for him to reverse.

He followed the man's directions and then headed for the exit, where the other guard raised the barrier and waved him farewell. He returned the wave and turned out of the car park and onto the road, immediately looking into the rear-view mirror. He saw some kind of vehicle far down the street. It was stopped. He couldn't identify its colour in the poor light. He accelerated away to a junction.

He turned the corner to join a line of slow-moving traffic. He looked back for the car again. It didn't appear to be moving. Maybe it wasn't the red sedan. As he drove he looked in every direction for signs of the car. He couldn't see any. He exhaled deeply and sat back. Told himself to relax. He was towards the next and penultimate phase. He needed to compose himself.

His thoughts went to Stratton again. Would his old protégé pick up the baton and run with it? He hoped he would. But he couldn't be sure, of course. Stratton would quickly get an inkling as to how dangerous a game it was. The problem would be for him to find a good enough reason to risk his life. It wouldn't be an official mission. He would have little or no support. And probably no thanks for his efforts if he were to die trying. It might even be the opposite. Chandos wondered if, in Stratton's position, he'd do it, based on what he knew and his experience of the game. He didn't think he would. The thought didn't make him feel any better. But there was always Bullfrog. Bullfrog would work some charm on Stratton.

He consulted the map and checked the street ahead. A kilometre to go. The street he was in was bustling. There were more people on the road than vehicles, crossing and walking down the sides, flitting through the headlights, selling and begging to the slow-moving traffic. Everything was grimy, the buildings dirty and poorly constructed. He saw several fires either side of the street, used for cooking or providing warmth for the homeless. The people were poorly dressed, in dirty clothes, yet most looked as if they had places to be. Those who noticed Chandos gave him a double take. A white driver in Lagos was not unheard of, although it was unusual. But a white man always had money. And white people were usually buyers of whatever they were selling. Crap, most of it, thought Chandos. Bought out of fear or charity. He wished the car had tinted glass.

He saw a break in the traffic, pulled into the gap and turned down a side street. Five minutes later he was driving through a quiet, dark neighbourhood and slowing as he made his way along a deserted street. There were few lights on in the dwellings. Cables, electrical or phone wires, hung in tangled bunches, sometimes hanging down between them. He was looking for a particular house.

He watched a couple of men walk down the street. Talking together. They paid his car no attention. There were a few cars parked. All were dirty. Battered. Chandos pulled in behind one of them and killed the motor.

He sat still. The street was mostly silent. A sound now and then. A howl from somewhere. He looked over at a large detached house across the road, bigger than the others. Alleyways running down both sides. Lights were on in some of the windows. He saw movement past a window in an upstairs room.

He wound down the window to hear better and got a nose full of rotting garbage. It smelled like sewage. The warm stinking air felt thick enough to cut with a knife. He could pick out sounds in the mixture. Music, distant traffic, car horns. A cry went up somewhere. Or perhaps it was laughter.

Chandos checked the description of the house once again. The location was right. It was the one. An Islamic headquarters. An al-Qaeda operations cell in the heart of Lagos. It was ideal. Precisely what he wanted. He removed his jacket and put it on the back seat. He took his laptop from his bag. There was evidence on it that experts might find. The rest he'd leave. Especially his passport and return air ticket to London. That had to be found. He climbed out of the car with the laptop and looked up and down the street. A couple of people were walking along the pavement from the far end towards him. They seemed innocent enough.

He closed the door and went to the sidewalk. There was an opening into a storm drain beneath the pavement. Grey, stinking water flowed down the side of the road and into it. He crouched down and pushed the laptop into the opening. When he let it go, it fell into the drain and out of sight. It would only be found if they dug up the pavement. But it would be unreadable within minutes.

He opened the Civic's passenger door and

took out the backpack. Pulled it onto his back. He tucked two of the machine-gun magazines into his pockets and held the gun in his hand. Memories of holding such a weapon all those years ago came back to him. The Sterling was one of the first weapons he'd ever fired as a Royal Marine officer recruit. At that time it had been nothing more than an introduction to various weapons in use in the regular Marines. A familiarisation with a basic weapon built during the Second World War that little could go wrong with.

He eased back the breech against its large, heavy spring and locked it into place with a clunk. He took one of the curved magazines and eased it into its housing. It clicked home. He tugged on it to be sure it was firmly in place. He didn't apply the safety catch, and placed his trigger finger along the guard. It was ready to fire at a touch. There was nothing safe about what he was about to do.

His confidence came back a little. He needed one more look at the diagram of the house. The sketch was plain enough. There were three floors. He compared the building with the sketch. It was correct. He wouldn't need to bother with the upper floors. Just the ground floor. The hallway and corridor. The stairs at the end leading down to a cellar. That would be it. Job done.

He stuffed the sketch in his pocket and crossed the road, looking left and right. The people who'd been walking along the street in his direction weren't far away now. Still walking. Two young men, locals probably.

Chandos stopped to watch them. More importantly, he wanted them to see him. They looked at him, suddenly shocked. It was probably the first time they had seen a white man in this neighbourhood. Then they saw the machine gun he was holding. They stalled, then moved on more quickly, their eyes remaining on Chandos as they hurried past. They carried on down the street without slowing down. A white man in this part of town was vulnerable, a gift to muggers, an easy victim. But a white man with a gun in his hands was all bad news. He was either fearless or insane.

Chandos turned back to the house and walked towards it, reaching the front steps — half a dozen of them leading to a wooden door in need of a paint job. Headlights flashed across the house, startling him. He looked around. A car had turned into the street, its headlights on full beam. It pulled to halt at the corner, about eighty metres away. Its lights went out seconds later. The doors didn't open.

Chandos stared at it, squinting in an effort to see the car better in the low light, and see inside. The light was so poor he couldn't accurately tell its colour. It could have been red.

'Jesus Christ,' he muttered. The more he concentrated on it, the more the car began to look red. How was it possible? If it was the assassin, how could he possibly know where to find Chandos?

Then it came to him.

Of course. A tracker. It had to be. It was the only way. His bag. His clothes.

But then, if the assassin had got close enough

to place a tracker on him, why hadn't he killed him? No matter, Chandos decided. This was the end of the road. The assassin wouldn't get to him before he went in the house. And if he wanted to follow, he was more than welcome. Chandos skipped up the steps to the door. A quick glance back at the car revealed the doors still closed.

He reached for the handle. Turned it and pushed a little. It opened. The arrogance of the bastards. No guards, no surveillance, no lock on the door. It would be their undoing. Sounds seeped through to him from inside. He pushed the door open wide enough to step in. A dim light glowed at the far end of the corridor. He closed the door behind him quietly and looked for a lock. There was a key in the door. He turned it and heard the gentle clunk as the bolt slid into position.

Sounds came from above and along the corridor. Music and voices. There were four doors on either side. One at the far end that he knew led down to the cellar. That's where he was headed. He levelled the machine gun, pointing the barrel straight ahead. He took a step forward and the floorboard groaned, making him pause. Bugger it, he said to himself. He put all his weight on it and it creaked loudly. He moved forward another step. The next one creaked just as loudly.

The sound of footsteps on a wooden floor came from his right. Inside a room. Someone was coming to the door just ahead of him. He aimed the gun at the door as it opened. A man stood there, his eyes wide at the sight of Chandos and the gun pointing at him. Chandos didn't hesitate. Everyone in the building was dross, al-Qaeda scum. Killers of the innocent for their own Neanderthal reasons. Nine/eleven back at you.

He pulled the trigger. He heard a heavy clunk a millisecond before bullets spat from the end of the suppressor. Sparks and flashes. The loudest sound was the metal breech block repeatedly hitting the breech face. He had aimed for the centre of the man's mass when he fired. The natural pull of the weapon caused the barrel to rise up and to the right. The first bullet went into his stomach and then diagonally up to his left shoulder, six inches apart. Chandos released the trigger and the weapon ceased.

The man dropped back to the floor, dead when he hit it. A shout came from inside the room, a woman's shout, more like a scream. Chandos stepped quickly into the doorway and saw two more men and a woman, one of the men getting to his feet. The other two sat on a couch. He didn't distinguish between male and female. That was a bygone age of chivalry. He squeezed the trigger. Rounds flew into them, starting from the man on the left, through the man on the couch and into the woman. Chandos didn't release the trigger, and brought the weapon back to the left to hit all of them again. The man on his feet dropped to the floor. The others went instantly limp. All were dead. The weapon went silent. The magazine had run out of bullets.

He tried to pull the magazine out but it

wouldn't release. He began to panic, then realised he wasn't pushing down the release button hard enough. He pushed it forcefully and the magazine popped out and fell from his hand to clatter across the hallway floor. He ripped another from his pocket and slammed it home. Snatched back the breech block and quickly aimed along the corridor, ready once again. His jaw clenched. 'Come on, scum,' he muttered. 'I'm starting to like this.'

No one was coming. He moved along the corridor to the cellar door at the end, passing a flight of stairs that led to the floors above. The cellar door was wide open. Stairs led down into darkness. He looked up the stairs, also in darkness. Sounds filtered down. Voices. A TV perhaps. His information had warned that there could be as many as thirty people in the house at any one time. Possibly more.

The sound of movement came from above. A creak. Maybe on the stairs. He stepped through the cellar doorway and went down into darkness. The stairs were made of concrete and were soundless. He put a hand out in front of him, afraid of banging his head. The hand found a wall. The stairs turned a corner. He touched another surface — a door. Halfway down he found a handle, turned it. The door opened. He felt around the sides near the frame and found a switch. He flicked it down and a red bulb glowed instantly inside the room.

It was a storeroom. Lots of boxes with black stencilled lettering. Some were open. Weapons were everywhere, some wrapped in grease paper.

Boxes of hand grenades, rocket-propelled grenades, mortar shells, belts of linked machine-gun bullets, and plastic explosives. Stacks of C4. Exactly what he wanted. Also bags of fertiliser and gallons of diesel fuel. Enough to manufacture thousands of pounds of Anfo — low explosives. It was the mother lode.

Chandos put down the weapon, removed his backpack and opened the top. He pulled out the plastic lump with the long fuse, ripped off the lighter and ignited a flame. He touched it to the end of the fuse. The fuse crackled to life. He checked his watch. The second hand was at the top of the hour. He didn't know too much about explosives but all members of the SBS had carried out a basic course on the subject. He guessed that the fuse gave him about a minute before it would burn down to the detonator and ignite it. Which in turn would set off the explosives. And which in turn would detonate the contents of the room. He had seen the devastation caused by a 500kg bomb. There must have been two or three times that amount in this room. It would be hard to imagine any of the building left standing after the explosion.

He put the bundle on top of the stack of plastic explosives. Picked up his gun and looked up the stairs. He thought he could hear voices above the sizzle of the burning fuse. He gripped the weapon and made his way up. As he neared the top, a figure passed the cellar door. Whoever it was had not paused to look down the stairs.

He stepped through the doorway into the

corridor. Movement to his right. He swivelled and saw a man and fired. Several rounds hit him in his chest and he fell back, a pistol clattering from his dead hand onto the floor. Chandos turned towards the back door at the opposite end of the corridor from where he'd entered the building. His exit, hopefully. People started coming down the stairs. He fired up at them, spraying the walls and the stairs. He heard a shriek. Someone fired a gun down at him, the sound deafening.

He headed for the back door, but as he grabbed the handle, a crashing sound came from behind. He turned to see the front door burst open. A figure stood in the doorway. All he could do was stare at it. The bomb had only seconds left. He pulled the back door and the wind rushed in, forcing it wide open.

His eyes remained on the front door. The figure held a gun. Was raising it up, aiming at him. Then suddenly a man landed in the corridor between them, a gun in his hand. He must have jumped down the stairs. Bad timing. As he raised the gun a silent bullet hit the back of his head and came out his eye. The man fell forward and Chandos turned to dive out of the building. He was halfway through the door when the burning fuse reached the detonator.

The explosion was enormous. Staggering. The crack and boom like thunder. The poorly constructed wood and brick building shattered into millions of pieces. The guts of it went skyward. The roof and every wall, floor, stair and stick of furniture disintegrated. Thirty-eight

Nigerians were ripped to shreds instantly or sent into the night sky.

The houses either side also got smashed and levelled. Every pane of glass within hundreds of metres was shattered. The shockwave blew in doors and smashed the windows of vehicles in the street, filling the sky with debris for a kilometre upwards. When it came back down, it struck vehicles and roofs blocks away. The raining debris lasted several minutes as the lighter objects floated to earth.

The explosion was heard across much of the city. When it subsided, a huge crater filled with shattered wood and rubble occupied the space where the house used to be. A fire burned.

It was morning before the first emergency services arrived at the scene. That was due to the fact that once the address was known the police were afraid to investigate for fear the explosion was the start of some wild attack by the Islamic revolutionaries. They wouldn't approach the site until the Army had been brought in to support them.

The building wreckage was still smoking when the sun came up. There had been several injuries in the neighbourhood. The serious ones had been taken to the nearest hospital by friends or relatives. What was left of the destroyed house had already been looted by scavengers, young and old. Anything of value had been taken. Not that there had been much left.

Once people realised that the house had been occupied by a good number of the terrorist gang when the detonation occurred, many concluded that the incident had been an own goal. Clearly an accident. However, a couple of witnesses came forward later in the day stating that they'd seen an armed white man outside the house not long before the explosion.

That piece of information significantly disrupted the earlier conclusions. But since no one could find any evidence of any nationalities killed in the blast besides Nigerians, it was placed to one side. A white man outside the house minutes before sounded odd, to be sure. But it didn't necessarily mean he was responsible for what had happened.

The Blue Honda Civic, badly damaged and half buried, was eventually examined and the holdall and weapons bag retrieved. The British were invited to examine the evidence. Scotland Yard sent their findings to the Ministry of Defence. It included evidence of explosives in the small backpack.

The Nigerian government never received any details of the man they knew only as Berry Chandos who had entered their country that day and several hours later was last seen armed in the immediate vicinity of an Islamic fundamentalist headquarters that was blown to smithereens.

They found no evidence of a second white man.

9

Stratton, in workout gear, ran hard along a residential East London Docklands street, turned a corner into a road lined with apartment blocks of various sizes and went in through the entrance to one of them.

He jogged up a flight of stairs, reached a front door on the fourth floor out of breath, and supported himself with his hands on his knees while inhaling deeply. He took a key from his shorts, opened the door and entered the hallway, closing the door behind him. He switched on the TV, before getting down onto his back on the carpeted floor and proceeding to do some sit-ups.

The news channel was playing a report about an alleged missing Pakistani atomic weapon. The Americans were accusing the Pakistan military of failing to report a missing nuclear weapon. The Pakistan military were insisting that no such incident had occurred and that the Americans had created the story to discredit Pakistan and its military.

Stratton had little interest in the news, as per usual. He received daily international intelligence updates by email produced by military intelligence analysts. The reports included conflict analysis, as well as general governance news. The more salient points. The only interest he had in televised news reports was the occasional video coverage. The media tended to get their hands on eyewitness material before intelligence organisations could.

He stretched his hamstrings and lower back, carried out a series of tension releases and took a moment to relax and clear his head. He sat up to look out of a ceiling-to-floor window. He watched an old wooden boat head slowly along the Thames, its sails puffed out by the wind. It must have been a couple of hundred years old, Stratton thought. Majestic. He fancied the idea of spending a few weeks on board something like that. Working hard, purely for the fun of it. He wondered when he would ever have the time for such things.

He went into the small, modern and well-equipped kitchen to make himself a cup of tea. The apartment was owned by the Ministry of Defence, for the purpose of temporarily housing members of military intelligence and other short-term visitors to the city. As essentially a non-commissioned member of the Special Boat Service, based in Poole, Dorset, Stratton wouldn't have qualified to use such lavish premises — but he was also a part-time Secret Intelligence Service operative. It was one of the rare perks of the business. This particular apartment, which was quite luxurious and in an expensive area, was far above his SIS pay grade too. It was supposed to be for the use of the equivalent rank of colonel and above only. But the old Army quartermaster responsible for running and maintaining the MoD apartments in the city had a bit of a soft spot for Stratton. From their first meeting Stratton treated the old boy kindly and with respect. And therefore he was always assured plum accommodation whenever he stayed in London, if one was available.

He had arrived in the city for an MI6 communications and coding refresher course. It had been a good excuse to get out of Poole after his tour of Afghanistan. There had been nothing much going on after the hamlet-clearing operation. On completion of the comms course he was looking forward to taking some leave. But he hadn't been able to get his old boss off his mind. Most frustrating was not being able to get in contact with him. Stratton wanted to know how he was getting on. It had been less than two days since their meeting. Obviously, if Chandos was concerned about an assassin monitoring him, he was unlikely to have an open line of communication with anyone.

Stratton stirred his tea. He took a sip as he tried to put Chandos out of his thoughts. Burns had recommended him for leave after the op. It would be nice to take a girlfriend somewhere. But there was a minor problem with that idea. He didn't have one. No old flame came to mind who he might call either.

He went into the bedroom to get out of his PT kit and take a shower. As he reached to turn on the shower, he heard a faint beep come from his laptop which he'd left open on the living room table. He chose to ignore it for the moment. If the SIS or SBS wanted him urgently, they would call or send a coded pin message to his mobile phone. That was a tone he'd usually respond to right away.

Ten minutes later, he stepped from the bedroom wearing a shirt and a pair of casual trousers and returned the empty mug to the kitchen. The TV in the living room had changed from news to sports and he paused to watch an excerpt from a recent rugby game. His computer on the desk gave a reminder beep. It was a distraction he couldn't ignore for long.

He went over to it and touched a key to bring the screen to life. The subject message to the email window was profound and to the point.

CHANDOS DEAD

He didn't recognise the email address. Stunned, he tapped a key to open it. A message appeared: DOWNLOAD Z-CRYPT SOFTWARE — OPEN Z-CRYPT FILE IN SECURE, OFFLINE ENVIRONMENT. There was an attachment. Its extension showed it was a Z-Crypt file. Whoever sent it didn't want to risk it being read by anyone else.

His secure memory stick was on the desk and he plugged it into the computer and typed in the password. He accessed the browser and found the Z-Crypt software. He downloaded it. The secure stick allowed him to access any internet site and read the data without leaving a trace on his laptop.

He looked at the message again as the software installed itself and wondered who could possibly have sent it. The software opened and invited him to select a file. But there was no password on the message. He examined it again, wondering if he had missed something, and the laptop pinged again.

Another email from the same sender. He opened it but all it contained was a series of numbers, letters and symbols. The missing password, Stratton presumed.

He copied it into the password window and hit enter. The attachment promptly opened. It was a letter addressed to him. He sat down in front of the computer as he read it.

I KNOW MUCH OF THE CIRCUMSTANCES THAT LED TO OUR FRIEND'S DEATH, THE ONES THE AUTHORITIES WILL NEVER FIND. THEY REMAIN A GREAT CONCERN. ANYONE WHO INTERFERES RISKS FALLING UNDER THE GAZE OF THOSE WHO SANCTIONED HIS DEATH. IF YOU WISH TO KNOW MORE I AM PREPARED TO MEET WITH YOU. BUT TELL ME THIS: WHAT WAS CHANDOS'S FIRST COMPLAINT ABOUT YOU?

PLEASE DESTROY THIS LETTER AND THE EMAILS ASSOCIATED WITH IT IMMEDIATELY.

BULLFROG

Bullfrog. The codename Chandos had given to him regarding a trusted friend. Stratton sat back, shocked by what appeared to be confirmation of Chandos's death. There was every possibility that it was misinformation. But he suspected he was clinging to a false hope.

He wondered how the man had died. Until he heard otherwise, he would assume Chandos had been killed by the assassin. He looked at the email again. The address and details. He wondered if the invitation was a trap of some kind. Perhaps it was from those behind Chandos's death, cleaning up anyone he was associated with. If they were so smart, they would have known he had met with Stratton that day in the pub. But then, why would they want Stratton out of the way? Chandos had told him nothing of any significance.

And the messenger asked for a proof-of-life question to which only Chandos would know the answer and who had supposedly told them. Stratton asked himself why he would actually want to get involved in any of this. Much as he had admired Chandos, he didn't want to risk his own life for something that was of great importance to his former boss but not him.

He looked out across the Thames. The river had turned dark-grey, reflecting the clouds that were gathering. To walk away and show no interest in the cause of Chandos's death was not something he could easily do. He wondered if there was anyone he could confide in. Hand it over to. There would be an investigation into Chandos's death. Stratton was not an investigator. Furthermore, if the assassin was real, then Stratton would be well out of his depth. As indeed Chandos had been.

He couldn't think of anyone he personally knew and could trust who was qualified enough to investigate the incident. And even if he could have, he'd precious little to hand over to them anyway. He wondered who this Bullfrog character was. If Chandos died as a result of what he knew, why was Bullfrog still alive? He apparently knew the same things. Whoever killed Chandos possibly didn't know about Bullfrog. Despite himself, Stratton was intrigued by it all.

But not quite enough to get involved. He deleted the emails and the Z-Crypt file and password and ensured there were no further traces of them. He opened the saved addresses file. In it was Bullfrog's. It was the only way he could reply to the curious individual. His finger hovered over the DELETE key.

He couldn't push down the key.

He started to close the laptop but was unable to do that either. He couldn't turn his back on Chandos. Not as coldly as that. He had to find out more at least. Once he had all the available information he could decide what to do. He owed Chandos that much. Meeting with this Bullfrog character wouldn't commit him to anything. If Bullfrog wasn't a target of those who had killed Chandos, Stratton could expect a meeting between them to be safe. There were holes in the logic. But then he could hypothesise all day.

He initiated an email addressed to Bullfrog. CHANDOS COMPLAINED I WAS A SCRUFFY BASTARD ON THE PARADE GROUND.

He sent it, got to his feet and walked to the window. He tried to remember what it was he had been thinking about prior to the email. It came to him. His vacation. An idyllic Mediterranean fishing village. A pretty girl beside him. The image was becoming blurred, though. Interference from his sudden sense of obligation.

His laptop beeped again.

He walked over and looked at the screen. Another encrypted attachment. The message said, SAME PASSWORD. He sat down and opened the file through his secure memory stick.

THE CHESTERFIELD HOTEL. MAYFAIR. 1400. AT RECEPTION YOU WILL USE THE NAME MR BOUYANC AND ASK FOR A KEY TO YOUR ROOM.

There was no date. That meant today. Stratton looked at his watch. It was almost midday. This Bullfrog was keen. That suited him — he was due to return to Poole that evening. He could get the meeting out of the way and be home for the evening. With luck he could be packing a bag that night and heading for an airport to somewhere the following day.

Think positively, he told himself. He couldn't get involved in anything to do with whatever Chandos was into. That was pretty obvious. But he still couldn't accurately recall the image he'd had of the idyllic Mediterranean village.

10

Stratton took the Underground into the centre of the city and got off at Hyde Park Corner. He walked past Wellington's old house and along Park Lane in the direction of the Dorchester Hotel. Before he reached it, he turned into the backstreets of Mayfair. A few blocks later he arrived at the Chesterfield Hotel. It was a tastefully appointed Victorian structure with an attractive frontage.

He walked into the lobby and to the reception desk. A portly lady in a smart uniform jacket looked up at him from her paperwork. Her professional expression hinted at a smile — she asked how she could be of help.

'Mr Buoyanc,' he said. 'I'd like a key to my room, please.'

She checked her register and then took a key card from a box, programmed it in a machine and handed it to him. He looked at it. There was no indication of the room number. He looked at her.

She seemed unsure why. 'Room twenty-seven,' she said, hoping that was the answer to his look.

'Yes,' he replied, as if it hadn't been the reason he'd glanced at her. 'Thanks.'

He made his way through a sitting room towards the elevators. Before he reached them he stopped, turned around and looked back at the entrance. He had instinctively carried out a fundamental anti-surveillance procedure intended to reveal if anyone was behind him.

There were four people in his immediate view. He discounted three quickly as potential monitors: one was sitting in a chair sipping a cup of tea, a pot and several sandwiches on a small table in front of her — she would have had to know he was coming. Another was a doorman entering the hotel with a suitcase — that would have to have been planned too, and way ahead of his visit. The other was a waiter passing through the sitting room — as before, implausible. The fourth person was a man who had just walked into the hotel — a possibility. The man was walking directly to the reception desk without as much as a glance in Stratton's direction. He spoke briefly to the receptionist, who handed him an envelope. At that moment the man looked towards a lady coming out of the restaurant, beamed a smile. They embraced lovingly and went into the restaurant together.

Stratton wasn't sure why he had carried out the drill. It was the sort of thing he did automatically on operations, but in his head he was practically in rest mode. Or at least trying to be. It was evidence, if he needed it, that he was starting to get edgy about the whole thing.

He walked into an open elevator and pushed the button. The doors closed and a few moments later opened on the second floor and he stepped into a plush corridor, which was quiet and empty. The thick-pile carpeting silenced his footsteps as he walked along it.

He arrived at room twenty-seven and placed

the key card in the slot. A small green light flickered and he pushed down the handle, opening the door.

He remained in the doorway at first, half-expecting someone to be in the room. The instructions had been brief. Then he stepped inside, closed the door and remained where he was as he surveyed the room. It was expensively furnished in an antique style. A bed, desk, armchair, television. But no person. No Bullfrog.

Everything had been so precise. The coding, the timings, the key waiting for him. He told himself to be patient, the meeting would happen. He walked into the room and sat in the armchair, waiting in silence. The place was really quiet, the passing vehicles outside near silent.

He checked his watch. Bullfrog was six minutes late. He asked himself how long he would give it before leaving. Ten more minutes would be good enough, he decided. A sound came from the far corner of the room. A click. His eyes shot to a door near the window. It must lead to an adjoining room. Another click. It was being unlocked from the other side.

The handle turned and the door began to open. A figure stepped into the room — a woman wearing a formal business jacket and matching skirt. She looked to be in her fifties, hair short and red. She wore a little too much makeup. Stratton suspected she would have been attractive in her younger days.

She smiled slightly. It broadened her narrow face. Her mouth was big. She looked intelligent but tired.

'John Stratton,' she said, taking a step into the room and remaining there, keeping the adjoining door open.

He got to his feet and crossed over to her, offering his hand. 'That's right,' he said. She didn't appear remotely threatening. In fact she had a pleasant, welcoming look about her.

'I've heard a lot about you for many years,' she said, taking his hand. She held his fingers lightly for a few seconds without shaking them. 'It's a pleasure finally to meet you.'

She had a strong Russian accent, but otherwise her English sounded perfect. Stratton said nothing else. He was waiting for a name, her codename in particular, or proof that she had sent the email.

'I'm Bullfrog,' she said. 'A nickname. A private codename from Berry.' She pronounced his name softly. As if the taste of the word invoked fond memories.

'You knew him? I mean, personally?' Stratton asked.

'Yes. Will you come next door please?'

She walked back through the adjoining door and Stratton followed, closing the door behind him. The room smelled of fresh cigarette smoke. She waited for him to move out of the way before locking the door.

'These rooms are used for private meetings,' she said. 'The room you were in is for examination. Once the attendees have been swept and examined for any kind of recording or monitoring device, they come in here. There are no monitoring devices of any kind in this room.

119

The sensors indicated you have a phone on you.'

'Yes,' he said, taking it out of his pocket.

'Remove the battery please.'

Stratton did so and placed it on the dresser.

'You have no transmitting devices on you, but it's very difficult to detect electronic passive recording devices that can be downloaded afterwards. You have three coins in your breast pocket.'

He removed his wallet from inside his jacket and opened it to reveal the money.

She took the coins and dropped them into a glass of water.

'It's not you I don't trust, Mr Stratton. Someone could have placed them on you to retrieve them later. Your watch please.'

He removed his watch. She took it and held it over the glass. 'I take it your watch is waterproof,' she said with a thin smile.

He nodded. She put it in the glass, which she then covered with what appeared to be a tea cosy. A sound-proofer.

'Please sit down,' she said.

He sat in the armchair, taking a quick look around. The room was just like the other one.

'Would you like a drink? Some water?'

'No thanks.'

She remained standing, took a cigarette from a pack and a lighter off the table. 'I hope you don't mind.'

'No.'

She lit the cigarette and stood at the window as if contemplating what she was going to say. 'I work for the FSB,' she began. 'Berry suggested

I tell you a little of my past and how he and I met. Is that of interest to you?'

'Very much,' Stratton said. He wondered if she might shine some light on Chandos's lost years after he left the Service.

'I started my service life in the Army and a few years later I joined the Spetsnaz. You've worked with them, I understand.'

'I wouldn't exactly say *with* them,' Stratton said.

'Of course.' She smiled. 'I was one of the handful of female operatives in my division at that time. I did a lot of surveillance work. Mostly in Moscow. Have you been there?'

'Once or twice,' he said.

'It was interesting in those days,' she said. 'In particular the relationships we had with the Americans. Some of those relationships among the senior members of both countries were truly special. Many people remained close after the Berlin wall came down. When that happened, a number of powerful KGB men moved into the private sector. It wasn't that they didn't approve of the new capitalist order. Or of the FSB. On the contrary. Most of them thoroughly embraced all of the changes. Why shouldn't they? With Russia turning to capitalism, there was much more wealth — and power — to be had in the private sector.

'I first met Berry Chandos in a hotel bar in the city not long after the wall came down,' she went on. 'By then I was an apprentice handler in the FSB.' She paused as if waiting for Stratton to contradict her, but he didn't move. 'It wasn't a set-up. It was natural. We didn't know anything about each other. I allowed myself to be consumed by him.

'But I had to report the relationship. The usual investigations were made. When I read his profile I was not too surprised to discover he was MI6. The next time we met I confronted him. I told him I was a member of the FSB. He had not known. He had not yet reported me as he was supposed to. He was still much more of a soldier than he was an agent. A risk-taker. To my surprise my boss allowed me to continue seeing him. Perhaps he thought I might recruit Berry.

'You must wonder why I am telling you this. Well, the beginning of the end came unexpectedly for us. And only a short time ago. I stumbled on a conspiracy. Quite by accident. It involved two men, one of them American, the other Russian. The American was a former member of the National Security Agency. He had been an advisor to three US presidents. The Russian had been a general in the KGB. They were both wealthy, powerful men who wanted even more wealth and more power.'

Stratton sat still, listening carefully.

'When you find a conspiracy of such magnitude,' she went on, 'among people like that, it is not a simple thing to expose. Something terrible will certainly happen to you within a short time of revealing your knowledge to the wrong person. But I trusted Berry. Strange perhaps that the only person I could tell was from the other side.'

She paused a moment, as if to collect her

thoughts accurately. Stratton did nothing to distract her.

'I was servicing a meeting room in Paris,' she said. 'A small hotel in Concorde. Two rooms together just like these. A cleansing room with an adjoining meeting room. As I was leaving the cleansing room by the connecting door, I heard the front door unlock. I quickly closed the adjoining door behind me. I was not seen. I thought it was the hotel cleaner perhaps or some other member of staff. The meeting room had not been booked and so no one was officially expected.

'I turned on the monitoring system to see who it was. To my surprise, it was not hotel staff but two men in suits. I knew them both by reputation only. My immediate thought, before anything else, was that I had not logged into the room prior to servicing it. An oversight on my part. I should have done so. The men would have checked the log. They thought the room was empty. It was the safest place in Paris for them to talk. Because they had something extremely serious to talk about.

'I wanted to leave but I could not without alerting them. Even if I had got away without them seeing me they would have eventually known it was me. I was the servicing officer, the only one with access control outside of meetings. There were also cameras in the hotel elevators and on the stairs. What I should have done was walk into the meeting room right away, before they started talking. It did not matter that I had seen them together. Meeting each other was a part of their job. I would have apologised. I would have been seriously reprimanded. And they could have found somewhere else for their talk.

'But I did not. I was worried. I could have been expelled from my job. And so I remained in the room. I could do nothing else but listen. After a few minutes it became very clear to me that I would be a dead person if they ever found out I was there. They began to talk about gold. Its great and increasing value. And how it was so simple to steal for people like them. They began to discuss something else. They talked about a bomb. A nuclear device that would soon be in the hands of terrorists. Terrorists who were senior officers in Pakistan's Inter-Services Intelligence. They mentioned a name. General Javas Mahuba. They talked about how ideal the Pakistan plan was. News had already leaked to the media about the missing device, but these two men had created other evidences. False, misleading information. They seemed pleased with their progress.

'They knew who had stolen the bomb, and from where. They knew where it was going. The Russian asked about the arming codes. The American said that they had already been secured and sent ahead into Afghanistan. They were in the hands of a trusted Taliban commander by the name of Kalil Rohami. He would personally deliver them to Bagram once the bomb had arrived there. The American said that side of the operation was about to be taken care of.

'After they left, I sat still for a long while. Maybe two, three hours. I was frightened for myself. But also of what these men were planning to do. It seemed to me that they intended to allow the bomb to explode in Bagram. Among thousands of the American's own troops. But why would these two men let such a thing happen? On the face of it, it was madness. But these men were not mad. All I could think of was the conspiracy theories surrounding the Twin Towers. There were always rumours that high-level members of American intelligence knew it was going to happen and did nothing. Just like Pearl Harbor. There are those who believe that could have been avoided but was deliberately allowed to go ahead to bring America into the war.

'If such a thing happened,' she said, 'if Islamists detonated a nuclear device and thousands of Americans died, it could unite the entire world to rise up against Islamic terrorism. America could ignore every legal and human rights obstacle to exact their revenge and wipe their enemy from the face of the earth, wherever they were — and Europe, Russia, even China would not stand in their way. It would be in their interests too. They are all cursed with the Muslim threat. I cannot think of any other reason why those men would allow such a thing to happen.'

Bullfrog stubbed out the cigarette which had by now burned down to the filter. Stratton wasn't sure if it was the end of her revelation. He waited, his mind full of questions.

Finally he asked, 'When did this conversation take place?'

'Five days ago.'

'What did Chandos advise?'

'He had the same problem as me. Who to tell? The bomb could already be at Bagram. Then there are the codes. Where are they?'

'Who were the two men?'

'Their names are Henry Betregard and Mikhail Gatovik.'

Stratton had never heard of either man before.

'Berry decided to track down Betregard immediately,' she said. 'He hoped to find a clue. Anything that might provide some evidence that he could take to his people.'

Stratton had to get out of the chair and stretch his legs. 'Do you know what happened to Chandos?' he said, going to the window, which was covered by a thick blind.

'He must have made a mistake. All I can think of is that Betregard found out Berry was investigating him and sent an assassin after him. He went to Nigeria. He asked for details of an al-Qaeda cell he knew operated in Lagos. He asked me to arrange a car for him. He asked for weapons and explosives. He didn't explain what he was planning to do.'

'Why Lagos?'

She shrugged. 'Neutral ground, perhaps. It suited his purpose.'

Stratton studied her for a moment. 'Do you expect me to take up where he left off? Is that why you're telling me all this?'

She didn't answer, as if she had her own doubts.

'Chandos was more experienced than me. What chance do you think I'd have?'

'Berry made a fundamental mistake,' she said. 'He focused on the cause when he should have been dealing with the symptoms. Those are more in your league.'

'What do you mean?'

'He could never get to Betregard,' she said. 'He's far too big a fish. But he might have been able to find the bomb.'

'Was the meeting recorded?'

'Only monitors. Sound recording is not permitted.'

'How could you find the bomb?' Stratton asked. 'Without inside information, that's a task for specialists.'

'A process of elimination,' she said. 'It will not be in the air base because they don't have to take that risk. My guess would be somewhere in Bagram Town.'

'I've driven through it a few times. It's not big. But it's spread out, a lot of outlying compounds.'

'Mahuba is taking responsibility for the placing of the device. We can be certain of that much. I have done my research on that man. He is determined. But also old-fashioned, and refined. When he went into battle he would get as close to the front as he could, to be seen by his men. And he was always immaculately dressed. Although he grew to hate the British, he admired them when he was a young man. He used to dress like them. He was known for wearing a clean cravat into battle. Tucked into a crisp, starched shirt. There are few houses in

Bagram where he would stay. He would refuse to live in a mud hut. And there would have to be servants. He has never cooked a meal for himself in his entire life or cleaned his own clothes. He would not start now, certainly not in his final days.'

'You'd base your search for the bomb on Mahuba's personal habits?'

'Of course,' she said. 'That's a fundamental.'

'How can you be sure he'd go to Bagram himself anyway?'

'He would not leave such an important task to a subordinate.'

'And the detonation?'

'It's an impact device. As far as I know — it has to be detonated manually. The ultimate suicide bomb, Stratton. It requires the ultimate suicide bomber. Mahuba knows he will die soon after anyway. No one involved in this massacre will survive the witch hunt. It will not be pleasant for those who do not kill themselves.'

'What about using technology to find it?' Stratton asked.

'I've considered that,' she said. 'The problem with our detection systems is you need to know more or less where the radiation source is. Most of the systems have to be close. Metres away. Our best detection system can operate from a thousand metres. But that would require a large team. Once again, I would need to tell someone. Even if we could organise such a team, it would be too late. The Americans have a detection system in Bagram. But once again, who can I trust?'

It was obvious she was expecting him to go looking for the nuclear device.

'There is no other way but to search for it,' she said. 'Look for signs. Mahuba will have guards, vehicles. I'm not asking you to go.'

He looked at her, wondering why he'd got it wrong.

'I would expect you to do it without being asked,' she said.

He should have been ready for that one.

She could see his resistance and looked disappointed. 'Berry was your friend. But not only that. Thousands of your allies will die if that bomb is initiated. Think of the repercussions. America would take Pakistan apart. And that would just be for starters. Thousands upon thousands of innocent people would die and suffer. The rest of the world might turn on the Muslims for fear of the same happening to them one day. It would be World War Three. The fundamentalists would be smashed to pieces. That is what they want. But how many innocents would die before it was over?'

Stratton began to seriously doubt Bullfrog. Perhaps she was the real nutter here. Maybe she'd been exposed to the business for too long. Her story had the hallmarks of a wild conspiracy theory.

'Do you have any proof at all about anything you've told me today?' he asked.

She hesitated and he saw the first signs of impatience. He watched her come to a decision. She went over to her briefcase on the desk and opened it. She removed an envelope and took several photographs from it.

'I am quite insane, you know,' she said.

He wondered if she was suddenly about to reveal her own startling psychology report and unravel this entire meeting.

'I must be to carry around material like this,' she said. 'If I had an accident and someone went through my things, or if my case was stolen and the items were found by the police, they might eventually end up in the hands of someone who knew what they were. And I would be dead shortly after.'

Stratton stepped closer to her to look at the photographs.

'I was unsure about showing these to you,' she said. 'But I am aware that my claims are quite extreme and incredible. You would have every right to question my sanity.'

She placed several photos on the desk in front of him. They showed two older well-dressed men standing in a similar hotel room to the one they were in. The men looked like they were deep in conversation in one shot. Another showed them sharing something amusing. In another they were leaning close to each other.

'These were taken in the hotel meeting room in Paris when I was in the examination room,' she said. 'That's Henry Betregard.'

Stratton studied the pictures. The man looked tall but it was hard to say. He had light-brown hair and deep-set eyes and his suit fitted him well. The other man, Mikhail Gatovik, was smaller, with darker hair, though more of a physical presence. It was hard to define the

130

dynamic of the relationship just from these few images.

'I got the images from the log-in scanner,' she said.

'Could anyone else access these?'

'No. I erased the scanner after I copied the images.'

Stratton looked at her. Too long for her liking.

'I suppose I wasn't prepared for you to doubt me,' she said, moving away from him. 'Berry didn't.' She looked back at him, unsure about what she could see in his eyes. 'Do you?' she said.

On examination, his feelings were entirely mixed about her. He couldn't accept that she was mad, but neither could he accept the same about the men in the photos. What she suggested was indeed madness. 'I don't know,' he said.

'Then you must think I'm insane. Do you think Berry was also insane?'

Chandos might have been a little gullible, Stratton thought, but not insane.

'Perhaps I fooled him into believing me?' she said. 'But what about the assassin? Or do you think that was a dream too?'

Bullfrog went back to her briefcase. 'I overestimated your loyalty to Berry,' she said, packing the photos away. 'And I suppose I can't blame you for doubting me. It's a lot to believe from a stranger.' She closed the briefcase and locked it. 'Of course, now I have a problem. I could die if you give this information to the wrong person. But then, you would too.'

He wondered if there was any hint of a threat behind the words.

She removed the cosy from the glass and went to the bathroom and poured the contents into her hand. She returned with his coins and watch, putting them on the desk in front of him. She picked up her briefcase and went to the main door to the room, stopping at the door without opening it. 'Can I ask you to leave first please?'

Stratton didn't move. If it was all true, he was turning his back on a most grave situation. If it was true, that Chandos had died because of these men, that would also be something he couldn't ignore. If his relationship with his old boss meant anything at all, he would have to follow up his disappearance at least and get to the bottom of his death. And also, if she was wrong, Stratton didn't have anything to lose.

'Where's the scanning equipment?' he asked.

Her jaw clenched and she looked about ready to tell him to get lost. Then she put the case down, removed a key from her pocket and went to a low cupboard against the wall. She unlocked it to reveal an empty shelf. She pulled a secret lever and the shelf came down and he saw what looked like a large hotel safe with a key code on its face. She tapped in several numbers and opened the safe, stepping back with a theatrical sweep of her hand, inviting him to take a look.

He could see several pieces of hi-tech equipment with Cyrillic lettering. A small monitor showed the empty room next door in x-ray mode — only the guts and framework of the furniture were visible. He'd seen enough. She closed the safe, replaced the shelf and locked the cupboard.

There was another reason he decided to accept. If there was an atomic bomb in Bagram, he owed it to the many friends he had who might be at the base — Brits, Americans and others — to try and save their lives. Not to mention the innocent Afghans in the town and the surrounding areas who would die.

'Can I have a picture?' he asked.

She studied him. The request didn't necessarily suggest he believed her. 'Why?'

'I'd like to know more about Betregard.'

'You'll be making the same mistake as Berry. Follow the symptoms, not the cause.'

'I won't make the same mistake.'

She thought about it for a moment, then opened her briefcase and gave him the picture that best showed both men's faces.

Stratton put it in his pocket.

'How can I reach you?' he asked.

'You cannot.'

He accepted that he would be on his own from this point onwards.

'Will you do it?'

He was on a knife edge, but leaning more towards sanity. 'Probably not,' he said.

Her expression remained the same. 'You're a more complex character than I was expecting. Berry never mentioned that about you. I can see why the SIS employ you. We must leave now.'

He went to the door as he put on his watch and placed the coins in his pocket. He paused to look back at her, to say goodbye. He decided to say nothing. He walked out of the room, closing the door behind him.

11

Thirty-seven minutes after leaving the Chesterfield, Stratton walked along a tunnel and in through the underground entrance to the MI6 headquarters on the River Thames. He was processed through several standard layers of identification recognition and detection systems and made his way up a flight of stairs. At the end of a broad, brightly lit corridor, he arrived at a communal data reception and research room.

He swiped his ID card through the scanner. Two suited men were talking to each other further along the corridor. One of them was tall, balding and athletic. He glanced in Stratton's direction. The security lock beeped and Stratton pushed his way inside. He was feeling a tinge of paranoia already. Not good. He needed to bring that under control.

The room was filled with all kinds of electronic data-processing systems. There were half a dozen cubicles around the room. Each contained a computer terminal for private use. About half of them were occupied. Stratton walked to one at the back and sat down in front of a monitor. He swiped his ID card.

The machine took a moment to identify him. A log-in window appeared. He filled in his name and pass-code. An elaborate MI6 homepage appeared seconds later. Stratton stared at the search window, thinking. Keenly aware that he needed to be cautious with his key strokes. He didn't want to throw up any red flags to the system monitors, which analysed every word typed and every document opened. He needed to be careful of names too. But also key words, phrases and combinations of searches. He needed to disguise any queries. But the system also flagged anomalies like individuals who rarely used it suddenly asking a lot of questions. And Stratton wasn't a big user.

He typed in NSA PERSONNEL, SENIOR REPORTING, <2000. After a few seconds he had a list. Just going back a little over ten years, he had come up with several thousand names. Almost all of them were hyperlinked. He scrolled down the list and quickly saw the name Betregard, in blue underlined. He didn't pause on the page for long and carried on to the end. He knew he couldn't simply click on the link. Although dozens of searches were probably made every month on any one of the names, Stratton couldn't afford to have a single, direct search of Betregard associated with him.

He decided to go down the list of names, checking the link to every one of them. Each opened a pop-up window with an official photograph of the individual, some history and current responsibilities. For more information there were further links.

When he got to Betregard's name, the picture that appeared looked recent. He took the photograph from his pocket that Bullfrog had given him and compared it to the one on the screen. It looked very much like the same person.

135

The information on Betregard was superficial. He had worked for the National Security Agency for thirty years, beginning as an analyst, and he had moved around a lot, but the biography stated that he had retired two years previously. Betregard's page had no drill-down links. That was it. Stratton closed the window and laboriously went through a dozen more NSA personnel, trying to give the impression of only a general interest in the organisation's past members.

Then he went back to the search window and typed KGB PERSONNEL, SENIOR REPORTING, <1985. He got an even longer list this time, pages and pages. But he couldn't find Gatovik anywhere. He clicked on a suggested link to the Politburo, narrowing his search to the years either side of the fall of the Berlin wall. A list of two dozen names appeared, GATOVIK was about halfway down.

As before, he went through the list in alphabetical order, maintaining a linear search pattern, as though browsing. When he clicked on the link to Gatovik, a picture window came up. There were several images, covering the man's military career from his mid-twenties to his last official post. There was a reference to Afghanistan. He'd spent five years there as observer for Marshal Nikolai Ogarkov, reporting directly to Sergey Akhromeyev, deputy general of the Army. He'd put on weight since then but in all the photos he had a similar hardline expression. The last, most recent photograph matched the one in Stratton's hand.

Stratton exited the link and, as before, waded through a dozen more names before closing the site. He sat back, unsure exactly what he had been looking for beyond verifying these people were who Bullfrog said they were. It was too dangerous to dig any deeper. He was already playing with fire. But a red flag of his own had flipped up on his way to MI6. Something that had come out of the Bullfrog meeting that hadn't registered while he was at the hotel. Bullfrog had mentioned an Afghan commander. The one responsible for delivering the arming codes for the nuclear device. Kalil something or other.

Rohami. That was it. He began to type in the name and then suddenly stopped himself. A sense of danger welled in him as he realised what he was about to do. The letters KALIL RO were in the search window, the cursor blinking, waiting for him to type in the rest. He back-spaced out of it, leaving the search window blank.

But he couldn't leave it alone. He had to check. There was something about the name, something about what Bullfrog had said about the codes. A recent operation. He typed in OPERATION LUSTRE and the Lustre file presented itself. Stratton paused before opening it. It wouldn't be considered odd for him to look at the operations file, since he had been one of the team leaders. He clicked on it and scrolled down the file contents. He found an annexe labelled AFGHAN PERSONNEL DETAINED & KIA.

He opened it. As expected, there were no names in the DETAINED column. There were several dozen under the KILLED IN ACTION column, though. Someone must have compiled the list after the event because no one from the assault party had remained or had enough time to search the dead. He scrolled down the list to KALIL ROHAMI. He felt a tinge of excitement on seeing the name. It was a connection Bullfrog didn't know about. Kalil's rank was listed as COMMANDER. There was no photograph or link to one or any other information on Rohami.

Stratton sat back and let his mind roll through the events at the hamlet. The documents he found. Had the dead man beside them been Rohami? Were the papers the ones Rohami was supposed to deliver to Bagram? To General Mahuba? Were the numbers he saw the arming codes?

Stratton wanted to do a search on Jeff Wheeland to check his links to the NSA. That would go a long way to help corroborate Bullfrog's version of events — but if it did, the red flags in the system would fly like starlings. He couldn't take the risk — he'd keep that one to himself, for now. He closed the page. If Betregard had gone for the arming codes, that suggested he wasn't going to sit back and let Mahuba detonate the device. In fact by capturing the codes, Betregard had prevented Mahuba from detonating it.

But the codes were just paper. They could be reproduced. He had to assume that Mahuba could get a copy. So maybe it was a delaying tactic. Which put Stratton back at the beginning, more or less.

He didn't want to be in the building any more. It was making him feel uncomfortable. He got to his feet and headed for the door. He stepped into the corridor, glad that it was empty, and walked to the stairs and down to the exit level. As he reached the exit doors he had a sudden thought and slowed to think things through once more before he entered the tunnel.

He needed better information about Betregard. And whatever the man's intentions were, someone had to find the bomb before duplicate arming codes could be delivered to Mahuba. He also needed to establish a link between Betregard and Wheeland. He wondered if Betregard knew precisely where the bomb was. If not, he would need to locate it. Finding it would mean one of two distinct kinds of operation: a full-scale search, utilising thousands of soldiers, or a clandestine one by specialist personnel. The former would be more effective. But the sudden numbers of men in the town would alert Mahuba and he might have a counter move. A clandestine search would be slow but its secrecy could be maintained. If Betregard was looking for the bomb, Stratton expected him to use the latter plan.

Stratton just couldn't come up with a plausible reason why Betregard and Gatovik weren't coming clean to their own governments about the bomb. Why didn't they want anyone else involved? What was the reason behind the secrecy? Unless of course Bullfrog was right and they wanted to start World War Three proper. If that was true, then why deny Mahuba the arming codes? An atomic bomb wasn't exactly subtle. And the reason for the plot would be equally blunt once it was uncovered. He just needed to find the missing clues.

He decided to go to Bagram. There was nothing more for it. He couldn't walk away. The journey would give him time to think it all through until he'd exhausted every possibility. He could always change his mind at any time and pull out. At least with the arming codes captured, the chances of the bomb going off when he was there were slim. It wouldn't be easy to come up with duplicate codes. He felt better about that at least.

But the fact was that as soon as he arrived at the base he'd be in range of a nuclear bomb blast — there was nothing attractive about that at all.

12

Stratton adjusted the collar of his leather jacket against the wind as he drove his Jeep north along the A11. The headlights illuminated the highway ahead and a dozen or so other vehicles in front of him. At a roundabout at the end of the dual carriageway, he took the exit signposted 'Mildenhall', towards the huge American air base.

Purely out of habit, he clocked the headlights of the cars behind as he headed away from the roundabout. One of them took the same turn. Not that there was anything odd about that. It was a popular route. But with a mile to go, the vehicle was still behind him. Stratton didn't feel anything in it but he increased his speed a little, out of mild curiosity. The car matched his speed. When he slowed down, the car maintained the same distance. That was more than enough to ping his senses.

He took a right down a country lane and the car followed. The narrow lane was otherwise empty. He felt certain it was following him, but there was something odd about it. It was way too obvious. He took another turn. The car followed. He grew irritated. Why were they being so nonchalant about it? He accelerated and the car did the same.

Sod this, he thought, and pulled a handbrake turn, coming to a screeching halt, the Jeep's headlights blinding the occupants of the car as it stopped abruptly only metres away. Stratton wasn't armed and quickly climbed out of the Jeep and stepped back and to one side, pretty sure whoever it was wouldn't be able to see him. The Jeep would be the target and therefore he couldn't afford to be in it. He waited. If a gun went off, he'd run. No point fighting a one-sided fight.

The car was black and looked new. It was a Lexus sedan. All of its lights went out, except the interior, which came on as the driver's door opened. A figure began to climb out.

Stratton selected his escape route: to his right, over a fence and into a wood.

The figure stood upright and stepped from behind the open door. It was a woman. She stepped fully into his Jeep's headlights and he saw that it was Bullfrog. He turned off the engine and killed all the lights, plunging the lane into darkness, except for the glow inside Bullfrog's Lexus.

'You followed me from the hotel?' he asked as he walked over. 'Why didn't you just call me?' He held up his mobile phone.

'From your apartment and from MI6,' she said. 'Don't feel so bad you didn't see me before I wanted you to. I've been doing it a long time. And I wanted to speak with you in person. Mildenhall makes perfect sense. I take it you have friends in the Navy SEALs.'

'What makes you think I'm going to Afghanistan?'

'Berry thought you'd do it,' she said, ignoring

his pathetic attempt to try and get her to doubt it. 'I needed to know. If you weren't going to go, I'd have a real problem. I might have to do something desperate.'

'If you know where I'm going, what are you doing here?'

'There's something else you should know. Have you ever heard of an 'integer' — as in related to our business?'

'Integer?' he repeated, shaking his head.

'I didn't think so. They're known only to those who operate directly behind the mantles of power. Your Prime Minister or the President of the United States may never have heard of them either.'

Stratton had no idea what she was going on about and elected to shut up and wait to hear the point of it.

'The integers were apparently formed in the 1920s,' she said. 'Between the World Wars. They have diplomatic immunity and they are state-sponsored. They originally worked for the UK, Germany and France, and the USA and Russia, as clandestine diplomats. The integer was created to act as an unbiased middleman, their task to assist in the unsavoury chores of high diplomacy. They belong to no single country. No allegiances. They are incorruptible and unbending in their tasks. They are not arbitrators either. They have no voice. And, most importantly, they have no conscience. They do what they are asked without question. If the American President wanted to send a private message to a North Korean general for instance, but didn't know how to contact him without exposing his own intelligence or spy network, certain persons in the intelligence services who are able to would summon an integer.

'I first came across them by accident in Norway a year after the wall came down,' she said. 'I escorted a man to a remote Norwegian fjord, where I dropped him off, as ordered. I worked out later by piecing together intelligence reports that he'd gone to meet a Ukrainian-born defector from a Russian submarine somewhere in that fjord. I was on standby to pick him up, but the call never came, so I contacted my handler for the operation and he simply said, 'Never question an integer.' It was a slip of the tongue. I never saw the man again after I dropped him off but the defector was turned back. The integer had succeeded.

'Somewhere along the way,' Bullfrog continued, 'around the time the Americans declared the end to their assassination programme, the integers were employed to fill that gap. No one knows who requested the first assassination from an integer. Or when. But it happened.'

'You're going to say an integer killed Chandos, aren't you?'

'They are the best there is. When it comes to assassins there is no finer academy. None more accomplished. In fact, they never lose. It's an explanation that fits the puzzle. Betregard was at a high enough level in the intelligence services to have first-hand experience of integers. I wanted you to know,' she said.

'That's the kind of story that might talk me

out of doing this job.'

'Some, Stratton. But not you. In fact, if my instincts are correct, a part of you is more than just curious about these individuals who challenge your lofty opinion of yourself.'

He didn't deny it.

She smiled ever so slightly before climbing back into the Lexus. 'Good luck,' she said, closing the door. She started the engine and turned the car around, before driving back the way they had come up the lane.

Stratton stood watching until the rear lights disappeared. His head was full of the notion of these ultimate assassins. And she was right. He was curious about them, and also slightly miffed at the thought of the existence of such supermen. But she wasn't entirely correct in her assessment of his idea of a challenge. There was enough to put him off doing the task. The bomb put it on a knife edge. This assassin stuff was more than enough to put him over the other side.

Or perhaps not quite enough.

He climbed into his Jeep, started it up and headed back along the lane towards the US air base.

13

Stratton walked down the ramp of the C-17 Globemaster transport aircraft along with a couple of US Navy SEALs. He'd called an old SEAL buddy in Virginia to ask if there were any flights into Bagram he could jump on. He was in luck. He knew he could have done the same through the Brit system but someone might have asked questions. A message could have been left for him at the SBS HQ. Any number of small things like that could have ended up with someone at the Service wondering what he was doing. The Yanks were far more laid back about that sort of thing and the old boy network worked well.

He had spent most of the flight talking to lads from SEAL Team Two, out of Norfolk, Virginia. They had friends in common. They were on their third rotation to Afghanistan, replacing a couple of injured buddies who had been caught in a roadside mine. The injured guys had been lucky and would be back in a couple of months.

They headed across the tarmac of Bagram Airfield towards the terminal. It was early afternoon and there was a distinct chill in the air. Stratton decided it was several degrees colder than it had been the week before. In the distance snow-capped mountains made up practically the entire surrounding panorama beyond the Shomali plains. It was dramatic. Sparse. Vast and with a feeling of isolation, despite being on a busy air base.

He watched another C-17, painted completely black, taxi to the far side of the pan. It had no markings other than a series of numbers, unreadable from where he was without binoculars. The ramp lowered and he watched two Suburbans drive out of the belly, one behind the other, away from the terminal. Whoever they were, they were a law unto themselves.

Stratton carried on to the terminal building. The processing was conveniently short, made simpler for him with his special forces ID pass. After he was through, he headed out into the vast camp. Bagram Air Base was a sprawling mass, nearly ten square miles of barracks, hangars, offices, dispersal areas and two giant runways, home to over a hundred different US and NATO units. But there was still space and large gaps of nothing between some of the organisations that occupied the place. Stratton was not entirely sure where he was going, other than eventually to the checkpoint nearest to Bagram Town. He had a loose plan, but to execute it he had some urgent requirements, namely clothing and transport.

There weren't an abundance of Afghans on the camp. Not simply because of security issues. Stratton knew the US military and the civilian contract construction companies had initially hired as many locals as they could manage — an obvious source of cheap, unskilled labour, and politically a good idea — but the numbers eventually had to be reduced because of theft.

147

Some companies got rid of Afghans entirely because anything of value that could be stuffed inside clothing or into a vehicle without being seen would be. On a previous visit, Stratton remembered a construction engineer in the PX store complaining bitterly that his entire operation had ground to a halt because just about every single vehicle they had in their compound had had its battery stolen during the night, despite the compound being surrounded by a high fence topped with a twirl of razor wire.

Stratton guessed Afghans would still hang around the civilian media centre. It was separated from the more sensitive parts of the base by fencing. Journalists hired Afghan drivers and translators who often stayed in the camp while their employers went on trips with the military, often for days at a time. He had been there only once before.

It was a long walk around various perimeters, some of which had changed since his last visit. Half an hour later he saw the media building, a lone brick structure two storeys high with a flat roof, the colour of sand like most of the offices on the base. The nearest buildings to it were a line of hangars a hundred metres away. He was covered in a film of grey dust by the time he reached the location.

He stood opposite a fenced compound of rows of military ten-man tents. The tents were used to quarter journalists, many of whom turned up in numbers for significant press conferences or visits from US officials. Much to his disappointment he could see no activity at that moment. It all looked quiet, almost deserted. He could hear a distant aircraft taxiing.

He walked in through the door of the media building and stepped along a dusty corridor in the direction of voices he could hear. He went through a door into another corridor, glass-panelled to waist height on one side. Through it he saw a woman in BDUs head from one room to another. He didn't want to meet any soldiers. It was of no consequence if he did: he would simply flash his ID if challenged — but questions would require answers and it could get tedious.

He walked to the end of the corridor, to an open door into a large room with a few tables and chairs. Ragged maps were taped to walls in places. A few Army signs, clearly ignored, asking for the place to be kept clean. He guessed it was the civilian media room where journalists hung out. There was a stack of military ration boxes against one wall and a corner table with tea and coffee, and an electric kettle. A cheap tin cooker.

He headed back outside and scanned around, focused on the only movement in front of him. The tents. They weren't completely empty, it seemed. Three Afghan men came out of one and headed away. They were wearing long linen shirts with linen trousers underneath and thick jackets on top, and heavy scarves wrapped around their necks. He watched them head to the far end of the compound and through a gate and along the road towards some far buildings. When they were out of sight, Stratton swung his bag over his shoulder and crossed the deserted road to an open gate in the fence.

The tents were air-conditioned as well as heated, with a wooden-framed airlock door as an entrance. He walked to the one the Afghans had just left and paused at the door to listen. All was silent. He knocked.

There was no reply.

He pulled open the rickety door and walked in. Another door was immediately in front of him. He pushed it open and paused to look inside. Warm air bathed him. There were a dozen beds and no sign of life. On three of the beds he saw open suitcases. Stratton moved quickly. He found a shirt big enough for him and trousers to match. He had a rummage in another suitcase and found a scarf. He took a heavy Afghan coat from a coat hook, inspected it and pulled it on. It was a little tight under the arms but would do. He bundled up his booty into his bag, which was just big enough to take it all, and stepped out of the tent.

He managed to find his transport within minutes of leaving the tent compound. As he walked along a broad dirt road towards one of the base's main entrances, he saw a bicycle leaning against the wall of an office building, just a few metres from the front door. It was precisely what he needed.

A convoy of civilian fuel trucks headed towards him, kicking up a minor dust storm, the sound of their heavy engines growing louder. There were hardly any pedestrians around, but there were plenty of vehicles, parked or moving. Mostly civilian, a few military. The brick building stood all alone and had no signage to indicate its purpose. It looked run-down and behind it ran an endless internal barrier of HESCO containers. Stratton knew it wasn't the perimeter because it had no watch towers. There were literally miles of HESCOs throughout and around the camp. Bomb-proof, bulletproof, ram-proof, and topped with hundreds of miles of razor wire.

As he got closer he could see a yard alongside the building of empty, folded HESCOs and piles of metal stakes, and a bulldozer with a large bucket. The first of the fuel trucks rumbled past, coughing out black fumes that mingled with the dust cloud they kicked up. Stratton upped his pace without running, hoping anyone wanting to leave the building at that moment would wait until the trucks had gone.

He threaded both his arms through the handles of his holdall and pulled it onto his back like a pack. He grabbed the bike, turned it around and slung a leg over it and got going. It wasn't the finest example of its make but it worked. He rode along the edge of the road as more trucks passed him, heading in the opposite direction into the camp. He had to squint to keep the dust out of his eyes and spat gritty particles from his dry lips.

The road here was open and there were few structures either side. After several hundred metres he saw an opening in the HESCO wall — a deserted yard, rubbish everywhere. He cycled in, then jumped off and ran the bike into the yard out of sight of the road. He leaned the bike against the dusty HESCO wall, took his holdall off his back and dug out the clothes and, other than keeping on his trousers, exchanged the rest for his own. He wound the scarf around his neck a couple of times. He was reasonably confident he could mingle with the Afghan populace without drawing attention to himself. He had done it many times before and as long as he didn't have to open his mouth he'd get away with it. He could have done with a few more days' worth of stubble. His hair was dark enough, although his complexion was pale, but then, so were many Afghans, especially at that time of year.

He stuffed the holdall under a board and piled on dust and rubbish. He planned to be back for it no later than the following day. Satisfied, he wheeled the bike back onto the road and headed for the camp exit. Going into a local Afghan community in disguise was going to be different this time in several ways. In the past he'd been armed and had the support of people on the end of a radio. In the event of a situation, they were never far away. This time the only emergency plan he had for a serious incident was to use his mobile phone. He would make contact if his life depended on it, of course. But the response would be slow and then there would be the aftermath. London, and indeed the SBS, would want to know what the hell he was doing in Afghanistan, let alone outside the secure base on his own disguised as a local. He wouldn't know what to tell them. It got to the point where it didn't bear thinking about and so he put the whole contingency plan idea to the back of his mind in the hope he'd never need it.

He had cycled less than a kilometre when he arrived at the back of a line of vehicles waiting to leave the base. Beyond it, to one side of the checkpoint, he saw dozens of Afghans. The checkpoint was a complex construction of walled channels for incoming and outgoing vehicles and pedestrians. It had buildings for ID processing, a bypass for military vehicles, and isolation bays where vehicles could be parked to one side for inspection, with a soak area beyond packed with trucks. It was bustling with US soldiers and trusted Afghans in US fatigues who acted as interpreters and traffic coordinators.

Stratton joined a line of pedestrians, which included a couple of other people with bikes. Egress from the camp looked far less complicated than entrance. There were still inspections of personal ID cards and bags and vehicles for any stolen items, but otherwise it looked a formality. As he closed on the exit, an Afghan in BDUs shouted at him. It was the one thing he wanted to avoid. His Farsi was pretty poor despite the amount of time he had spent in Afghanistan.

Unable to speak English in front of everyone, he didn't say anything. The guard kept shouting, walking briskly over and demanding something, by now inches from his face. Stratton groaned as if he couldn't talk, then pointed to his ears. The guard was gesturing for an ID card.

A US soldier, dressed in full camouflage fatigues, helmet, webbing, body armour and cradling an M4 assault rifle in his arms, came over to see what was going on.

'He looks to be a mute,' the Afghan guard said.

'Where's his ID?' the soldier asked.

'That's what I'm trying to get from him.'

'Well, he got into the camp so he must have an ID. Let's see your ID,' the soldier said to Stratton. 'ID,' he repeated and formed his gloved index fingers and thumbs into a rectangle.

Stratton smiled at the soldier and began to fumble around his pockets as if looking for it. He moved his bike away from the line and placed it down on the ground. He continued his pantomime of searching his pockets. The Afghan guard walked away to remonstrate with another of the people on foot. Stratton kept it up until he was happy the guard wasn't coming back and the line of locals were no longer taking much notice of him. All looked eager to get out of the camp themselves.

He produced his ID and handed it to the soldier, hoping he wouldn't give him away. For an instant the soldier looked surprised, but he held his composure as he compared the headshot to the man in front of him. He looked into Stratton's eyes and Stratton looked right back at him, unmoving but asking for calm.

The soldier handed him back the card. 'I don't give a fuck if you're dumb, deaf or stupid,' he said, getting louder the more he talked. 'When you come to this gate you have your ID ready! Now get the fuck outta my camp!'

Stratton humbly obeyed.

14

Stratton rode through a crowded marketplace of makeshift wooden stalls and unfinished buildings and as soon as he was able turned off the main base road towards the residential part of Bagram Town.

It was a kilometre or so square, with several hundred mud houses organised haphazardly on its winding streets. He saw a few concrete block compounds and others that were a combination of both. Most had been finished off in plastered mud. There was a lot of exposed blockwork. The main road through the town had been tarmacked but the rest were dirt or gravel.

He kept to the side streets, which were mostly empty of people. He saw a few pedestrians and another cyclist. No one gave him a second look. He decided to be systematic and cycle across the town from one end to the other, north first, then south, skirting the perimeter to the next street and across the town again, until he'd covered all of it. At the same time he would take Bullfrog's advice and focus on the compounds and the largest of the houses. He guessed it would take him until the evening.

He stopped outside the first gated home he came to. It had a front courtyard and a few pots of flowers. There seemed to be little in the way of flora anywhere in the town other than geraniums. Red flowers on the ends of long, straggly, knuckle-like limbs. Most of the homes seemed to have some of them, in pots or growing from patches of dry soil that melded seamlessly with the roads. There were no clues that suggested it was occupied by anything other than a small family.

After several hours he'd made a dozen runs across the north section of the town and had found nowhere with any signs of Mahuba and the bomb, like suitable vehicles or a guard force.

He came across a gap in a wall with open ground on the other side and decided to take a break. He walked the bike behind the wall, sat down and dug down inside his Afghan trousers to the side pocket of his own trousers. He pulled out a fruit drink bladder and a nutty bar, care of the US Air Force inflight lunchbox. He had packed a similar meal into the same pocket on his other trouser leg. They'd do him for the day.

He decided if he hadn't found the place by morning he wasn't going to and would head back. An untethered goat walked over to investigate, watching Stratton munch on the nutty bar. He wasn't in the mood to share. Beyond the animal the endless line of unassailable, snow-capped mountains hovered. The sky was clear. It would be a cold night, he decided. He didn't even want to think where he might spend it.

The goat walked off and Stratton emptied the bladder of fruit juice into his mouth, then buried all his litter. He looked at the sun and took a guess at the time. It was well off-centre and towards the western horizon. Around 1600, he decided. He checked his watch. It was 1623. Not bad, he thought. He got to his feet and looked around the edge of the wall to check it was clear.

It took him another half-hour to complete the northern and largest section of the town, after which he crossed the main tarmac road and began to criss-cross the southern section. As the sun went behind the mountains and the light started to fade he headed along the first of the outgoing roads to check the few lone houses on the edge of this part of town. He could see a number of isolated compounds of various sizes, some of them medieval-looking. He knew many families built their houses close together and shared the safety of a single high wall and gated entrance. There were quite a few here and he was prepared for a long night's work.

He stopped outside the metal gates of the first compound to have a look inside. There was no one about. The gates were buckled where they met, as if someone had forced an entry without removing the chain that held them shut. The place had no outside lights and only a handful inside the houses that he could see. It didn't possess the credentials and he moved on.

Darkness fell quickly. Without street lights, he felt safer in the glow from just the distant houses. The brightest lights came from the base, which glowed like a city, its perimeter marked by powerful spotlights on the top of tall poles. After going a few hundred metres beyond the compound it became obvious there was nothing else along the track so he turned around and went back. This next phase of the search would be like exploring the spokes of a wheel. He would go to the end of one, turn around, go back down it to the town and find the next one.

When he reached the main road again, he turned left and kept going until he came to another track heading away from the town. Within a few hundred metres he saw another compound. It didn't look promising so he carried on. Another compound appeared half a kilometre after, but it was also disappointingly small. Once again, a few hundred metres beyond it the darkness took over and he turned back towards the town.

He continued methodically in a clockwise direction around the town's periphery. In some ways, he thought, it should be easier checking for the place at night. He'd expect it to have security lighting for a start. He wondered if Mahuba was clever enough to avoid anything that might point a finger at him. Such as lights and guards. If so, Stratton had little chance of finding him.

By nine he estimated he had covered about half the circumference of the town's outer reaches. He went a way up the next track and lifted the bike off the road, up a short bank and through some bushes to take another break. The air had chilled noticeably. He noticed fires had been lit in every occupied house. A noisy vehicle passed by along the main road. As he ate he stared at the distant mountains. They were always impressive. Jagged teeth in black gums.

The stars shone brightly in the heavens. Clear and crisp. He felt the chill as a breeze found its way through his open jacket.

As he buttoned up his front, the sound of engines drifted to him on the night air. Whatever it was turned off the main road and onto the dirt track he was sitting alongside. Lights flicked across a nearby house and the treetops beyond it. He decided he was fine where he was. There was a low wall not far away, beyond that open country. The engine grew louder, the lights stronger. The track was suddenly bathed in a strong white light as the vehicle came around the bend.

It was a 4×4. A Suburban. And it was not alone. There were two of them. They were dark, probably black, with tinted windows. The second had a light on inside and he saw figures, or their foggy outlines. It also had some kind of technological apparatus on its roof.

There was a third. The same as the others but without the roof apparatus. They had to be coalition troops. His thoughts flashed to the vehicles he had seen earlier in the day, driving out of the back of the black Globemaster. The convoy continued along the road, its headlights illuminating the trees and houses ahead. Stratton walked down onto the road to watch the red tail lights disappear around a bend. They weren't going into the camp. The track was headed in the wrong direction.

He quickly went back for the bike and dragged it onto the road and pedalled after the Suburbans. Quite quickly he couldn't hear the sound of the engines but he could still see the glow of the rear lights, moving further away. They weren't going that fast but after a few moments the lights disappeared too. He kept up the speed as well as he could, hoping to see the lights again. His ears were pricked for any distant sound but there was nothing.

As he took a wide bend he stopped pedalling when he saw a red glow up ahead, about a couple of hundred metres away. The light went out and he eased on the bike's brakes, which squeaked, released them and dropped his boots to the road to stop the bike.

He didn't get off right away and remained still. All he could hear was a distant aircraft taking off. Whoever they were, and whatever they were up to, despite their proximity to the camp, they were still in hostile territory. They would take the usual precautions, like sentries to cover obvious arcs and routes into their position.

Stratton got off the track and hid the bike, before moving deeper into the open ground. A low wall appeared to follow the track for a distance and he crossed over to the other side of it, walking lightly, his ears and eyes focused as far ahead as he could. His first worry was thermal imagers. Any sophisticated lookout would be scanning their arcs with one. But the vehicles had only just stopped. Perhaps the sentries hadn't deployed yet.

He focused his attention on a large spread of bushes and small trees that he estimated the vehicles to be just beyond. He wanted to be in among them as soon as he could. He speeded up a little, stepping silently across the dry earth. As he approached the dark foliage, a goat bleated and scampered off a stone's throw to his right. It paused him. Judging by the direction the animal was going, it had been disturbed by something other than him.

He eased himself down and made his way quietly into the bushes. He heard a metallic sound from half-left ahead. He stopped. He realised he was close to the road and could see the rear of a vehicle about twenty metres away. The back doors were open. There was movement, figures walking on the road, one of them heading in his direction. He eased himself back into cover. The man came to a stop in front of Stratton's position. Then he stepped off the track into the bushes towards Stratton. He stopped again, only a couple of metres away. Stratton was surprised the man couldn't see him. He remained still as he studied the silhouette. It was someone holding an assault rifle in one hand. The man took a step forwards, then another, and his boot came down directly on top of Stratton.

Stratton reacted like a snake that had been stepped on, grabbing the leg. He got his entire weight behind it and twisted violently around so that the man fell under him, then he pulled himself on top, forcing a hand onto the guy's mouth to stop him squealing. The soldier went for a knife in a sheath on his thigh. Stratton planted his knees onto his chest as he grabbed the knife hand and they struggled with it. The man was strong and had the point up towards Stratton's gut, so he released his mouth hold and hammered on the soldier's throat with the heel of his hand. The man made a gagging sound and his limbs stiffened and he dropped the knife. Stratton hit him again and he shuddered before going limp.

Stratton felt for his carotid artery, concerned. He'd not intended to be discovered and certainly not to kill anyone. This man was more than likely an American. An ally, for Christ's sake. All he could hope for was that he wasn't dead. He searched for a pulse and when he couldn't find one, he kept searching. It wasn't always easy to find. He was also unable to fully concentrate, his senses were all about him. Someone might have heard. The others weren't far away. He would have been in deep trouble for being in Afghanistan beforehand. Now he'd gone and bloody well killed one of his own side.

Stratton kept his hand on the man's throat but could feel nothing. He felt around the soldier's equipment. He was wearing the usual webbing and belt order, the pouches stuffed with magazines, a pistol in a holster. He had a larger pouch on his hip, a radio clipped to the webbing. A wire led to his earpiece which had come off in the struggle. That would be a problem when the team controller asked for a communications check.

Stratton was curious about the large pouch and opened it. It held a gas mask. An odd piece of kit to carry. He went back to the man's uniform, which wasn't usual camouflage material but it felt familiar. The gas mask provided the clue. The man was wearing a chemical warfare suit. The material was made of several layers of carbon-impregnated cloth designed to absorb

162

highly toxic vapour elements in the air. Stratton felt for a pulse again just to be sure.

Nothing.

'Shit,' he muttered to himself. It could easily have been the other way around. But that didn't justify it. The soldier was only doing his job. Stratton removed the radio, put it in one of his pockets and clipped in the earpiece. He eased his way through the bushes until he was close to the edge of the road again.

He could just about make out all three vehicles. Most of the movement was happening beyond the furthest one, where a dozen or so men stood. All of them seemed to be wearing the same outfits as the man he'd just killed. Stratton took a good look at the centre vehicle with the unusual gantry fitted to its roof. It looked like a couple of metre-long probes. They were white and could best be described as giant cigarettes. One was pointing straight up and the other across the track into the darkness.

Two or three people sat inside the vehicle. It contained some kind of control panel with dozens of LEDs. Someone climbed out of the back and hurried to the lead vehicle. There appeared to be a brief conversation with the occupants, who then got out and walked to the back of the central vehicle and leaned inside. After a couple of minutes one of the men went up the track to the group. His conversation with them was brief. Whatever it was, they were suddenly energised.

Stratton watched as several of the men broke away and went to the backs of the front and rear vehicles. They collected several items each, the size of wine bottles, and headed along the road in both directions away from the vehicles. Two of the men were heading towards Stratton. He ducked back as they walked past. One paused a few metres away before continuing on for another thirty metres. They were placing the objects onto the track at intervals. When they were finished, they headed back to the vehicles.

Stratton strained to look at the object nearest to him. It looked like a canister. That might explain the gas masks. He plucked a piece of grass and released it into the gentle breeze. It blew from his back and across the track. His radio suddenly came to life, a man's voice asking for a communications check. Three other voices replied in sequence. They were all American and each used the letters Tango, Quebec and November. There was a silence followed by the controller asking a Victor call-sign to report. That had to be the man lying nearby.

'Victor, Victor, this is Solas, do you copy?' the voice asked again.

Stratton went for it, in his best American accent, and could only pray that it was even close to what it was supposed to be. 'Victor's good,' he said.

'You fallin' asleep, Victor?'

'Bad earpiece,' Stratton replied.

'Copy that,' the controller said. 'This is a general standby. Looks like we've had a positive read. Remote interdiction will commence within five. Out.'

A man left the lead vehicle and headed along

the track in Stratton's direction. He pulled his gas mask over his face as he went to the far canister and crouched by it.

'All stations, this is Solas. Commence lockdown,' the controller said over the radio. 'I repeat, all stations lockdown.'

Stratton didn't need to guess its meaning. He went back to the body, removed the gas mask from its pouch and pulled it on.

Back at the road the man initiated the furthest canister from the trucks and went to the next one to repeat the process. In less than a minute every canister, a dozen of them, had been activated. A loud hissing sound filled the air and a jet of vapour issued from every canister, rising up in an increasingly broad cone shape for several metres before bending under the influence of the breeze. The smoke dispersed into the darkness. Stratton leaned out of the bushes to get a better look at the activity around the vehicles. The group of men were still standing there.

The canisters steamed away for a couple of minutes. It suddenly occurred to Stratton that he might be missing an opportunity. For what, he was not sure. But his instincts urged him to go with the flow. All of them were in full NBC suits that included gloves, hoods and of course, gas masks. They were all identical. He quickly went back to the sentry, the sound of his movements now masked by the hissing canisters. He unbuckled the webbing and rolled the man from one side to the other to remove his jacket. By the time he had the suit off the canisters were almost out.

As he pulled on the suit he was aware of a different sound. A gentle voice. He paused to listen. It was distant. He suddenly realised it was coming from the earpiece that had fallen from his ear.

He shoved it back in, in time to hear his call-sign being called.

'Victor here,' he said in a low voice.

'You need to fix that earpiece,' the voice said. 'Stand by. The teams'll be moving, in one minute.'

'Copy that.'

Stratton tightened the hood around his gas mask and pulled on the webbing, weapons and ammunition, clipping the radio into a webbing strap. As he got to his feet and took a deep breath, he was reminded how much he hated gas masks. He moved to the track and looked at the Suburbans. The gas canisters had reduced to a fizz. He was just in time. The men were heading along the track away from him and he hurried to catch up.

As he went past the three Suburbans, he glanced in the centre one at the two men still inside. There was no one else about. The track took a sharp turn to the right. He guessed the gas would have gone along it at that point. He saw men up ahead and slowed as he reached them. He wanted to remain in the rear. Beyond them were lights and a high mud wall. The men at the front approached a pair of metal gates.

It looked like a pretty big compound.

15

The lead group didn't appear to care how much noise they made pulling the gates apart. Time seemed to be the factor. The team entered the compound and Stratton slowed so as not to get too close to the men immediately in front of him. No one looked back. They were all focused ahead and anxious to get into the compound. They had good reason not to care about their backs.

Stratton walked through the open gates after the rest of the team. A chain with a large padlock attached lay on the ground. The men were heading up the central path to the far end, past homes on either side. They seemed to know exactly where they wanted to go. As he walked across the compound, he saw an animal lying on the ground on its side. When he got closer, he realised it was a goat. Its eyes were open and its tongue hung from its mouth as froth bubbled out. Another goat was lying in the same condition a few feet away.

Stratton crouched to inspect it, putting a hand on its chest. The animal was dead. He looked further along the track and saw a man lying still against a wall. Stratton went over to him. He had wide-open eyes and slime oozing out of his mouth, just like the goats.

Stratton stepped to the nearest mud house, which had a light on, and he looked in through the window at a man seated at a dining table. A kerosene lamp in front of him lit his dead face on the table, his arms hanging limp by his side. Beyond him two children lay on a bed as though asleep. Stratton looked away.

He continued up the path past bodies on the ground to the biggest house in the compound. He could see the head and shoulders of a figure on the roof, slumped over the parapet in what appeared to be a gun emplacement. The front door of the house was open. The team were all inside.

Stratton understood the rationale of using gas. The compound was heavily guarded. A surprise attack, even with silent weapons, would be a risk if the guards were vigilant. But that was not enough of a reason to use a gas like the one that had been used here. It could only be warranted if those in the compound had the capability to react in dangerous ways if aware of an attack. But then, gas would never be used if there was a chance of killing innocent civilians. That could only happen if the risks were immediately life-threatening on another scale.

Stratton had a good idea what was inside the building.

Two of the men walked up behind him. He kept still, hoping they'd pass by. One of them patted him on the shoulder. 'Inside,' the man said, his voice muffled by the gas mask.

The soldier moved ahead to enter the house and the other waited for Stratton to let him go in. He was silent. Stratton walked through the front door and followed the first into a large, nearly empty living room. Dim electric lights bathed everything in an orange glow.

Two bodies lay on the floor, one a young boy, the other a man with a greying beard. Their eyes were open and saliva streamed from their mouths. Stratton looked to his left at another body slumped in a chair by the window. This one was well-dressed and wore a silk cravat. Stratton wondered how strong the gas was and how far it could travel before dispersing to a safe concentration. It had been virulent enough to be immediately effective at two to three hundred metres just filtering into these houses. That suggested it could remain potent for several hundred metres more at least. He wondered how many more innocent people had died. But then, if he'd guessed right about why the men were here, many more would have died anyway.

The man who had ordered him into the house stood on the other side of the room with several of the others around a large wooden table. He appeared to be the operation leader and was examining a substantial black plastic container on the table. He raised the lid of the container and, with the help of one of the other men, opened the sides.

Stratton got a glimpse of what looked like a beer keg connected to a smaller black box beside it with cables. He had never been that close to an atomic weapon before. One of the men, presumably a technician, set about unscrewing the panel. Everyone else waited patiently. The technician carefully raised up the panel flap to expose the shiny innards. A small keypad and a row of glowing LEDs indicated power.

Stratton looked behind him at the sound of wheels moving across the floor and stepped clear of a trolley being pushed by two more of the team. It had a more sophisticated-looking black plastic box on it. The technician took the ends of the cable attached to the black box on the trolley, brought it to the table and connected it to the nuclear device. He removed an electrical cable from a wall socket that was connected to the now-surplus small power box on the table.

The technician closed the panel on the bomb and set about returning the screws. When he was finished he nodded to the head man.

'Let's transfer it to the support habitat,' the man said.

Stratton couldn't be sure, but he thought he recognised the voice.

Four of the men surrounded the box on the table and reached inside to take hold of the device. Someone gave a command and they lifted it out of the box, grunting as they raised it off the table and shuffled it over to the trolley.

'Easy,' the commander said.

They lowered it down into the new box. It fitted like a glove. The men closed and latched the box tight, as the head man headed across the lounge and out through the door. The trolley followed him. The others walked behind as if in attendance and Stratton joined them.

The group went slowly back to the Suburbans and the box was lifted into the back and the technician gave it a cursory inspection before latching it to the floor of the car. The doors of the vehicle closed and the men began to disperse. A man who wasn't wearing a gas mask stepped from the centre vehicle, walked up to the leader, who was talking to another of the men, and tapped him on the shoulder. The leader turned, then reached for the bottom of his own mask and raised it up over his head.

It was Jeff Wheeland. He rubbed his face and took a cigar from a pouch.

The man he was talking to removed his mask. Spinter.

'You can take your mask off, son,' Wheeland said to Stratton.

Stratton reached for his mask, turned away at the same time as he took it off and walked away along the track. He heard a voice over his radio and put in the earpiece.

'All stations, close in. Copy,' the voice said.

He waited until the other sentries had replied before he did the same. He had to get going. He stepped off the track into the bushes and quickly found the dead man, as he had left him. There was nothing he could do about it. They would either search for him or not. It was possible, in the darkness, he might not be accounted for. They would be anxious to get back with their prize. Even if they did notice he was missing, they would hardly risk the bomb to search for him.

Stratton dropped the gas mask but kept the weaponry and collected his clothes. He left cover and crossed the patch of open ground to find the bike. He stuffed his Afghan clothes up under his webbing, slung the carbine on its strap over his head and carried the bike through the gap in the wall and down onto the track and got going.

Ideally, he'd like to follow them into the base and see where they went, but he would have little chance of keeping up. He'd just have to hope his intuition was right: they'd go back to the black Globemaster and get the bomb on board as soon as possible. He glanced back, wondering if they were searching for the missing sentry. It would confuse the hell out of them if they found the body, his clothes removed, weapons and webbing gone.

The track straightened up ahead. He could see lights from houses and traffic on the main Bagram-Kabul road. He looked back again and saw lights moving through the trees. Buildings appeared on both sides of the track and the main road loomed up ahead. Left went towards Kabul. Right to the air base.

He took station in the shadows of one of the buildings and watched a couple of massive fuel trucks rumble past on their way to the base, their engines growling loudly. All in all he was feeling relieved. Betregard must have learned of the bomb and confirmed or shared the information with his Russian friends. The arming codes had been captured to reduce the risk and to delay General Mahuba and give the Americans time to find and secure the bomb. It would probably be taken back to Bagram and flown to Langley, Virginia, where it would be made safe. And no doubt used as a bargaining chip in the dealings with Pakistan. Stratton could understand them keeping it all secret for political reasons. A lot of people, in many countries, would have been totally unnerved by the idea of a suicide atomic bomber on the loose. To the intelligence community it would completely alter the perception of Pakistan's role in the world, even after the bomb had been successfully retrieved. It was best all round that it was not public knowledge. As it turned out, Betregard had done a good job. Reluctantly, he had to say the same for Wheeland.

Stratton decided there and then not to bother trying to witness the bomb going onto the plane. There was no point in taking the risk of exposing himself. Wheeland would for sure have a concern about his missing sentry, and Stratton didn't want him making any kind of connection to him. First of all, he would never be able to explain what he had been doing in Afghanistan. And second, he would probably face court-martial. He'd call his buddy in the SEALs when he got back to the base and had disposed of the NBC suit and weaponry, and secure himself a flight back to the UK asap. With luck he could be back home by the end of the following day.

It felt good to, once again, think of a pleasant Mediterranean beach somewhere, a quiet café, gentle waves. He could practically taste the seafood already.

He still had Chandos's death to deal with. It remained unexplained. Perhaps the reason would become clear at a later date.

The lead black Suburban glided into the junction, the other two close behind it. They stopped at the crossroads to let a lumbering fuel

173

truck pass by, heading towards the base, and then pulled left onto the main drag one after the other.

Heading south, not north.

In the direction of Kabul, not in the direction of Bagram.

Stratton's first thought was that perhaps they were taking another way into the base. It had several other entrances for sure. The Suburbans would have to take a circuitous route several kilometres long to get to them. Which was why it made no sense. The main checkpoint was in a straight line less than a kilometre away. A clear and secure road. Surely they needed to take the quickest and safest route to the camp. The fuel trucks had been heading that way without a pause, which indicated no roadblock or traffic jam. Perhaps Wheeland had been warned of something else. A threat that had forced them to use another checkpoint.

Stratton stepped out from cover and ran up onto the tarmac to watch the tail lights of the Suburbans head away. A fuel truck spewing out filthy fumes as it went past him towards the base briefly blocked his view. He stepped off the road as another heading for Kabul came towards him. An empty one. It slowed to negotiate the junction and presented Stratton with an opportunity he had to take. He couldn't exactly say what drove him to do it but he ran at the fuel truck as it accelerated past and grabbed the fixed ladder at the back, pulling himself up a couple of rungs. He got his feet on a lower rung and climbed onto the top of the tanker and hung onto the handles of the hatch.

The road was busy but he could see the three Suburbans ahead. It was a single lane in both directions, which would make it difficult for them to pass any of the big tankers, especially in a group of three. He guessed they would stick together — the lead driver would only overtake if he saw enough room for all three. Stratton knelt on the hatch and squinted ahead, the wind buffeting him. None of the people in the street appeared to notice him.

He saw the last turn to Bagram coming up. As far as he knew, it was the only remaining track they could possibly take to go back towards the base. The Suburbans went right by the turning, still heading south. Towards Kabul. He couldn't begin to imagine why. Kabul had an airport, but why go all the way there? Maybe they weren't intending to fly it out of the country, not yet at least. But if not, why not?

Whichever, Stratton didn't want to go to Kabul, certainly not on the back of a fuel truck and wearing a US military camouflage suit. It was nearly seventy kilometres. He'd never keep up with the Suburbans anyway because eventually they would overtake. He would have to get off the truck somewhere and he'd be alone and vulnerable. There was nothing for it but to jump off and head back to Bagram.

The truck wobbled as it went over a bump and Stratton had to hang on tightly. He could still make out the Suburbans ahead. Their distinctive tail lights were hard to miss. The last of the houses gave way to the open ground of the Shomali

175

plains. The mountains continued to form an endless barrier to his right. In front of him the land unfolded into a plateau, like massive, rolling waves, leading down onto the arid flatlands that stretched as far as he could see. The air was cold on his face and hands. It was time for him to quit this task and let it go.

The driver changed down a gear as the road began a steep descent, slowing noticeably. Stratton crawled to the rear ladder and began to make his way down it. Way out in front along the road, a massive, thunderous explosion shook the night. The flash was enormous and the shock-wave followed immediately, a powerful pulse travelling out from the centre of the blast. It came up the road and smashed the fuel truck's windows. The vehicle rocked as debris filled the air.

Another, slightly smaller explosion followed, and Stratton saw a giant ball of flame balloon upwards, plumes of bright orange, red and yellow scarred with black.

Every vehicle swerved, unable to stop quickly enough, but the steep hill drew them down towards the cauldron. He heard crunching collisions all around. In front of them a fuel truck swerved and turned over on the steep verge, rupturing its huge tank. Stratton watched raw fuel spill out to flood the road and hillside. The truck immediately in front of Stratton's jack-knifed and skidded off the road, swiping an oncoming truck. The gasoline from the burst fuel truck was washing down the road and somewhere flames caught and raced back uphill, spreading as they went, to the source. The fuel truck disintegrated in an almighty boom.

Gunfire followed all of this mayhem. The staccato bursts came from the high ground to the right of the road. Stratton felt the searing heat of the fireball sucking the air from his lungs. The truck beneath him left the road and bounced to a stop in a ditch with a screech of tearing metal.

The nose of the cab came round as the driver desperately tried to control it, the brakes fully applied. It began to tip. Stratton hung onto the ladder, riding it, waiting for the right moment. The truck tipped violently over. Stratton was catapulted off. He managed to land on his feet and rolled forward, before hurrying to cover.

He watched the mayhem from behind a rock. It had been an attack. An ambush. The enemy was close. He reached for his rifle on his back but it was gone. He glanced around but couldn't see it. There was no time to waste looking for it. He pushed off at the run as he pulled the pistol from its holster.

Tracer rounds were flying down from the high ground into an area of road about a hundred metres from Stratton. He watched an Afghan driver scramble from his vehicle and stagger a short distance before dropping to the ground. There were several more explosions. Much smaller ones. Stratton thought they were grenades or RPGs.

He found better cover behind a tree and decided to hold his position. He wanted to see what was happening. In particular to the spooks, if they were still there and hadn't pushed on through. He wondered if the Suburbans had been the target. But they couldn't possibly have been because the Taliban knew of the bomb. They had probably set the ambush and waited for the first target. Three shiny black Suburbans travelling nose to tail would have been irresistible. The regular military didn't travel like that. The Kabul to Bagram road wasn't a very popular ambush site because of the number of military vehicles that moved along it. A night attack like this reduced the Taliban's risks.

The sporadic gunfire continued. It appeared to be moving down the hill towards the road. Stratton moved off, keeping to the higher ground. He had to skirt the fireball but needed to keep in the darkness. The enemy was closing on their target. There didn't appear to be any return fire.

Another explosion on the road. Muffled, like a fuel tank. Stratton kept moving forward and saw figures running, illuminated by the fires. A dozen or so of them. Then he saw two vehicles appear, driving towards the fire from the direction of the higher ground. They were pick-up trucks. They stopped on the road and more gunfire came from that same location. Stratton was still unable to see beyond the fire. He moved quicker, his pistol in his hand. Not a match for AK-47s but he had the darkness. The attackers wouldn't hang around long anyway. Someone would respond to the attack soon enough and they knew that. They had the weapons and numbers for an ambush but not to take on a sustained attack by any substantial force.

He looked back in the direction of Bagram, wondering if a military convoy might be on its way, pushing through the disarray of abandoned and crashed vehicles. There was nothing. It was too soon. An engine revved loudly from beyond the flames. One of the pick-ups bumped off the road back into Stratton's view. The driver gunned it as if trying to get the pick-up out of a rut. It jolted forward, turned back onto the road, crossed it, went over a bump the other side and carried on across country. It soon disappeared from view.

The attackers were leaving.

Stratton headed down the hill. The flames were still unfolding in great sheets and the heat coming towards him was intense. As he got closer in he saw men clambering into the other pick-up. They looked like Afghan fighters. The vehicle started up and accelerated off in the same direction as the first. The gunfight was over.

He felt confident the ambushers had gone. As he moved further around the flames, he saw the black Suburbans for the first time since the explosions, all three of them. Two were lying on their sides off the road. The other was upright on the edge of the highway with all of its doors open. The armoured windows had been cracked and punctured and the skins twisted and torn like paper. He could see a shredded body in the front of the upright cab. Off the verge, the vehicle with the gantry holding the cigarette-like probes had sheared away and lay in the dirt, buckled beyond recognition. The upright Suburban, as far as he could tell, had been the lead vehicle and had contained the nuclear device.

As he approached it, he saw a body lying on the grass. One of the spooks. He wasn't moving. Stratton got to within a couple of metres of him before having to stop due to the searing heat. He pulled his hood over his head and made a lunge for the man, grabbing hold of his harness and dragging him away.

Stratton tried to find a pulse. If there was life in him, it was beyond what Stratton could do for him. Hopefully a military ambulance would get here soon. Stratton looked around for others but couldn't see any. They were probably still in the vehicles. He went to the lead Suburban with its rear doors open. A couple of men lay inside the back, both dead, shot several times through their heads at close range. One of them was Mike Spinter. He had his eyes open, looking directly at Stratton. He looked the same in death as he had in life.

The large black-plastic container had gone.

Stratton looked for it around the immediate area, then remembered the clips the technician had used to secure the box. He went back to the Suburban and saw that all four had been undone. The box didn't fall out of the vehicle. Someone had unclipped it and lifted it out.

The Taliban had taken it. Probably because it looked expensive. It wasn't possible they knew that this convoy was carrying a nuclear warhead. The Taliban always inspected their victims if they had the time, and they took what they could.

They would never have known what was in the box.

'Don't move,' a voice said from behind him. 'Stand perfectly still.'

It was a woman's voice, American. The odds against her being anything other than friendly forces were extreme but Stratton did as instructed. His pistol was in his hand by his side. He had his back to her. He heard her moving above the sound of the fire. He caught a glimpse of someone in his peripheral vision. She was looking about the scene and inside the vehicles.

'Turn around,' she said.

Stratton obeyed slowly, until they were facing each other.

She was almost as tall as him, wearing grey US Army fatigues, no hat with short hair. She had intense, intelligent-looking eyes and was holding a large semi-automatic handgun. A Magnum 0.44 or 0.50. An unusual weapon for a regular soldier to carry. She wasn't bulky but she looked strong. There were no markings on her uniform. No insignia, rank or unit.

'Any other of your team survive?' she asked.

Stratton had a choice to make.

'I can't find any,' he said.

She looked around at the dead men. 'You were lucky.'

It didn't sound like a question so he didn't say anything, until she looked at him as if waiting for a response.

'I have no idea how I survived,' he said.

She looked into the back of the lead vehicle. 'The device was in here?'

181

Another surprise. She not only knew about it, she knew which SUV it had been in. He wanted to ask her who she was. Why she hadn't been with the team.

She was looking at him, aware that what she'd asked had surprised him. 'We work for the same people,' she said. 'My job is to monitor the device.'

'What do you mean?'

'What I said. My job is to ensure the device is secured. Nothing else.'

'The Taliban must've taken it,' he said.

'Which direction did they go?'

'That way,' he said, pointing south-east.

She walked to where she could see the open country, holstering her gun. After a moment she walked into the darkness without a word or a look at him.

Stratton stepped away in search of cooler, less acrid air to breathe. The land dropped away in front of him. The vast panorama looked dramatic in the starlight. Kabul was far out of sight due south, where the icy mountains on his right headed towards. He saw lights along the base of the mountains, a line of tiny white pinpricks. They were vehicles heading along the highway towards Bagram. But the ambushers hadn't used that road. They had cut across country because they didn't want to run into any roadblock set up by coalition or Afghan security forces.

As he looked across the plain south-east of where they stood, he saw a sudden distant flash of red, well away from any roads. It appeared again. Vehicle tail lights. It had to be the Taliban who had stolen the warhead. The frustration welled in him. He could only stand and watch them get away, unable to pursue them.

Someone was going to be very upset about this.

16

A vehicle started up and pulled onto the road and stopped level with Stratton. It was a standard, dirty, drab-green US Army Humvee with armoured door panels, extended front bumper, long whip antenna and spare wheels on the back with fuel cans and shovel. The woman was at the wheel, looking at him through the narrow opening of the driver's window. There was no one beside her in the passenger seat.

He wondered if she was about to offer him a lift back to the base. No doubt she'd called in support. The priority for him was the bomb. It was still close. An air asset would be perfect, with an assault team. But by the time they had organised all that the Taliban and the bomb would be long gone.

She was a hard arse, or at least she put on a convincing act. He wondered just how tough she was.

'I don't suppose you'd consider lending me your Humvee,' he said.

She gave him a blank look. He took it to mean 'Get lost'.

'Aren't you interested in pursuing them?' he asked.

'That is my directive,' she said. 'To ensure the device remains on track.'

'Directive?' he muttered to himself. It was time to see how tough she really was. He looked back in the direction of the lights he had seen in the distant sea of blackness. After a few seconds they flickered again. 'There,' he said, pointing. 'That's them.' He looked back at her for a reaction. 'You up for it?'

She looked past Stratton where he had pointed. Then she looked back at him, as though studying him. 'Get in,' she said.

It would seem she was up for it, in principle. But he knew saying and doing were two very different things. As was chasing Taliban and then catching them. He walked around the vehicle to the passenger side, opened the heavy door and climbed in. He glanced into the back. Other than some body armour and what looked like weapons boxes, it was empty. He had travelled in Afghanistan on his own but always as a local, and rarely without the support of other operatives not far away. She seemed to be totally alone, in military fatigues, in a US military vehicle. And a woman.

As he slammed the door shut, she shoved the heavy vehicle into gear and it shunted off, its headlights cutting into the darkness.

'See those tracks,' he said, pointing at tyre marks leaving the road and going downhill. She followed them. The vehicle jolted heavily as it went over an edge and down a gentle incline. She grabbed a pair of night-vision goggles out of the dashboard and pulled them on. Then the vehicle's lights went out. For Stratton, everything turned black.

There was another pair of NVGs in the dash. Stratton pulled them on and the ground ahead appeared in a contrast of white and grey. He could make out the tyre tracks but no further sign of lights in the distance. Judging by the marks, the Taliban had been travelling at speed. They had failed to avoid some dangerous-looking lumps. He hoped they continued to be as reckless.

'How long've you been with the DL unit?' she asked.

It was a question Stratton hadn't prepared himself for. He had no idea what a DL unit was, for a start. If he knew anything about her, it would help. She couldn't be an integral part of the team, not directly. Otherwise she would have known he wasn't a real member of the team. He was going to have to blag his way through.

'I joined them a week or so ago,' he said. 'What were you doing hanging back on your own?'

She slammed on the brakes and Stratton had to grab the dashboard to stop himself from hitting it. She had her gun out before the Humvee had come to a halt and levelled it at his head. She removed her NVGs.

'Tell me what you're doing with the team,' she said. 'Start with your name. Then explain your accent.'

He had a bad feeling about how serious she was and so decided to stick as close to the truth as possible. He slowly pushed his goggles onto the top of his head. 'My name is John Stratton. I'm from British special forces. SBS.'

'Who's the DL commander?'

'Wheeland,' he said. 'Spinter was second in command.'

'What's a Brit doing with the team?'

'I helped Wheeland secure the arming codes. It was a joint SBS-DL operation. A week ago in Helmand.'

'Who had the codes?'

'Kalil Rohami,' Stratton said. 'He died on the op.'

She kept the gun level, as if he hadn't given her enough.

'I was later involved in a surveillance operation against certain figures in Pakistan's ISI,' he said. 'I was part of the team that tracked the device to Bagram. Wheeland invited me to stay with the team when they confirmed it was in area.' He'd taken a leap and could only hope it wasn't too much of one.

'Who does Wheeland report to?' she asked.

'I'm not entirely sure, to be honest.'

The gun remained rock steady in her hand.

'I suppose it must be Betregard,' he said. 'Wheeland said he gave the OK to let me stay on.'

She lowered the gun. It went back into its holster and she pulled on the NVGs and accelerated the Humvee down the hill. He felt relieved, to say the least. She seriously looked as if she would have pulled the trigger if he hadn't come up with the answers. He brought his NVGs back down over his eyes.

'Do you mind if I ask a question?' he said.

She didn't react. She wasn't the chatty type, that was for sure. He took the silence as a positive.

'Do you have a name?'

He was met by another wall of silence. She turned the wheel sharply to go around an abrupt ridge then rejoin the tracks on the other side.

'Hetta,' she said eventually.

That was a success, he thought. She was dry, to be sure. 'Everyone calls me Stratton,' he said. 'That Magnum would've blown my brains all the way to China.'

She didn't respond and just changed gear heavily as the hill got steeper.

No sense of humour, he decided. Perhaps she liked more direct talk. 'Why'd you bring me along?' he asked.

'We have to take the device back. You would be up for that, right?'

Maybe she did have a sense of humour. 'Sure. Do you think they know what they've got?'

'No. It was a coincidence. They ran into some bad luck.'

'We certainly did.'

'I didn't mean your guys,' she said. 'I meant the Taliban.'

He hoped she was as full of bravado when the time came. 'I estimate eight to ten of them. A dozen at the most,' he said.

'Don't worry. I'll take care of it.'

That's pretty big talk, he thought. But the way she was driving, her body language, he had a feeling she wasn't going to turn back.

'No more questions,' she said. 'I don't like talking.'

That suited him perfectly. No talking meant no more questions about him. He settled back and studied the way ahead. The ground was beginning to level out, more or less. Lights appeared over to their right a couple of miles away. Judging by the brittle cluster, it was a village. The Taliban tracks didn't appear to be heading in that direction. He saw similar lights further to the left. Straight ahead, in the direction the tracks were going, he could see nothing but blackness.

Stratton raised the NVGs from his face to look at the internal console. The navigation system wasn't working. The monitor that should have been attached to it was missing. He looked around: the vehicle was a mess. Ration-pack wrappings littered the floor and inside the dash. It looked like it had been taken from a regular Army patrol.

They had been driving for nearly two hours in silence when the Humvee bumped heavily and the terrain suddenly changed. The middle-ground seemed to disappear, as if it dropped away steeply. It was hard to tell with the NVGs. They didn't provide great depth of field. The image gave the impression they were heading towards a cliff. The tracks continued to head towards it. She slowed the vehicle enough so that she would have time to react if it was too steep.

She dropped a gear as they approached what was looking like a steep edge, then another until they were moving slowly. Then she stopped them completely. Not because it was a cliff — the incline was navigable for the Humvee. They could see pick-ups at the bottom of the slope. Hetta turned off the engine and opened her door. Both of them climbed out and walked to

189

the front of the Humvee. Hetta removed her NVGs, placed them on the hood and raised a thermal imager to her eye. Stratton had to make do with his NVGs.

It looked like there were four vehicles altogether. He could see a fair bit of movement, perhaps a dozen or more people. One of the vehicles looked much larger than the others. A truck perhaps. A hundred metres further away, near a fire, he saw kerosene lamps and a couple of structures that could have been tents.

'Nomads,' Hetta said.

She was able to make out the various images better than he could. Other figures near the tents were animals. Goats or sheep. 'Any idea what's going on?' Stratton asked.

She didn't reply.

'Taliban and nomads don't usually mix well,' he said. 'You ever met any?'

'No.'

'They've little respect for anyone. They'll make a deal with the Taliban one day and sell them out to the coalition the next. And the same goes for any coalition people they stumble on.'

'The people with the pick-ups, the Taliban, they're changing a tyre,' she said.

That made more sense. The Taliban must have had a flat and caught the attention of the nomads. Stratton lifted the NVGs, wondering what his new-found friend was planning. If it was up to him, and it clearly wasn't, he'd take the opportunity to skirt around the hold-up. They knew the Taliban's track, their general direction, so all they would have to do was get

190

back on it and find a good site to ambush as the Taliban came on through. Give them a taste of their own medicine.

Several flashes suddenly fired below them, followed by the distant crack of rifle fire. It was around the vehicles. Figures were running but a couple had dropped. He watched others run but they didn't get far. The shooting ended as quickly as it had started and several figures walked in. There was another flash and bang. He watched the figures go from body to body.

Back at the tents, more figures were emerging, some very small. Women and children. The families looking on at their proud sons and fathers. Stratton removed his NVGs. Things had suddenly changed and he wasn't sure if it was for better or worse. The nomads had taken the booty for themselves. There were a lot more of them than there had been Taliban. But they wouldn't be in a hurry to go anywhere. They were by nature slow-moving. And unconcerned about being pursued. If the Taliban had no idea what they had been carrying, the nomads certainly wouldn't.

A fire began where the attack had taken place. Stratton held his NVGs to his face again. The flames quickly became fierce. It was one of the Taliban's pick-ups ablaze, the one that had got the flat. The other was being driven away. His first fear was that they were burning the box as well — but that would have been uncharacteristic. Nomads were scavengers and wouldn't leave a thing like that without inspecting it at least. They were destroying half the evidence of the attack and stealing the other half.

He watched the nomads toss the dead bodies onto the flames and head back towards their camp.

Hetta turned and walked to the back of the Humvee, opened it up and rummaged through the box inside. When she came back she was carrying an M4 assault rifle and wearing a chest harness, its pouches filled with magazines. She wasn't wearing any bulletproof vest or ballistic helmet.

'Everything you need for a fight is in that box,' she said. 'Help yourself.'

'Do we have a plan?'

'Two. One with you. One without you.'

Ouch, he said to himself.

He went to the Humvee and looked in through the open rear door. There was another M4 and webbing, along with an assortment of grenades. He took the gun and webbing but couldn't find any body armour. He wondered whose oversight that was. He slipped the chest harness over his head and tightened it, put a couple of first field dressings into a pocket and grabbed a flashlight. There were a couple of hand radios. They reminded him that she had not made radio contact with her controllers, whoever they were. They had been on the road for several hours and she had made significant decisions that would normally warrant informing a higher authority.

He checked his watch. It wasn't yet midnight. They had six more hours of darkness. If she called her people now, she could have an assault team in the area before dawn. He couldn't see any satellite communications anywhere.

There was no mobile phone coverage in the area. She must have something with which to communicate with her bosses. Perhaps the spook team was all there was. Maybe she really was on her own in Afghanistan.

It reminded him of the number of times he'd been at the sharp end without support, trying to surmount a problem on his own. Maybe she was in the same boat. She also seemed to have a similar attitude as he did to working alone.

He walked back to her as he used a soft cocking technique to load the weapon quietly.

She looked at him, as if judging the way he wore his hardware. 'You had much experience of fighting?' she asked.

'Some.'

'I'm talking about open field combat.'

He decided not to answer and let her think he was inexperienced. Perhaps she would take more of the lead. Get shot in the process. That might not be a bad idea.

'If you don't feel up to it, don't push it,' she said. 'I don't need you.'

'I'm looking forward to the experience.'

She loaded a magazine into the breech of her M4 and silently cocked it.

The cold wind stroked his face as she set off down the slope. Stratton let her get a few metres ahead and followed, walking to the side. They moved at a steady pace towards the nomad camp. The ground was powdery underfoot. The wind blowing towards them would mask any sound they made before it reached the camp. And unless the men were sitting in complete silence, they wouldn't hear the pair until they were close.

Hetta raised her thermal imager while they walked. She was obviously content with what she saw since her pace and direction didn't alter.

As they closed in, the camp began to take better shape, illuminated from two locations — the burning pick-up and the campfire. They saw three large tents in all, animals beyond them. Each tent had a light inside from a kerosene lamp. He counted fifteen men around the campfire, but no women or children. They had gone back into the tents. The men's voices drifted to them on the wind. The Afghans were deep in conversation.

Stratton and Hetta slowed as they got closer. There was a large box near the fire and a couple of the men were inspecting it. He couldn't be certain but it looked like *the* box. He wondered what they would do if they knew what it was. Probably tear off in their vehicles at a fast pace, leaving it behind.

Fifty or so metres from the fire Hetta came to a stop. Stratton kept a strategic distance. They took in the encampment: the burning vehicle on the far left, the nomads' truck and pick-up on the right, the tents left of centre, the men around the fire, the box right of centre.

The men's voices were clear, though Stratton couldn't understand a word. As well as some Farsi, he spoke a little Dari, but many nomads spoke Gujari, a dialect of which he knew nothing.

'Move right beyond the truck,' she said. 'Check anyone trying to use them as cover.'

'What's the plan?'

'Kill them. Take back the device.'

Brilliant, he thought. How subtle. He looked at the attack angles. She needed to maintain the element of surprise, and, ideally, kill as many as they could before the nomads reacted. He sighed, did what he was told and walked away from her, keeping his footsteps quiet. As he moved behind the truck, it masked his view of the men around the fire. He kept walking until they were back in his line of sight. He stopped when he had a clear view of all the nomads. The three tents were now beyond the fire. Stratton hoped the women and children would remain inside when the fighting started.

He could no longer see Hetta, the truck being in the way. The fire seemed to illuminate him but he knew from experience he was still in the blackness as far as the nomads were concerned. He could even afford to get a little nearer and improve the accuracy of his fire. As he took a step, he heard her voice. She wasn't going for any kind of surprise attack.

The nomads' conversations stopped instantly and they got to their feet to face her, every one of them holding a rifle, though none yet up on aim. Stratton could see her moving slowly towards them out of the darkness. She held the M4 in both hands, with the end of the barrel pointing at the ground in front. She was speaking fluently to them in Dari, too quickly for him to understand much, but he was impressed.

The nomads might speak Gujari but they would understand Dari well enough.

Stratton stepped closer as the nomads moved apart. They must have been highly confused. It would have come as a big surprise for anyone to walk into their camp in the middle of the night. Alone would have been unheard of. A foreigner, impossible. But a foreign woman alone. That would be beyond their comprehension.

Stratton wondered what she was saying. Maybe she was simply asking for the box. He didn't think she had a chance of convincing them to hand it over — but surely she knew that? He wondered why she was taking the risk of even speaking to them. Standing alone and facing them with a gun in her hand was akin to holding a red cape in front of a bull. Knowing her even as little as he did, he doubted she was being at all polite and humble.

Whatever she was saying, she finally succeeded in getting a rise out of them. One of the older men, probably the tribal elder, seemed to have had enough of the intrusion and let out a wail as he raised his weapon. That was as far as he got and where his life came to an abrupt end. Stratton watched as she fired a controlled burst at him and he went flying back, his arms outstretched, the weapon released into the air.

Before he hit the dirt the others had gone into action, and before any could return fire two of them suffered a similar fate to the elder. The nomads quickly spread, several towards the nearest cover, which was the truck.

Hetta crouched and fired before quickly

getting up and changing position. She moved deliberately, without great haste, not staying in the same spot for more than a second. She hit another, judging by the way he doubled over while dropping his rifle. Two of them were coming towards Stratton. It was time for him to join the fray. He fired two single shots into both, enough to drop them for good.

Two others headed away from both shooters. Neither got far. Stratton dropped both of them. When he looked for any other targets, Hetta had stopped shooting. For a second he thought she'd been hit, but it was only because there was nothing more to shoot at. Every nomad was down. He couldn't help being impressed with her. She had not fired her weapon on fully automatic, which was the Hollywood version of a gunfight with an assault rifle. Like him, she'd fired single shots in rapid succession. It saved ammunition, retained accuracy and reduced the need to change a magazine, during which time the shooter was most vulnerable, especially out in the open. But shooting at a crowd was the ideal time to use fully automatic firepower. To select single shot when so outnumbered had been audacious. It displayed serious confidence in her own ability. That or she'd selected the wrong setting. Somehow he didn't think that was the case.

Stratton remained where he was, content to wait. If you don't need to move among the victims then don't, was one of his many mottoes. There was always the chance one of them would be wounded. No point in risking a bullet or a grenade. As he looked at the men lying motionless in the dirt, he couldn't help feeling a tinge of regret. They would have been brought up with guns all of their lives, to shoot and hunt like natural. And they were fearless. But they'd obviously never come up against someone like her before. If they'd had time to think before they died, it would have been devoted to utter stupefaction.

Hetta evidently didn't have the same philosophy as he did about moving among a recently fallen enemy. She marched towards the fire. One of the nomads moved and she took care of that immediately and fired once into his head. She stopped among the bodies and Stratton watched her. She shot another nomad, who'd apparently shown a sign of life. She was clearly aware of the dangers and had a simple solution to it. She continued to the box.

Stratton moved forward, past the men he'd felled. They were dead. He kept an eye on the tents in case anyone inside felt like coming out to have a go, and joined her to look inside the box. It looked like the same device to him — cable still attached to the battery, inspection plate screwed shut and a faint glow of LED light visible through several pin holes in it.

She closed the box lid and glanced at him. He couldn't say he saw approval in her eyes, but the look of disapproval she'd worn since they'd met seemed to have mellowed a little.

'Bring the pick-up over here,' she said.

The adulation was over.

He suppressed his irritation and walked over

to the pickup, wondering what she was going to do.

It was a Toyota Hilux. He wasn't surprised since it was the most popular vehicle in Afghanistan for both the Taliban and Afghan civilian security forces. The key was in the ignition, so he put his weapon inside, climbed in and started the engine, which fired first time and sounded in good condition.

He put it into gear, steered it around towards the fire, and reversed up to the box. Then he went round to the back, where she was unlatching the tailgate and dropping it open. She took hold of the handle on one side of the box and waited for him to take the other.

They lifted it together. It felt like a couple of hundred kilos and they had to put all their effort into it. She managed her end, though only just. After a massive effort they got a corner of the box onto the bed and Stratton quickly repositioned himself to take some of the weight off her end and together they heaved it into the back.

They took a moment to catch their breaths.

'Am I allowed to ask a question?' he said.

She looked at him in a way that appeared to indicate permission.

'What's the plan now?'

She looked at him as if weighing him up.

He thought about pushing her a little, telling her he had a right to know what was going on. If he had been a real spook, by now he would have insisted on knowing who she worked for and by what authority she was in charge. But he didn't

199

want to give her cause to dig any deeper about him.

And he doubted somehow it would get him anywhere.

He decided to go for a nudge regardless. 'Look, we know you've got a big gun that you like to shove against people's heads if they say something you don't approve of, but technically this device is my responsibility,' he said. 'I don't know who you work for or what your job is, but considering all that's gone on, I'd appreciate a little more respect.'

'You talk a lot,' she said.

'Actually, not normally. But you don't talk enough.'

'I told you my job. It's this device and nothing else.'

'Except if anything gets in your way.'

'That's right.' She said it as if to remind him. 'Nothing gets in the way of that directive.'

There she went with the directive thing again.

A noise that sounded like crying came from one of the tents and Hetta called out something in Dari. Stratton got the gist of it and the crying instantly stopped.

'Do you know why Wheeland wasn't taking the warhead into Bagram base?' she asked.

He hoped he wasn't expected to know the answer to that. She'd probably have her Magnum out again. But considering the spooks' move along the Kabul road, Wheeland clearly had no intention of taking the bomb to the base by another route. If he was taking it to the US ultimately, which was only to be expected, Kabul would have been the next obvious choice. But why he hadn't taken it to Bagram, Stratton had no idea. Unless there was something about Bagram that wasn't like anywhere else.

And then the answer struck him. It was something Bullfrog had said. There were radiation detection systems operating at Bagram. And Bagram was under the control of the Radiation Detection Agency, not the CIA or NSA. If any of those systems picked up radiation traces, the balloons would go up. This was a nuclear device and part of a highly secret operation. Wheeland didn't want anyone in Bagram to know about the bomb.

'The detection systems,' he said. 'Bagram would have discovered we had a nuclear bomb.'

'That's right. They don't have radiation detection equipment in Kabul, and Wheeland and his vehicles could get the device through the security inspections without question and onto a cargo flight back to the US.'

Stratton knew Kabul airport well enough. It was pretty much completely in the hands of the Afghan authorities and they liked nothing better than to make life difficult for the invaders, despite all that was going on. Wheeland clearly had the clout to overcome those obstacles. Most likely that meant money, and in the right hands.

'So, we're headed to Kabul?' Stratton asked.

'Can you get the box through?' she said.

That single question told him a lot. She didn't know the airport, so asking him must have been tough. It also suggested she didn't know Afghanistan well. And it meant she didn't have the same kind of authority Wheeland had to get the box through. He sensed an opportunity to wrest some control and also give himself some value. He didn't know exactly why, but he wanted to stay in this game. He was intrigued. She was dangerous and, strangely, that intrigued him too. He wasn't sure if it was the challenge. She certainly was.

Yet there was something decidedly odd about her concept of operations. He felt he had some latitude to dig deeper. 'Why don't you just call in some help?' he asked.

'Because everyone involved in the operation was in that convoy,' she said. 'There's only you and me left. There is no one in Afghanistan I can trust. Not right now. I could hold up for a few days until assistance arrives, but my orders are to get this back Stateside as quickly as possible.'

He thought that was interesting. It confirmed a few points.

'If you can't be of help, I'll find a way,' she said, picking up her carbine and walking to the front of the vehicle. She climbed into the cab, shut the door and started the engine.

For a second he thought she was going to drive off and leave him, but she looked out the window at him. 'You seem to know this country,' she said.

He thought it odd she could speak Dari yet know so little about the place. But then, military language courses were often like that. Intensive without ever going to the country of origin. She'd probably only ever been to bases or camps. Like most of the coalition forces — only

202

a relatively small percentage of them knew the ground in any great detail. And only special forces knew a wide variety of bases and operational arenas, things like the roads and country in many of the provinces.

'Pretty well,' he said.

'Can you get the box into Kabul airport and onto a flight?'

By now he'd thought about it. 'I don't have any contacts in Kabul right now. It would be high risk to try without the right assistance. Do you have any money?'

She shook her head. 'Not enough.'

'Can you bring in a spook flight if we could find an airfield somewhere else?' he asked.

'I want to do it with as little assistance as possible.'

He assumed that was because of the need for secrecy. 'Then you need an air base with a Western civilian administration to fly this box back to the US.'

'That would be best.'

Stratton considered the options. A boat would obviously require crossing borders, which would be fraught with problems. Too long on the road in any direction meant too much exposure to the authorities and numerous bad guys. Air was the best way.

It came to him without much further thought.

'Kandahar,' he said. 'It's a large coalition base but also with a number of civilian contractors and commercial flights.' He wondered if she knew how to get there and what to do when she arrived. Probably not. He could see she was uncomfortable about something. He thought he could guess what it was. 'You ever been to Kandahar?' he asked.

She shook her head again.

He guessed this was the tough part for her. If she accepted the suggestion, she would have to let him manage it. That would mean handing him the controls. She wouldn't like that one bit.

'I want you to come with me,' she said.

'We can't take the Humvee,' he said, not making a meal of it, though he knew how hard it had been for her to say it. 'The Hilux will be perfect. We'll need to get into local clothes, and I'll drive. Outside the cities, you'll only attract attention if you're driving.'

She didn't waste any time deliberating his advice and turned off the engine. Everything fell silent except for the cold wind blowing across the open plain and the tents flapping louder than before. The wind was picking up. She climbed out, leaving her M4 in the cab, and walked over to the largest of the three tents and pulled back the entrance.

He heard a woman beg for mercy in a loud wail. Hetta shouted back at her, telling her to shut up, and the hysterical voice went silent. Minutes later Hetta emerged carrying a pile of clothing, all of it black cloth and lace, and walked back to the Hilux, where she began to remove her webbing.

Stratton went to the truck and looked inside the back. There were several crates and a couple of old suitcases. He climbed inside and set about searching for clothes. When he returned to the

Hilux he was wearing a pair of light cotton trousers over his fatigues, a linen shirt over his T-shirt, and a large three-quarter-length goatskin jacket.

Hetta had simply pulled a full-length burkha over the top of her fatigues, the hood thrown onto her back for when she needed it.

Stratton was holding a small cloth bag. 'I found this bag of Afghan passports,' he said, taking a bundle from the bag. 'The nomads were obviously in the false document business. I might need one if we get stopped by the police. Could you choose one for me?'

He held them out to her — since she could speak the lingo, he expected she could read it too. She took the bundle and quickly went through them, flicking to the identity pages, comparing the photographs to Stratton.

'This will do,' she said, handing him one. 'Your name is Mustafa Dinorani.' She put the rest in the bag and gave it back to him.

'Mustafa Dinorani,' he said, making an effort to remember. Then he tossed the bag on the fire.

'We should pack the vehicle with household items,' he said. 'And fuel.'

They collected baskets, cooking pots and rope and piled them into the back, covering the large plastic box with a rug. By the time Stratton had returned from the truck with several cans of fuel, she was busy lashing down the contents of the flatbed with line.

He topped up the Hilux's tank and fitted as many spare cans as he could into the back. Kandahar was several hundred kilometres south of Kabul but they had enough to get there. Then his eyes fell on a water container, which reminded him to look for some sustenance. The more self-sufficient they could be the better. He felt suddenly hungry.

He spotted some pots around the fire and a lamb stew of some kind, with unleavened bread. He made a quick sandwich and filled one of the smaller pots with bits of everything and brought it back to the vehicle. While he ate, he took another scan around in case there was anything else he'd forgotten. He realised she was looking at him with her usual blank expression.

He wondered what she was thinking. Perhaps she was unhappy that he'd taken over, to a degree. Stratton didn't doubt that when the opportunity came for her to take charge again she would. He held the pot out to her.

'You want some lamb?' he said. 'It's pretty good.'

'Let's go,' she said, walking around to the passenger side of the pick-up.

He wondered how deep he'd have to dig to find a human side to her. He wasn't particularly interested in making much of an effort. He climbed into the driver's seat, placed his weapon muzzle to the floor with the butt on the seat beside his leg for easy access and covered it with a scarf. She climbed in beside him on the bench seat, sorted out her flowing burkha, placed her carbine beside her like he had and covered it in a cloth.

'All right, dear?' he said, starting the engine.

She sat looking coldly ahead.

He turned on the headlights, put the engine into gear and eased the vehicle along the hard ground, using the compass on his watch to provide a rough direction. Due west would cut the Bagram-Kabul road that ran north-south. He had little idea how far away it was — thirty, forty, fifty kilometres maybe. He looked ahead for any steep hills that would be better avoided sooner rather than later, but all he could see was blackness, with the far mountain range beyond. It would be nice to reach the road by sunrise.

With his partner being such a bundle of fun, it was going to be a long drive.

17

Twenty-five minutes after the Hilux left the camp a dozen Taliban horsemen rode into the clearing. They were outriders, tasked with keeping the smaller, more remote villages in constant touch with the fanatical organisation. They achieved this by running hot and cold in temperament and understanding. They could be magnanimous one day and ruthlessly punishing the next, depending on what a particular village had been up to. If, for instance, a coalition military unit had passed through an area and the Taliban learned that the tribal elders had been tolerant of it, the Taliban would mete out punishment. And usually disproportionately to the crime. There would usually be executions, since they were the most effective instructional tool. These would include a draft from the families — men, women and children — and the method of execution would depend on the mood and taste of the Taliban leader.

The commander of this particular squadron was Alba Tushani, an Iranian-born Pashtun. He liked to tear his victims apart using horses. He would use two, three or sometimes four of the animals, tethered to the limbs of his victim. It was a visually horrifying MO that Tushani found most persuasive when it came to convincing Afghans where to focus their loyalties.

Tushani rode around the camp inspecting the

place, in particular the dead nomads around the fire. One of his men called out and he rode over to inspect the still slightly burning Hilux with the bodies on it. His men confirmed it was one of theirs and they identified the men who weren't too disfigured.

Tushani had been waiting for his men to return from their ambush on the Bagram road. They should have been at the rendezvous by the time one of his men reported the distant fire. He was able to form a general idea of what had happened, but only up until the nomads were killed. He was well aware that nomads would take what they wanted from passing travellers regardless of whether they were Taliban or not. They had clearly made an effort to burn the evidence.

Tushani wasn't an excitable man. Everything had its course to take as far as he was concerned. A distant fire wasn't something to get overly excited about, even if he had suspicions that all was not well. As soon as he'd finished his evening meal, he ordered his men to mount up and they went for a late ride to take a look.

Another shout came from one of his men, who'd found the women and children huddled inside a tent. Tushani rode over and questioned the nomad leader's wife.

She told him what had happened, to the best of her knowledge, although she lied about her men killing the Taliban. She believed the people who'd killed her men, and Tushani's, were Americans. All Westerners — especially military — were considered Americans by these people.

Tushani asked her what had happened to the other Hilux. She explained that her men were helping the Taliban fix a flat tyre when the Americans attacked. Two of the Americans had left in the Hilux and headed west. Tushani asked how many Americans there were altogether. The woman stumbled on the answer, mainly because she couldn't tell him just two had done all of that killing, and especially that one of them had been a woman. So she told the Taliban commander she had no idea how many Americans there were altogether. She'd been hiding throughout and heard the fighting from within the tent.

Tushani knew she was lying about something, but he didn't have time to cross-examine her further or use more persuasive methods to exact the truth. The important facts were that Americans had attacked and they weren't all that far away. His men found the tyre tracks, which went some way to proving what the old woman had said about the pick-up being stolen.

Tushani loved to fight. Or rather, to kill. He particularly loved to capture Americans and torture them before executing them. That gave him immense pleasure. But revenge was even more important to him. They'd stolen his property. Killed his men. He knew exactly how far the Kabul road was. He knew how long it would take the Americans to reach it in the Hilux. If he was swift, he could reach them by the time they arrived at the Kabul road.

He cried out to his men and they rode their horses along the tyre tracks made by the pick-up.

* * *

The Hilux bumped along, its headlights seeing far into the darkness. Stratton steered it over and around a seemingly endless field of dips and bumps. The terrain was sometimes stony, sometimes dirt, with frequent patches of hardy plants.

Stratton was able to maintain a westerly direction for most of the route, but some of the ground was so undulating or steep that he had to divert north or south to navigate around. At times the vehicle bounced from side to side so violently the pair of them had to hold on tightly to prevent bumping heads.

They'd been driving for almost two hours when Stratton first began to experience a subtle yet disturbed feeling. Long experience had taught him that, even though it was not a certainty, he was wise never to ignore such feelings. He glanced continually in the rear-view and side mirrors, looking for something, though what he had no idea. He could see nothing but total blackness behind them.

He noticed Hetta looking into her side mirror and wondered if she was experiencing something similar.

'You feel it too?' he asked her.

She nodded.

It was enough for him to put the brakes on. He turned off the lights, stopped the vehicle on the soft, gravelly earth, killed the engine and climbed out.

She also stepped out and used her thermal

imager to look back into the darkness.

Stratton found a rock and smashed both tail lights. They stood silently, listening, watching. All he could hear was the wind against their backs, which didn't help.

'Let's go,' he said.

They climbed back into the Hilux and got going, without lights. Hetta handed him the thermal imager. The sense of an encroaching threat never left either of them. They continued to check the mirrors but nothing was ever visible. Stratton would have liked to know how much further it was to the road. He would feel safer once they were on it. Maybe it was the ghosts of the nomads.

Another hour went by and the first hint of daylight began to break over the mountain range behind them. Stratton could see well enough without the imager, which was fortunate since its power was waning. He thought he could make out a scar running across their front a mile away. He hoped it was the road. There would be little or no traffic at that time of the day. He didn't know the curfew times in Kabul but it wouldn't be raised before full daylight. Any early morning traffic would be from the villages between Kabul and Bagram.

He negotiated a tight dip that rocked the vehicle violently. As he pulled back onto level ground, Hetta grabbed her carbine and pulled her webbing belt with its attached magazine pouches off the floor. Stratton's eyes flashed to the rear-view mirror. He saw riders coming down the broad slope towards them.

He hit the accelerator hard. He knew he couldn't outrun them on the terrain but he had a chance on tarmac, if they could reach it in time. As he flew over a bump he was reminded they couldn't lose anyone with broken suspension.

He estimated a dozen riders. Armed Afghan cavalry was not to be taken lightly. The Hilux went airborne again over a rise, landing with a heavy jolt, and the road appeared a few hundred metres ahead. The riders would reach them before they made the road. They needed a more immediate solution.

They'd have to debus and take them on. But good cavalry could divide quickly and come at them from all angles.

Hetta pulled off her burkha. 'Sharp turn left,' she said as they bumped furiously along.

Stratton wondered what she meant, since he could see no great obstacle in front.

She opened her door and held it open. 'Turn now!' she ordered.

He realised her intentions and made the turn in front of a fold in the ground. She leaped out and Stratton kept the new heading to draw the riders. Hopefully they hadn't seen her debus. He caught a glimpse of her rolling to cover.

After fifty metres he brought the pick-up back round towards the road. He flashed another look in her direction and couldn't see her. At that same instant a bullet slammed into the side of the Hilux. Several more shots came from the riders, another striking the vehicle's door. The sound of gunfire increased over the engine and creaking chassis. Two more bullets hit the pick-up, one cracking the windscreen. It was pointless heading for the road. It was time to play his part.

Stratton slammed on the brakes, turning the wheel hard over. The Hilux skidded as it turned and the engine stalled. While the pick-up was still moving, he grabbed his carbine, webbing, opened the door and dropped out to land on his back. The landing wasn't too bad on the stony sand and he rolled through a patch of low grass.

The pick-up slow-wheeled on for a few metres before coming to a stop with both its doors open. Stratton brought his carbine up on aim as he viewed the battle zone. Hetta was on one knee, her rifle in her shoulder, and firing single shots into the riders.

Stratton watched three of them fall one after the other. He quickly sighted a rider heading towards him, aimed high in the torso and fired. The rider fell sideways off his horse. The group had divided up, some engaging Hetta while the rest bore down on Stratton. He got up on one knee and fired again, hitting one of them in the chest, and the man came down hard. A round struck the ground near Stratton's foot. He moved to fire again and another rider tumbled off his horse. A bullet went through the side of Stratton's coat. There were two riders left and they parted to pass either side of him. Instinctively, he knew he couldn't get both with no reply. He aimed at the one on the left and fired, then dropped, rolled onto his back, and aimed right and fired.

He hit the first but missed the second. The

214

first had fallen from his horse but the second was firing — the bullet struck close to Stratton's head. He scrabbled and aimed and fired.

Stratton watched the man drop his rifle but he stayed on his horse, galloping past Stratton, who had to roll away to avoid its hoofs. The Taliban commander stayed in the saddle for only a few moments before sliding off to a dusty stop.

Stratton quickly scanned in every direction. There were no more riders, just empty horses. He looked at Hetta, who was doing the same. She lowered her rifle and walked towards the Hilux, without a glance his way. He watched to see if she was injured or suffering any after-effects, not that he expected to find any signs of the latter.

She appeared to be her same mechanical, cold self.

He looked at the men they'd killed, spread around the plain. Several of them lay twisted in awkward positions after their falls. All were unmoving. The bodies would likely begin to rot before anyone found them. There didn't appear to be any villages nearby and so the stench wouldn't be offensive to anyone. If a passer-by discovered them and told the police, there might eventually be an investigation. The police might make some effort to identify them, although the cadavers no doubt would have been relieved of any valuables by then. The bodies would end up being tipped into a single grave. Like so many Afghans had been in this conflict.

Stratton went to the vehicle and gave it a quick onceover. The tyres looked OK and there were no holes in the engine compartment that he could see. He climbed inside and started it up. It fired first time and sounded fine.

Hetta climbed in beside him.

'You OK?' he asked, if only to get some response.

'I'm fine,' she said.

She seemed uncomfortable with his concern and looked away.

★ ★ ★

When they reached the road, he pointed the vehicle south. The tarmac was in moderately good condition for Afghanistan. There was no shortage of potholes or chunks missing at the sides, but it could have been a lot worse.

Traffic was reasonably quiet, with a vehicle passing the other way every five minutes or so. It wasn't long before they caught up with other cars. As the morning passed, the road rose gradually and traffic rapidly increased, mostly commercial trucks in both directions, interspersed were locals heading to work.

The sun poked its way into the sky as they reached their first Afghan police checkpoint a kilometre from the outskirts of Kabul. Traffic had come to a standstill. The police waved the cars through one by one while they scrutinised the occupants, relying on instinct and anything suspicious catching their eye. Hetta had pulled the hood of her burkha over her head long before they approached the checkpoint. All that was visible were her piercing, dark eyes.

An officer waved on the car in front of them. He looked at Stratton and Hetta and didn't hesitate to signal them through, his eyes quickly darting to the car behind. A hundred metres on they drove past stalls lining both sides of the road and joined the early morning traffic into the bustling city. Stratton was thankful they'd arrived early because the normal daytime traffic in Kabul could be much worse than it was now. He didn't know the city well, though enough to navigate around the outskirts. There were sections of it that looked quite normal and void of any signs of trouble or military occupation. Few of the houses were more than three storeys. Many were well maintained but they were outnumbered by the dilapidated. The roads were in poor condition, the pavements broken. Sewage ran down every gutter, coming from the buildings.

The traffic got heavier as they approached the Kabul gates, which was normal for that time of the morning. The gates were the rendezvous point for the huge fuel and food convoys that crossed the country. They mustered along the sides of the road, meeting up with their armed security escorts prior to journeys out to the dozens of military camps and outposts through-out eastern and southern Afghanistan.

Stratton and Hetta passed a long line of heavy fuel trucks parked nose to tail. Dozens of Hilux pick-ups were parked in-between the trucks or in groups across from them. Every Hilux seemed to be manned by security guards, each carrying an AK-47 and ammunition. Some carried RPG7s.

217

They saw PKM belt-fed machine guns mounted on the beds. The guards were nearly all bearded, and dressed for the low temperatures that would get even colder on the journeys, especially for those headed into the mountains' military camps. Truck drivers were checking their engines and tyres, filling fuel tanks, sharing tea or coffee. Garbage was everywhere and the smell of fuel and sewage filled the air. Despite the millions of gallons of fuel that surrounded them, practically everyone seemed to be smoking.

Horns blared as they joined the creeping traffic moving past the convoys. Bicycles and motorbikes weaved in and out. Sirens sounded as heavily armed police vehicles used them to force through the bustle. They were largely ignored, despite the shouts and gesticulations from officers standing through the sunroofs and leaning out of the cabs.

When they reached the southern part of the city, a police checkpoint indicated that they were leaving the built-up area and heading out into the country. The officers waved them through, anxious to keep the traffic flowing, and Stratton was able to speed up as the road opened. The city was soon out of sight in the rear-view mirror and he settled in for the next leg of the journey. His thoughts went briefly to the night to come. They wouldn't reach Kandahar before midday the following day and he wondered where they might catch some rest. It wasn't a good idea to drive at night. Like most places in the world where internal security was unreliable or non-existent, with darkness came the evil ones.

Bandits mostly, and sometimes Taliban. Afghan security forces would be few and far between on the road between Kabul and Kandahar, often too frightened to pass along it. And for good reason. They were targeted day and night. A pair of headlights on the road would attract a lot of attention, none of it good.

By late morning they'd reached Ghazni, a hundred and fifty kilometres from Kabul. The traffic slowed again to a crawl through an Afghan Army checkpoint. Stratton and Hetta watched ahead as they approached it. She was wearing her hood again. The soldier on duty appeared to be halting every vehicle and looking inside it.

Stratton got his passport ready. When it was their turn to stop alongside, the soldier, who was dressed in a new set of khaki fatigues and carrying an AK-47, held out a hand to Stratton. He handed over the document. The soldier glanced through it, looked at the couple and waved them on. Hetta stared ahead. It would be unusual for a woman to be checked if she was with a man.

They drove on through the town and out the other side. When they were clear, Hetta removed her hood and veil which, judging by the way she took it off, she didn't like wearing. An hour after leaving Ghazni, Stratton found a deserted place to pull over. He needed a stretch and a pee. Hetta went for a walk behind a thicket while he refuelled the pick-up.

They were back on the road quickly. He didn't want to stop anywhere for too long. Stratton felt hungry and remembered the food they had taken from the nomads. He looked at her. She was looking straight ahead, as usual.

'I don't suppose you'd like to play mummy and make me a sandwich,' he said.

She appeared to take a moment to consider. Then she reached back for the pot that contained the lamb and bread and put it on her lap. She removed the lid, grabbed a handful of meat, unceremoniously dumped it into a sheet of the bread and handed it to him.

'You were never a short order chef,' he said, examining the mess. 'I'm gradually working you out by a process of elimination. You weren't a nun, peace worker, or a Junior McDonald's Happy Face.'

She ignored him and helped herself to some of the food.

'Where're you from?' he asked.

She kept looking ahead, as if she hadn't heard him.

'You can tell a lot about a person's military background by the way they soldier,' he said. 'Your background isn't military, is it?'

She started to glance at him but changed her mind.

'I can tell by the way you changed your rifle magazine. You didn't eject it directly to the ground. You pulled it out first before you dropped it. That's a regular military technique to save damaging the magazine. But you're obviously not regular military because of the way you shoot. You do a lot of instinctive shooting. Regular military don't do that.'

'What if you don't want to leave the magazine

behind?' she said. It was as though she were reluctant to get into a conversation with him but couldn't resist defending herself.

'You mean leaving it behind as evidence? OK. Maybe. But what about all your casings? They're evidence. You can't go round picking all of those up after a fight.'

She didn't respond.

'And your pistol. Why a Magnum?' he asked.

'People stay down when hit,' she said.

'A pistol isn't a primary weapon. For a gangster, maybe. But not for a military specialist out in the middle of nowhere. It's a secondary weapon, in case your primary has a malfunction. You need more than eight rounds, though, which is all you have in that monster.'

'Fourteen,' she corrected. 'I have an extended magazine.'

'Twenty would be even better. Even in a lower calibre.'

A frown began to crease her brow but she remained looking ahead.

'Another thing that gives you away is the way you hold it. You look through the sights,' he said. 'Special forces operatives should be pistol specialists. And a pistol specialist doesn't use sights.'

'That's rubbish,' she said.

'You're right. Not all special forces operators know what they're doing with a pistol. In fact few of them do.'

'The weapon is made with sights,' she said. 'The manufacturers can't all be wrong.'

'Sights are for target practice, not for combat.

221

A kid's bicycle comes with stabilisers. If you know how to ride a bike you don't need them.'

She appeared to be growing irritated. He decided to ease off her.

'Having said all that, the way you engage your targets while under fire, and at close range,' he said. 'You can't teach that. Very impressive. I was only curious about your background. Sorry if that offends.'

Her expression didn't change.

Stratton decided to shut up.

Within half an hour they'd caught up with the rear end of a civilian truck convoy, mostly fuel trucks and therefore slow. The last vehicle was a Hilux just like theirs but filled with private Afghan security. For half a mile Stratton contemplated overtaking, but decided against it after seeing the way the rear gunner reacted to any encroachment. It wasn't worth the risk. The gunners were jittery on this road. If they thought Stratton was any kind of threat, they'd open fire. The convoys were popular targets for the Taliban, and for bandits on occasion, although the criminals rarely took on the larger security companies, preferring the more vulnerable target such as a lone vehicle or one that had broken down.

Stratton settled back a hundred metres behind the convoy and relaxed. There was no great hurry. The land was still barren but hillier than it had been further north. Clouds had covered the clear skies of earlier and it looked like rain. The sun had been on their left side when they started and during the journey had crossed the skies to settle on their right. The large orange ball began to lower onto the distant Chopan Hills. Darkness would soon be upon them.

It was time to look for somewhere to rest for the night. Stratton didn't fancy the idea of a large town. Not only would their own security be challenged, the contents of the vehicle would be at risk. They had a couple of choices: the first was to pull off the road and find somewhere secluded where they could sleep in the vehicle. Security would remain an issue. One of them would have to be awake at all times in case they had visitors. The other option was to find someone who'd put them up.

The latter option was more attractive.

The world was quite suddenly plunged into near-complete darkness as the sun disappeared. The land rose up on their left, where it turned into a series of low, overlapping hills. Beyond the second fold Stratton saw a light, like the window of a building, and a track up ahead leaving the main road in that direction. When they arrived at the turn, he took it. The edge of the tarmac ended abruptly and it was a considerable step down onto the dirt track.

'I thought we could find a hotel for the night,' he said.

She didn't respond to his facetiousness and studied the ground ahead instead. The track cut around the side of the first hill and climbed the next one for a couple of hundred metres before it levelled out at the crest. A few mud and stone huts appeared up ahead with smoke issuing from the larger one. They drove past a wooden corral containing a dozen or so goats. A pair of camels sat beneath a tree on the other side of the road.

Stratton pulled the vehicle to a stop a dozen metres from the buildings, more out of caution than anything else. He turned off the lights and the engine, and silence descended.

Country Afghans weren't unlike country folk the world over, but after decades of misrule by the Russians, the Taliban and now the Western invasion, they'd tempered their natural goodwill with caution. But neither was it unusual for travellers to purchase comfort for the night. As they sat there, the front door of the main building opened and orange light from a kerosene lamp streamed out to divide the darkness.

'You're up,' Stratton said. 'We need a room for the night.'

Hetta pulled on her veil and climbed out as a man stepped into view holding the lamp. She walked towards him. It would be unusual for a woman to make such a greeting when she was with a man who would have to be either her husband or brother — but the farmer would understand once she explained that her husband couldn't speak or hear.

Stratton watched them talk for a moment, the farmer looking congenial, nodding and smiling. A woman came out of the house and became involved in the conversation. She looked more serious but otherwise the meeting appeared to be going fine. Hetta held out her hand to the man, who took what she was offering. He checked the notes and appeared to be more than satisfied with the deal. He tried to hand some of it back. Hetta refused, and returned to the Hilux.

'He's welcomed us for the night,' she said. 'They have a hut that their son used to live in. They didn't say, but judging by his expression when he mentioned the son, something bad happened to him. His wife's going to prepare it for us.'

Stratton climbed out, stretched his aching back, and looked out over the country. The main road they had come along was visible, some headlights still moving along it. Lights shone from several other farmhouses dotted about the low hills on both sides of the road.

A kerosene lamp announced the farmer's wife stepping from the house. She beckoned Hetta over and together they went around the back of the main building and out of sight. Stratton opened the rear cab door and took out a blanket, placed it on the driver's seat and wrapped his carbine and webbing inside it.

Hetta returned holding a kerosene lamp and led Stratton back around the corner, between a couple of mud huts to a smaller one a few steps from the main building. Chickens scattered to let them pass. It was a dilapidated, single-room dwelling, but a coal fire had been lit inside a large cauldron in a corner. A rusty, crooked flue directed the smoke through the roof. The place wasn't as warm as it looked but it soon would be.

On the floor lay a makeshift straw mattress. The only furniture was a rickety chair that didn't look strong enough to take the weight of an adult. Stratton placed down the blanket bundle beside the bed. The farmer's wife appeared at the door carrying a wicker basket. She stepped inside and placed it on the dirt floor beside the cauldron and then left with a short glance at Hetta only.

Hetta followed the woman outside and Stratton walked around the small room, inspecting the walls and ceiling. It was similar to the hut in Helmand he'd stayed in prior to the attack on the hamlets, other than that the roof looked effective in this one. Before long Hetta returned, carrying her own weapons bundled in a blanket, and placed it on the floor at the foot of the bed.

'You up for dragging our toy in here?' he asked in a soft voice. It was a question he already had an answer for and hoped she'd agree. He doubted they'd both manage to carry it the distance without dropping it. He thought it would be secure if left on the back of the Hilux.

'I'm OK with leaving it there,' she said. 'It will need a vehicle to carry away and we'd hear one if it arrived.'

Stratton was happy with that and closed the door. He rubbed his chilly hands together. 'Home from home,' he whispered.

As he expected, she didn't acknowledge him.

Stratton went to the basket and pulled back the cloth cover. Inside was a bowl of rice, vegetables, fried tomato halves and pieces of roast lamb. A large, thin sheet of unleavened bread was rolled up beside it all. It seemed like a lot of food. He wondered how much of their own

226

supper the family had given up. It would have been typical of the household to be generous, to give the impression they had an abundance of food.

He spooned some of it into one of the bowls and tore off a piece of the bread. Hetta was sitting on the blankets on the floor, removing one of her boots. He took the food to her. She wasn't a team player but he wasn't about to pick up any of her bad habits.

'It looks pretty good,' he said, holding it out.

She looked surprised, then uncomfortable, and took the bowl without saying anything and put it on the floor while she took off the other boot. Stratton sat against the wall between her and the fire to eat, wondering how the sleeping arrangements might work. It was a hard floor but he'd slept on worse.

He heard a noise outside and paused. His hand went under his jacket to his pistol. Hetta had done the same, under her burkha. There was a knock at the door and a voice followed. It was the farmer's wife asking if she could come in.

Hetta put her food down as she replied and the door swung open. On the ground outside they saw a large cauldron. The woman picked it up. It looked heavy and Stratton contemplated helping her but she was already on her way and Afghan men didn't help the women anyway, even with a painfully heavy load.

She placed it on the floor by the fire cauldron. It was filled with hot water. The woman went back outside and returned with a couple of towels and a cloth with a piece of soap on it. She looked apologetic as she closed the door behind her.

Hetta took off her burkha and settled back against the wall to eat. The room was warming up nicely and Stratton removed his coat. They ate in silence.

'The water's for washing,' she said.

'Why don't you go first,' he said.

She didn't stand on ceremony and got to her feet. Stratton sat on the edge of the bed and unrolled the blanket that contained his carbine. Hetta began to undress, while Stratton removed the magazine from his rifle, quietly ejected the round from the breech and slid out the stock pin to open the weapon. As he pulled out the working parts, he glanced around at her to see she'd removed her shirt and T-shirt, leaving her naked from the waist up.

He raised his eyebrows as he looked away and stripped the breech block parts down. He produced a cloth he'd pocketed from the Hilux and cleaned the breech. He couldn't help taking another look at her, by now completely naked, standing on her socks and washing herself as if she was all alone. She had the body of an athlete. Her skin glowed orange, bathed in the light from the fire. She was stunning.

He looked away as she doused her hair and he went back to cleaning the rifle. He had a realisation: it wasn't a case of her being shy. It was more that he was of no consequence. He didn't exist beyond his purpose as a tool, and a temporary one at that. He was fodder, something to assist her in getting the bomb out of

Afghanistan. He didn't even warrant a look or a second's thought as she stood there in her birthday suit washing herself.

He looked down the barrel of the carbine while aiming it at the kerosene lamp. It could have done with a pull-through, which he didn't have. The shiny rifling was speckled with tiny bits of dirt. Not enough to cause a problem when fired, though. It would do.

'You can wash now,' she said matter-of-factly.

She was drying her hair with one of the towels, naked and carefree.

He replaced the parts of the weapon, closed it, pushed home the stock bolt, loaded a magazine and quietly cocked it to place a bullet in the breech. Then got to his feet. She walked past him to the mattress. He went to the cauldron. As he looked at the water he asked himself what he was doing there. In the past he'd gone days without a wash, weeks even. He didn't need one, not in the field. On the other hand, he was going to have to sleep near her since there was nowhere else. It would only be polite to wash. Despite his manners, he still felt a hint of internal resistance.

Bollocks, he decided. He took off his clothes and his boots and his socks and crouched in front of the cauldron. The heat from the fire felt good. A contrast to the chilly air coming from under the door. He washed himself, but much as he wanted to, he couldn't detach himself from her presence.

He glanced at her. She was wearing her T-shirt and reaching for her carbine without looking at him. Should have expected her not to take any notice. He heard her unload the weapon and strip it down. After he'd finished, he pulled on his shorts and looked in her direction again. This time she was looking at him and she didn't look away. He couldn't read the look. No desire or cheekiness, but she watched him for a moment nevertheless. Then she turned and lay down, facing the wall, leaving space for him.

He put the lamp on the floor by the bed, lifted up the heavy blanket and sat on the mattress. The straw crunched softly under him. He straightened his legs beneath the cover, lay back and covered himself in the blanket. He turned down the wick in the lamp until the light faded and died, but the room continued to glow red from the fire in the cauldron.

The wind had picked up outside. The air in the room was warm but it would be cold by morning. He pulled the blanket up and closed his eyes, acutely aware of her beside him. He fought to put her out of his thoughts and fall asleep. It had been an odd twenty-four hours.

An atom bomb lost then found.

And the strangest woman he'd ever met, and without doubt the most accomplished, battle-wise. He no longer doubted that the Amazons existed.

He exhaled slowly, waiting for sleep to envelope him.

She disturbed him by rolling over onto her back, her body brushing against him. She rolled onto her side so that she was facing him. He could feel her breath against his face.

'Stratton?' she said.

'Yes,' he said, turning his head to look at her.

'You're pleasing to the eye.'

He didn't know quite what to say. Her going from cold as ice since he met her to suddenly warm was unexpected, to say the least.

She reached across and, even more to his surprise, moved on top of him. She lay there for a moment, supporting herself, looking at him. He couldn't refuse, couldn't help himself. She was beautiful, but there was something else. A strange attraction to her, despite her attitude. She pulled off her T-shirt and he did the same with his shorts. She closed her eyes and went somewhere inside her head. He put his arms around her. Her skin was soft, her muscles firm.

But the pleasure soon began to dwindle for him. She was in her own world. Once again, he felt like he was simply a tool for her. With a powerful heave, he turned her over onto her back. She half-resisted, but he was the stronger. There was a look of shock in her eyes. He had taken control, again. His face was close to hers. Their noses touched. She was still a little resistant. This wasn't what she'd intended.

She'd wanted to be disconnected, inside her head. His lips moved down to touch hers. She turned her head to one side. He found her lips again. This time she let him kiss her, as if she were curious. Then she held him tightly.

They moved as one. Their breathing quickened. They stopped and held each other. Tightly. Their grips eventually loosening. Stratton rolled off her onto his back and they lay still in silence. She turned onto her side with her back to him and didn't move.

She was a strange girl, he thought. And for a brief moment, that's precisely what she had been. A girl. She certainly liked to surround herself in her armour.

The wind was still blustery outside and fighting its way through the gaps in the door. A cosy sound from within the mud walls, the fire nearby. He closed his eyes, looking to feel content. But he couldn't. His senses were tingling again. A distant threat perhaps.

Not close yet, but it was there.

18

Stratton woke suddenly in the darkness, wondering where in the world he was. He didn't have any clothes on and a woman was lying beside him.

Then it came back to him.

Hetta seemed to sleep soundlessly. The fire had gone out and the air was cold. He sat up and felt around the floor for his clothes. His hand touched the butt of his rifle leaning against the wall. He found his shorts and pulled them on. The room slowly took shape as his eyes grew accustomed to the light.

He got up and dressed quietly, not wanting to disturb her. Early mornings were his favourite time of day and he preferred to experience them alone. Besides, she bothered him in so many ways. A moment without her was welcome.

The wind outside had stopped blowing, the air silent. He put on his boots and eased the door open to look outside. The first thing he saw was white. Everything was white. Snow fell from the door and the cold air took hold of him, his first breath outside thick. The sun was still behind the mountains but its glow crept into the cloudy sky.

The snow was pristine and about six inches deep. No one had been by the house since it had fallen. He took a walk to look at the Hilux. The snowy blanket that covered it was undisturbed. The land was white as far as he could see in every direction. He had seen the sight before and it was the only time Afghanistan ever looked clean and peaceful.

He looked towards the Kandahar road but all trace of it had disappeared. No vehicle had yet been along it that morning. Nothing had ventured along the track either, save a fox or dog. He went back inside the hut. Hetta was sitting up, pushing her fingers through her short hair. She looked at him, for an instant only. Her expression was the same as usual. He thought he'd caught something slightly different in her eyes. He couldn't say what it was. Softer than usual, whatever it was.

'Morning,' he said.

She glanced at him in response. That was more than he would have received the day before.

He took his blanket, wrapped his gun in it and carried it outside to the Hilux, stowing it in the footwell covered by his scarf. He set about clearing the snow from the windows.

Hetta arrived in her burkha and carrying her gun in its blanket. She climbed into the passenger seat and placed her gun as before.

Stratton climbed in and started the engine. It fired on its second attempt and he let it idle while it warmed up.

'I don't like to be the first vehicle down any road in Afghanistan in the morning if I can help it,' he said. The people who liked to lay mines along busy roads usually did so under cover of darkness in the early hours. They often waited to detonate the mines in the morning, either by command wire or mobile phone. He didn't expect his Hilux to be an attractive target to a Taliban bomber, but some of the mines were triggered by the passing vehicle itself. Those were the ones he was concerned about. There was no point in taking the risk if they didn't have to.

She didn't disagree and so he took his time. He put the pick-up into gear and turned it around so that they were facing the Kandahar road. He noticed movement near the farm buildings and looked in the rear-view mirror to see the farmer step into view. Stratton wound down his window and waved. The farmer waved back.

They drove slowly down the track through the fresh snow and Stratton brought the Hilux to a halt a hundred metres from the main road, keeping the engine running. It wasn't long before a couple of vans came along from the direction of Kandahar. That was good enough for him. As long as there were tyre tracks on the road, he was happy to drive it.

He pulled out onto the road. The back wheels slid a little in the snow and he took it nice and easy and settled into a steady speed. The sky looked as if it might be ready to deliver more snow. Stratton wound his window up against the cold air.

He checked his watch and studied the way ahead. He reckoned they'd reach Kandahar in two or three hours.

It was midday by the time they saw the outskirts of the city and here the snow had largely disappeared. Patches of it had gathered on the sides of the road but it was melting under the early afternoon sun.

The traffic slowed as they approached the city. Pedestrians appeared on the sides of the road, along with markets and stalls.

Hetta pulled her hood over her face.

The buildings increased in density either side of them, the usual run-down, brick and concrete block structures. Most were single-storey, a few were higher. The roads were busy, noisy and polluted, packed with vehicles of all kinds. A smattering of police and Afghan Army maintained a presence. The Hilux passed a British military convoy coming the other way, a string of sand-coloured armoured vehicles.

Stratton avoided the centre of the city, bypassing the bulk of it to the east. The huge coalition base with its civilian and military airfields lay a few miles south. He kept with the flow of traffic, overtaking where possible without causing other drivers stress. Soon they arrived at a junction where an old Afghan Air Force jet fighter was positioned at a take-off angle on a plinth to one side of the road. It signified the turning to the airport.

Stratton took the turn and within a kilometre the broad, recently surfaced road became a HESCO-lined approach to the entrance and perimeter of the base.

The checkpoint had been divided up into pedestrian, civilian, truck and military entrances, much the same as at Bagram. Stratton decided to go for the military entrance despite being in a civilian Hilux. The civilian line usually took hours to get through and he didn't care about Afghan civilians noticing them. Not this time. It was the end of the road for the Toyota pick-up.

Hetta took off her burkha and tossed it aside with some relief.

As Stratton pulled the Hilux in behind a military convoy horns blared and whistles blew in the hands of a couple of the Afghan soldiers. Stratton knew the pick-up might be considered a threat and brought the vehicle to a stop.

The guards had their guns in hand and looked aggressive as they approached. Stratton had the window wound down and held out both his hands as well as his identification card. The soldiers stopped short, keeping their guns aimed at him.

'British soldier!' Stratton called out.

The guard shouted something in return.

'He wants you to get out and show yourself,' Hetta said tiredly.

Stratton turned off the motor and climbed out.

The lead vehicle of a British military convoy had stopped several metres behind the Hilux and the crew were waiting patiently. A jam at the first outer entrance checkpoint into the base wasn't remotely unusual.

Stratton removed his Afghan coat and opened up his arms to show his body.

It wasn't enough for the guard, so he opened up his shirt and raised his T-shirt to show his naked chest, beginning to wish he'd taken the civilian entrance. These things usually depended on who was manning the checkpoint at the time.

Either this bunch had had a recent scare or intelligence had warned them of a potential attack. That or they were just in an officious mood.

One of the soldiers approached and Stratton kept his arms outstretched, holding his ID, so as not to unnerve the man. The guard took the ID and inspected it, before handing it back. He lowered his rifle, shouting something at Stratton to direct him towards the checkpoint hut.

Stratton got back into the Hilux, drove to the hut and stopped. A private security officer arrived with a sniffer dog, letting the animal lead the way around the vehicle. When they'd completed a circuit, the pair of them walked casually back to a chair beneath a shelter. The man sat down, the dog beside him.

Stratton was beckoned forward and he drove to the next part of the checkpoint, where another soldier inspected his ID card. The soldier took Hetta's and gave that the onceover. Satisfied, he waved them through. They drove around a bend lined with HESCO walls to yet another checkpoint, this one run by US soldiers. Their IDs were inspected again, after which Stratton and Hetta finally drove into the vast complex.

Inside a ten-mile security perimeter, Kandahar Air Base, or KAF as it was known, was a mixture of military compounds, civilian contractors, and military and contractor air terminals, as well as an Afghan civilian airport sharing the same airfield and runways.

They made their way along a busy main drag lined with contractor compounds, warehouses and vehicle parks, both military and civilian. There were several large, tented areas used for surplus military accommodation. They could see no evidence of the snow that had fallen that morning. Stratton pulled the Toyota off the dusty road into a car park beside a large warehouse-type building familiar to him.

'You hungry?' he asked her.

Her way of acknowledging was to climb out of the pick-up.

They took off all their Afghan clothing and joined a line of soldiers and contractors filing in through a gap in a staggered line of concrete blast walls. Inside the building, they showed their IDs to a US Army administrative clerk, who let them through, and they walked through a pair of doors into a vast hall.

The place echoed with the conversations of hundreds of men and women. It was like a food fair, with more than a dozen stalls, each along a different theme: grills, sandwiches, salads, Chinese, roasts, pizzas and burgers, fruits, ice cream and drinks of all kinds excluding alcohol. The tables and chairs, placed in rows and sections, could seat a couple of thousand people.

Stratton made for a stall providing fresh salad and filled a plate. Then he looked for a table, and not an empty one. The clientele were mostly men, civilians and soldiers, and mostly soldiers. The obvious difference between the soldiers and civilians, apart from their clothing, was the amount of hair on their heads and the size of their bellies. Most of the civilians looked fat and unfit, an indictment of the unlimited food, little

239

of it on the healthy side of the line.

He hadn't chosen the mess hall just to get a meal. He saw a dozen civilians seated at a close group of tables, one in particular catching his eye: a man in a jumpsuit with a pair of wings on a chest badge.

A good starting point.

He looked around for Hetta, who was attracting the attention of several young soldiers at a nearby table. They were more than curious. Her fatigues were not regular military and her belt and holster were unconventional. And there was the Magnum semi-automatic cannon sitting in it. Regular soldiers were restricted to carrying standard-issue weapons. A Magnum wasn't even special forces issue.

She had a plate of food and was looking around the room for Stratton. She saw him looking directly at her and nodded towards an empty row of tables. He shook his head and motioned towards the table of contractors he'd singled out. He headed over and placed his tray down at the end of the table, where there were a couple of empty seats.

'Do you mind if I sit here?' he asked the nearest of the men.

'Sure thing,' the man said politely in an American accent.

Southern, Stratton guessed. He pulled out a chair and sat down. The others at the table glanced at him, some taking a second look. Stratton presented an unusual sight in the generally conventional military base. His hair was much longer than a regular soldier's and he had several days' worth of facial growth. His chemical warfare fatigues were unusual, as well as being grubby. He had his shirt unbuttoned halfway down his chest, his sleeves rolled up to reveal the tattered long sleeves of his T-shirt, the cuffs of which had long since failed. If a regular soldier were to turn out in such a manner, he'd risk getting charged for being improperly dressed.

Several of the men gave each other glances but Stratton didn't look up at any of them as he ate. When Hetta placed her tray on the table beside him, the men visibly paused to look at her. In her case, they were not just impressed by the unusual fatigues and the monster gat hanging from her hip. To a gun-toting Southern militia-man, which several of these gentlemen seemed to be, she was a dream.

One of the men, a large individual with a beard, dark glasses and a pony tail, who was sitting across from Stratton, couldn't contain his curiosity.

'How you folks doin'?' he asked. 'Name's Larry.'

'Fine, Larry,' Stratton said with a smile and an interested look. He noticed several of them were wearing the same shirts with a company badge on the breast and 'CAMCO' emblazoned across the top. There were several baseball hats on the table bearing the same badge.

'You new here?' Larry asked. 'Pardon me for askin', I ain't tryin' to poke my nose in. It's just that we've all been here quite a few years and I ain't seen you guys before.'

241

'We are new here,' Stratton said. 'What do you guys do here, if you don't mind me asking?'

'We're in construction. Jack here runs the cement-making machines.' Larry indicated the largest of the men, who must have weighed 150kg, most of it fat.

Jack gave Stratton a polite nod while he ate.

'George runs transport,' Larry said.

'How'd you do,' said George, a grey-haired man in his sixties.

'Hank's our engineer, Bob's our site manager. And Doug here visits once in a while,' Larry said, referring to the man with the wings and the one of most interest to Stratton. 'And the rest of us, well, we join in where we can.'

'Sounds like you're the lucky one,' Stratton said to Doug. 'You only get to visit.'

'Well, sometimes I get to stay overnight,' Doug said. His voice was soft and his accent mellow.

'If we don't screw up the load or the weather don't close him in,' Larry said. 'If you haven't already guessed, Doug's our favourite pilot.'

'That's only because of the contraband I smuggle in,' Doug said with a wry smile.

'Hey, that's supposed to be top secret,' Bob said.

Everyone found the comment amusing.

'Just in case you're thinkin' bad things,' Larry said to Stratton, 'Doug's referring to beer and pirate DVDs.'

'And the occasional case of Jack,' Doug added.

'And the occasional case of Jack,' Larry agreed. 'And if the 27th's commanding officer who lives down the road from us doesn't get his cut, there'd be hell to pay.'

'Where do you fly to?' Hetta asked.

'Dubai mostly,' he said. 'We also go Stateside sometimes. CAMCO's Mid-East office is in Dubai but our head office is in Houston.'

There were dozens of civilian contract companies on the base and most had their headquarters in the States.

'I guess you're heading out soon?' she asked.

'Yep,' Doug said. 'Tomorrow morning. You want a ride?' He was smiling, getting a few winks and smirks from the others.

'Might do,' Hetta said, forcing a smile. 'Depends where you're headed.'

'Houston. Soon as I can get these guys to finish unloading and reloading.'

'We'll unload tonight and reload first thing in the morning,' Larry said. 'The thought of you sittin' in Hooter's, sippin' a cold one by tomorrow night, don't make us want to hurry none.' He grinned, as did most of the others, including the pilot.

Stratton had finished eating and now he stood. 'Well, gents, it was nice to meet you all. We have to be going.'

'Good to meet you too,' Larry said. 'Sorry, I didn't get your name.'

'Stratton,' he said. There was no point in hiding it. Anyone who cared to ask for his ID card would see it and every checkpoint he passed through would be aware of it. 'And this is Hetta,' he added, since all of them seemed much more interested in her than him.

'You be safe now,' Larry said. 'You too, Hetta.'

'We will,' Stratton said. 'All the best.'

He picked up his tray, noting Hetta was walking away and had left hers behind. He picked it up, disguising a frown. The men were all watching her go.

'That's one helluva lady, I'll tell you right now,' Larry said.

There were no disagreements.

Stratton followed her out of the mess hall, through the trash room, where he dispensed with the trays, and outside into the warm, dusty air. They sat in silence for twenty minutes before they saw Larry and the other CAMCO men file outside. The contractors walked through the crowded car park to a couple of company 4×4s. The large CAMCO logo on the doors matched the ones on their shirts and baseball hats. When they headed out of the lot, Stratton followed, keeping a couple of military vehicles between them. The main drag was relatively busy and the severe speed restrictions in the camp meant everyone drove around at a sedate pace.

He had a rough idea where he was in the camp from previous trips. They were heading towards the airfield. A Boeing 737 suddenly appeared, climbing above a line of hangars directly ahead. The CAMCO convoy reached a T-junction, the hangars and warehouses running across their front in both directions. They turned left, following the perimeter of the airfield. Less than a kilometre from the T-junction, Stratton watched the vehicles slow and turn sharply in through an opening between a couple of three-metre-high blast walls — reinforced concrete slabs two metres wide with a large, flat base.

Stratton and Hetta looked in the entrance as they drove past. It had a gate but it wasn't closed after the vehicles went inside. And since there didn't appear to be a sentry on duty, it had to be assumed the gate remained open, during the daytime at least. He took the next left up ahead, around the corner of the CAMCO compound. The compound perimeter extended along the line of the road about thirty metres in, on the other side of a machinery park full of cranes, generators, flatbeds, bulldozers and other bits and pieces of machinery. The CAMCO compound was noisy. It stretched for another couple of hundred metres to a minor road that separated it from its neighbour to the rear. Stratton didn't take the turn.

'I take it you have a plan?' she asked.

'Kind of.'

She glanced at him, wondering what that meant exactly.

'The pilot's leaving in the morning,' he said. 'The CAMCO guys are unloading the plane tonight and reloading it early tomorrow. Which suggests whatever they're loading will be in their compound overnight.'

'You hope.'

He shrugged. 'If it doesn't work out with this outfit, we find another one. I can go to the air movement office and find out every cargo flight leaving this week and who's chartered them. I take it we're not exactly in a rush, right?'

She didn't reply. He got the feeling she didn't agree with him.

They came to another T-junction. Left meant

245

back into the built-up part of the base, right seemed to head out towards the bottom end of the airfield, where there were few structures and little activity. He took the left, following the road for a kilometre before pulling into a busy car park surrounded by several large, modern, prefabricated buildings.

'We should get out of these clothes,' Stratton said. 'Slip into something less war-like.' He pointed to their front. 'Home from home shopping.'

The building was a US Army PX store filled with everything they could possibly need.

'Do you have money?' he asked.

'Some.'

'Would you mind taking me shopping? I'm travelling a little light.'

Half an hour later they emerged from the store, each carrying several plastic shopping bags.

'You're fun to shop with,' he said as they walked through the lot. 'Most girls take for ever choosing clothes. You're like a bloke. You see it, grab it, pay for it. I like that.'

She ignored him while they got into the pick-up and he drove them back the way they'd come. When they reached the junction that led right to the CAMCO compound, he went straight on. From that point on, they were the only car moving on the road, which led to nowhere in particular.

A large stretch of ground opened up on their right, with layers of razor wire stretched across its outer reaches. A couple of hundred metres up ahead, the road came to a dead-end, blocked off by concrete barriers and razor wire, so Stratton turned the pick-up into the open ground in front to an old, empty hangar that appeared abandoned. He carried on around the back of it and pulled the car to a halt. The engine went quiet.

All of the building's windows had been broken. A large pair of doors were open, piles of trash inside, the roof partially collapsed. A line of razor wire ran past them to the edge of the airfield. Much of it was hidden by a million plastic bags caught on its barbs and flapping in the breeze.

Beyond the wire he could see one end of the airfield. It looked dusty and unused. It was the world's busiest single runway airport, but aircraft rarely ventured that far. Further beyond, several hundred metres away, he could see the main airport perimeter of HESCO barriers topped with razor wire, and beyond that a vast, open plain of grey sand framed by rolling hills, the crests of which were miles away.

They both changed their dirty clothes for new, nondescript earth-coloured trousers, T-shirts, shirts and fleeces. Before Stratton tossed his trousers, he searched the pockets. There was something in one of them and he dug it out — a large coin on a chain. Chandos's SBS stone. He'd forgotten all about it.

He put it in a pocket of his new trousers and checked his face in the Toyota's side mirror. His straggly hair and beard would continue to be useful in civilianising his look. And if challenged for identification, they would also pass as off-duty soldiers.

Stratton watched a big transport aircraft come

in over the airfield. Looking at the clear skies, he guessed it was around three in the afternoon, and his watch confirmed it. They'd have to wait till dark before he could crack on with the next phase of the plan. He climbed into the rear seat of the Hilux and lay down. Daytime dozing wasn't something he was good at, but the night could be a long one and since there was nothing else to do, he might as well try and get some sleep.

He exhaled and let his body relax, as Hetta climbed into the front passenger seat and reclined the seat as far back as it could go. The air was still. Few sounds in it. They were in a safe place and it was peaceful.

'Why'd you join the military?' she asked.

The sound of her voice surprised him, as well as the fact she'd asked him a personal question. He wondered why.

'You don't have to answer. I know how it feels when people ask personal questions. I'm not passing the time. I'd like to know.'

'Quid pro quo?' Stratton said.

'I doubt it. Yesterday you sounded like you knew all about me anyway.'

'I was only testing some theories.' He thought about her question. 'Because I'd nothing better to do,' he said. 'I was young and lost. So I joined the Marines. The Royal Marines to you Yanks. I'd no idea what I was good at. If I was good at anything.'

'Didn't your parents help you with that?'

'I didn't have any. And there was no one else close enough to share those sorts of things with.

One day I went for a walk in the city, London. I found myself looking at a shop window. A sign was offering careers in the Marines. To this day I don't know quite why, but I just walked in and signed up.'

'It was your destiny calling.'

He glanced at her. Her eyes were closed. 'I didn't have you pegged as the destiny-believing type,' he said.

'I'm not sure if our lives are already written, but I do believe we have a calling in life. There's something that each of us can do better than most others. We're all unique enough to have a purpose. Some of us get to discover what that calling is. Most of us don't.'

He thought about what she had said.

'You don't agree,' she said.

'Where were you when I was seventeen?'

He glanced at her. Her eyes were still closed, but he thought he could detect the very slightest of smiles on her lips.

'I take it you had the benefit of good advice when you were young,' he said.

'Yes.'

'And did you discover your true calling?'

'No. I was taken to it.'

'How'd you know it was the right choice?'

'It was my father who showed me. It had been his calling. And he told me it would be mine too.'

'Your father was a soldier?'

She hesitated. 'Yes,' she said finally.

'So, where'd you grow up?'

She didn't answer.

He looked at her again, with her eyes still

closed, but her expression had changed. It was one question too many. But it was more conversation than he'd expected from her.

He closed his eyes and did his best to wash everything from his mind. The high-pitched engines of an aircraft intensified for a few moments as it accelerated along the runway and grew muffled and less intense as it took to the skies.

He heard few other sounds after that. No birds or flies. It was peaceful.

19

Stratton opened his eyes and looked at the ceiling of the Hilux cab. It was dark.

Hetta had gone.

He sat up, surprised that he'd fallen asleep deeply enough not to feel or hear her leave. He looked around outside through the windows. The stuff in the back looked undisturbed, in particular the device box secured beneath the rug. He saw her silhouetted by the security lights on the airfield perimeter, standing near the razor wire, hands in her pockets, looking into the distance.

He climbed out and stretched his legs as he looked around. The camp was well lit by street lamps and every compound seemed to have security lights on its perimeter, as well as internally to illuminate entrances and walkways. The camp veritably glowed in most places.

'It's time,' he said.

'So do you have a plan?'

'Kind of.'

They drove straight to the CAMCO compound and past the main entrance. The large gate was drawn across it, secured by a heavy chain and, like everywhere else, the place was well lit. But they saw no sign of any security. They continued around the corner and into the machinery park, itself illuminated by the security spotlights along the top of the CAMCO perimeter fence. But the trucks and plant provided many dark areas.

Stratton steered the Hilux between a pair of flatbeds and stopped alongside a mobile crane. He shut off the lights and engine and wound down his window. Several large generators were thundering away, powering CAMCO's facility. Another line of generators across the road kept the location extremely noisy. While they waited, a truck passed by on the main road, its headlights bathing the machinery park.

The CAMCO compound perimeter was constructed of solid metal fencing three metres tall and topped with a triple spool configuration of razor wire that stretched along its entire length.

Stratton climbed out of the Toyota and went to the fence to give it a closer inspection. Hetta got out and looked around.

'Why don't I take a look inside the compound and you wait here,' he said to her, loud enough to compete with the generators. 'It'll be easier for one person alone.'

'Go ahead,' she said.

The compounds tended to rely on the military units within the base for security and therefore didn't always employ guards. And if any Taliban did manage to sneak into the base with a bomb of some kind, there were far more important military targets to hit than a civilian contractor like CAMCO. He followed the line of the fence in the opposite direction to the main entrance.

When Stratton reached the corner where the minor road followed the length of CAMCO's perimeter fence on that side, he turned with it and followed the fence. The noise from the generators was greatly reduced. After about forty metres he came to a broad gate chained and locked to its post, made of robust alloy bars and chain-link fencing. He could see inside the compound.

He caught a strong smell of sewage and he could see why. A row of collection tanks stood on the other side of the internal road. That was the purpose of this particular entrance. These compounds tended to have their sewage emptied at least once a day and had a gateway purely for that purpose. It had been banged about by the heavy vehicles that came in and out and when Stratton gently pulled at the gate it twisted on one of its hinges, which was broken. The gate would have to be lifted to open it once it was unchained. He pushed against one end and a gap opened up at the support post, large enough for him to squeeze through.

He eased his way inside, stepping into the shadows to assess things. Sounds came from every direction. A toilet flushed and music drifted from a prefab behind the sewage containers. He headed along the inside of the same fence he had just come up on the outside. As he reached the corner a door opened in the prefab a few metres away and light shone across his front. He stopped dead.

A man stepped out of the door and tossed a bucket of water onto the ground. He was wearing a white jacket and hat. A cook. Inside the room behind him, Stratton glimpsed lines of steel racks filled with tin cans and vegetable racks. The cook went back inside and it went dark again.

Stratton passed through a narrow gap between the fence and a prefab building and when he emerged the other end found himself in a large parking area, looking at a line of pick-up trucks with their rears to the fence. The main buildings had to be fifty or sixty metres away. The sound of the generators seemed to have got louder again. Someone left one of the buildings, and a broad shaft of light shone through the open door into the car park. Stratton heard the door close and the man's feet crunching on gravel. Then the creak of another door opening and closing.

Stratton studied the pick-up trucks. Two of them were laden with shipping crates. When he got to the first he could read the cargo labels:'Destination: CAMCO Houston'. But the crates looked a little small. He had better luck with the second pick-up, where he found one more than big enough for the warhead. He took hold of the side and tried to move it. It wouldn't budge even a fraction. He wouldn't be able to lift it even with Hetta's help.

Another door opened beyond the car park and someone stepped outside. Stratton kept still and watched the person, confident he couldn't be seen in the darkness from that distance. Footsteps on the gravel indicated the person was heading away from him. He heard a door close and all went quiet again. He could detect no signs of sentry activity, which was good. But the main gates were still locked. Contractors had very regulated lives in camps like this. They worked long hours during the day and rarely worked at night, when everything was usually locked up. If they weren't working or eating meals, most would confine themselves to their rooms, where they had satellite TV, DVD and game players, and internet connections. So there would rarely be movement within the compound during the small hours.

The obvious solution was to drive the CAMCO pick-up with the larger crate on it out, place the nuclear device in the crate and then drive it right back to its start point in the compound. But that would require a lot of movement and opening and closing of gates. He doubted he'd get away with it without disturbing someone. Another option would be to remove a panel in the fence perhaps, but that was too big a job. Cutting a hole was another possibility.

He saw a length of plastic cable on the ground by his feet. He picked it up and tossed it up onto the razor wire directly above him. It would mark the spot at least while he tried to figure out a solution.

When he got back to Hetta she was leaning against the Hilux waiting for him. He stopped in front of her, looking at her but deep in thought. He looked beyond her, then above her. He walked past her to inspect the crane, climbed up onto the platform and looked inside the cab. Several heavy trucks went past along the main road, bathing him in light. He ignored them. No one except the owner of the crane would question his interest in it, and he expected the odds of that person showing up to be slim.

The cab was open and he checked the controls, which looked simple enough. He set about pulling the wires out from beneath the dashboard. Stratton wasn't experienced in hot-wiring vehicles but an MI6 course he'd taken on the subject a year before had explained the theory. It took several experiments before the dashboard lights came on. He pushed the starter button and the engine turned over and burst into life.

Now he looked through the window at the fence and the cable he'd thrown up that was hanging over the razor wire, about ten metres away. He applied the clutch, crunched the mobile crane into gear and pressed down the accelerator, and the engine stalled. 'Handbrake, idiot,' he said to himself. He released the brakes and fired up the engine again and this time the heavy vehicle moved forwards.

He carefully moved the crane to within a few metres of the fence, leaving the engine running as he climbed out. He took a moment to assess the noise. He could hardly hear the crane over the racket coming from the generators around them, so he went to the arm controls at the back. A period of study and experimentation was required to operate the various controls.

Hetta came over to look at what he was doing.

'You know how to operate one of these?' he asked her.

She shook her head.

'Well, pay attention. You're going to be operating this one in a minute.'

He pulled a lever and studied the steel arm above him.

The main arm started to rise up. He kept it going until it was at what he judged to be a good angle. He pulled another toggle and the arm turned. He stopped the move as it wasn't what he wanted at that moment. It would come in handy shortly.

He pulled another lever and the main arm began to extend like a telescope. He activated the winch and the hook descended. He halted it a metre off the ground and went around to the side of the truck where the strops were stored. He found a canvas one with loops on both ends, carried it to the hook and draped it over the crescent.

'OK,' he said loudly. 'I need you to raise me over the fence. That piece of cable hanging on the wire is the marker.'

She looked at him and then at the controls. After a brief study, she pulled on one of them and the arm started to rise up, the strop along with it. Stratton hurried over to the hook and placed his feet in the strop's loops as it came off the ground.

He ascended majestically. As the inside of the compound came into view he had a good look around it. He couldn't see anyone and he felt pretty sure the contractors wouldn't hear the sound of the crane's engine. He only needed to avoid being seen.

Hetta was a quick learner and yanked the correct lever and he moved towards the fence. She extended the main arm and the pick-ups came into view and he indicated her to move him to the right a little. He watched the top of the razor wire as he moved over it with inches to spare. When he was the other side, he held up his hand. The crane arm came to a halt. He was directly above the pick-up with the larger crate in it.

The buildings and pathways were so much more visible from his vantage point. Stratton signalled Hetta to lower him, and he descended. She watched and as he was almost out of sight his hand went up. She stopped him. He stepped off the strop onto the crate, removed the looped ends from the hook, threaded them through the crate's lifting strops and returned them to the hook.

He waved above the fence and the crane's engine revved a little as the hook began to rise. It rose up off the pick-up and once again he focused his attention on the compound. He could only pray no one came outside. It would greatly upset his plans.

And then, as if the gods had heard and decided to play with him, a door opened in one of the prefabs and a broad shaft of white light spread deep into the car park. Stratton watched the man walk out of the building, down the side of the structure and in through another. He appeared to have no interest in looking anywhere other than where he was going.

Stratton breathed a sigh of relief and Hetta swung the crate over the fence and brought him down to the ground. As the crate made contact, the strops slackened and he unhooked them. He unfastened the latches on the side of the crate and removed the lid. Inside was a piece of machinery he didn't recognise.

Stratton attached the lifting strops to a strong point on the machinery and signalled for her to raise it. The part rose out of the crate and Hetta swung it to one side and lowered it to the ground. Meanwhile Stratton removed the blanket covering the box on the Hilux. She was quickly repositioning the hook above him and he secured the black box to the strops and she raised it up, swung it around and positioned it above the empty crate.

He guided it down into the crate, which it fitted with room to spare, so Stratton removed the strops and replaced the lid. Then she swung him and the crate up and onto the back of the pick-up in the CAMCO compound. He removed the strop, took a moment to check everything was in place and nothing was left to indicate any disturbance, then he reached up an arm and was quickly sailing back over the fence.

'A tidy job,' he said, once they were back in the Hilux. 'Are you sure crane operating wasn't your true calling?'

She said nothing so he started the engine and drove them out of the lot, onto the main road that paralleled the runway, towards the opposite end of the airfield from where they'd waited earlier in the day.

It didn't take long to hit a military checkpoint — a small guardhouse beyond two vehicle dam systems built into the two road lanes and big enough to present a serious obstacle to all but the largest tanks. Five American soldiers dressed in defence of the cold, on top of full combat gear including helmets, stood around a coal fire in an oil drum.

One of the men put out a cigarette and walked over to the Hilux, cradling an M4 in one arm. Stratton turned on the cab light so that the soldier could see him and the vehicle's interior. The young man's expression hardened on seeing Stratton's unshaven face.

'This is a military checkpoint, sir. You need to back out of here and head around that way.'

Stratton held out his ID card. 'Excuse the scruffy appearance. I'm military,' he said.

The soldier took the card, inspected it and looked at Hetta. His expression changed on seeing her. 'Weren't you in the mess hall this afternoon?' he asked her.

She didn't respond, giving him the same silent treatment she gave everyone else as she handed him her ID.

'I need to put these through verification,' the soldier said. 'One minute please.'

He walked to the guard house, saying something to the others as he went inside the shack. They looked in the direction of the Hilux. The soldier came back out of the guard hut carrying a small device. He placed one of the cards into a slot and offered it to Stratton. 'Put in your pin code, please sir,' he said.

It looked like a credit card machine. Stratton punched in his code and thought he saw the clearance come up as he handed it back to the soldier. The soldier removed the card and handed it back to him. 'Thank you, sir. Ma'am,' he said, handing her the device after placing her card in it.

Hetta keyed in a number. The other soldiers had gradually closed in to get a better look at the 'specials', in particular Hetta.

The soldier studying the device looked surprised as it completed Hetta's verification. 'Wow. I've never seen a clearance that high before out here,' he said, removing the card and handing it back to her. 'You have a good day, ma'am. Sir.' He stepped back and saluted.

The vehicle dam slowly sank into the road and they drove through, watched by the soldiers. They went along the edge of the airfield, passing rows of US military aircraft: rotor wings, FA-18 jets, a squadron of Apache helicopters and several Predator drones in an open hangar. Stratton turned a tight corner to cut across the airfield on the designated vehicle route and they waited for the green signal light.

As they drove across the main runway to the other side of the airfield, they went past the row of hangars and warehouses they'd passed earlier on the road. Several large civilian aircraft were parked up on the broad skirt for the night. Stratton pulled the Hilux into a civilian car park and brought it to a stop nose-to the lot fence, the headlights illuminating pallets on the other side packed high with crates, all secured beneath large rope nets.

'This is where the civvy cargo gets processed,' he said, looking at a jet parked a few hundred metres away with the CAMCO logo on its tail.

'And that's our plane.'

He turned off the engine and lights, reclined his seat and made himself comfortable. 'We've got a few hours before this place comes to life.'

She sat still, looking at nothing in particular. He mulled over the next phase. If all went well, they'd be out of Afghanistan in a matter of hours.

'Where are you based?' she asked.

'Poole, in Dorset. You know where that is?'

'Yes.'

He wondered how. 'Where're you from?' he asked, doubting she'd answer.

She didn't speak right away. Stratton took it as her usual closed door. 'I like Switzerland,' she said.

It was a surprise that she answered. 'What's your favourite part?' he asked.

'There are many. Lake Geneva perhaps. Outside of the city. Towards the Alps.'

'I've driven to the French Alps from Geneva a number of times. I take it you like to ski?'

'Yes.'

'I don't like the resorts. Too crowded. I usually go cross-country.'

'It's the only way to ski,' she said, as she lowered her seat. 'You can sleep if you want. I won't.'

He took that as a signal her conversation moment had maxed out. He wouldn't sleep either, not after the long afternoon nap he'd had. They sat in silence for several hours. She seemed just as able as Stratton at waiting. They watched a single vehicle arrive and a woman in a heavy coat climb out and walk into one of the warehouses.

The place gradually came to life and by 5 a.m., even though it was still dark, the area was getting pretty busy. Two vehicles, nose to tail, drove into the freight compound in front of them on the other side of the mesh fence. They were CAMCO pick-ups, the logos on the door hard to miss. Stratton was pretty certain they were the two from the compound.

He watched the drivers climb out, both of them wearing thick coats. He recognised them from the chow hall. The pair had a brief chat with a man who'd joined them. He looked like he worked in the freight yard. They exchanged paperwork and the man walked to a forklift tractor. He gunned it to life and drove it over to the back of the first pick-up.

They watched the tractor lift the crate holding the nuclear device off the bed and carry it across the yard and deposit it on a large, empty pallet. Then it unloaded the rest of the crates onto the same pallet. The CAMCO men did some more paperwork before they climbed back into the pick-ups and drove off the compound.

The freight man secured a heavy net over the pallet then went back to the lifter, picked the pallet up and eased out of the yard with it, out of sight beyond several containers. Stratton and Hetta climbed out of the Toyota to watch the tractor go to the back of the CAMCO cargo aircraft and place the pallet on the rear ramp. A couple of crewmen rolled it into the belly of the aircraft and out of sight.

'Nice when a plan goes to plan, don't you think?' he said.

She didn't respond.

The forklift pulled away and headed back to the yard. All they had to do now was get on the plane. He felt the pistol at his holster. He'd keep it on him and leave everything else behind. Hetta kept her Magnum in its holster at her hip, which her new fleece largely covered.

Together they walked out of the car park towards the plane. They knew someone would eventually realise the Hilux had been abandoned and would find the weapons inside. But it would be just another Afghan mystery. They headed for the side of the aircraft in front of the wings where a set of steps led through an open door into the cargo hold.

'Why don't you do the talking on this one,' Stratton said.

The two crewmen were inside the cavernous cabin securing the pallet as Stratton and Hetta climbed in. Aside from half a dozen seats near the front, and the pallet lashed in the centre, the plane was empty. A crewman operated a switch and the rear ramp began to close with a high-pitched whine.

Both crewmen stopped as they saw the two strangers. Stratton didn't recognise either of them from the chow hall.

'Can I help you?' one asked, his accent American.

'Is Doug on board?' Hetta asked.

'Sure. I'll go get 'im for you.'

The crewman passed Hetta and Stratton and

went through a narrow doorway into the cockpit. A moment later the pilot stepped from the cockpit, dressed just the same as he had been the day before in his airman's jumpsuit, followed by the crewman watching on curiously.

The pilot looked surprised to see the pair of them. 'Hi,' he said. 'What can I do for you guys?'

'We decided to take you up on your offer of a ride,' Hetta said.

He didn't look too overjoyed at the prospect.

'I need to get Stateside and you're the first flight I can get on,' she added.

'We're going to Houston.'

'That's exactly where I need to go.'

Stratton wondered if Doug had been insincere and was now regretting the offer he'd made. It wasn't uncommon for Westerners to help out other Westerners, contractors or military, with flights in and out of Afghanistan. They were in a war zone and that's how things were done, as long as people had the right credentials. The contractors could circumvent Afghan bureaucracy while they were tagged alongside a US military base, and so it was entirely up to the pilot.

Stratton wondered what Hetta would do if he decided not to fly them out of there. The guy had a nuclear bomb on board. He doubted she was about to let it go without her. And offloading it to try someone else would be problematic for too many reasons. Stratton had the feeling that if the airman didn't play ball, things were going to turn out badly for him.

Hetta was looking into Doug's eyes, reading

him, waiting for a sign.

'I'll need your IDs,' he said. 'I have to call them in to the military and add them to the manifest.'

Stratton didn't think that meant he'd relented. It was as if he'd thrown down an obstacle that he hoped they might stumble on.

Hetta held out her ID for him. Stratton did the same. The pilot looked at them. Hetta's was from the US State Department and Stratton's was British special forces. Doug looked between the pictures and the faces in front of him. He would have no idea what such IDs looked like for real. They could be fake for all he knew. But on the other hand, the IDs stated that the two peculiar-looking persons, peculiar compared with the average soldier you came across in the camps, were VIPs. Unordinary. That would explain their looks. And her weapon. And how apparently they could go anywhere they wanted to go on the base.

The pilot's expression changed. 'I guess these'll do,' he said. 'No sense in going through all the palaver of manifesting you at the movements centre. You can do the paperwork in Houston.'

'Thanks,' Hetta said with a smile Stratton knew she'd forced.

Doug was still looking pensive about his new guests. 'You can both sit here,' he said. 'Jim will take care of the safety brief. I'll get us airborne and we can talk later.'

Doug left them to the crewman. Hetta and Stratton took a seat and settled back for the ride.

He looked at her for any sign of relief. He wasn't surprised to find no trace of any.

The four jet engines fired up, but the crew took another half-hour to prepare the flight. Stratton spent the entire time looking for signs that things weren't going as expected. When the heavy plane began to taxi, his uneasiness reduced. The take-off was a short one due to the lack of weight and the pilot took the craft into an immediate steep climb.

It wasn't long before the noise from the engines decreased substantially as the pilot hit cruising altitude. It was light outside and would be throughout the flight as the aircraft kept pace with the sun. The weather was clear and there was no turbulence. Stratton checked his watch.

'What time do we get in?' he asked one of the crewmen who happened to be passing.

'Winds look like they're in our favour,' the crewman said. 'Captain thinks we could arrive in Houston early afternoon. You guys want any coffee or snacks, just help yourself around the corner there.'

'Thanks,' Stratton said.

The crewman went to the back of the plane to check on the lines securing the pallets. Satisfied, he took a seat and made himself comfortable. Stratton looked over at Hetta, who'd closed her eyes.

He wondered how she was going to get the bomb off the flight and to wherever it was headed. He guessed that once they were on the ground, people from Langley or the State Department would take over. His name was eventually going to come up on someone's radar back home regarding his visit to Afghanistan. His details had been recorded at more than one checkpoint. The British SIS would learn of the part he'd played in the acquisition of the Pakistani bomb. The Yanks might openly thank the Brits for Stratton's contribution in getting it out of country. But at some stage he was going to be asked to explain, to both the Yanks and the Brits, how he knew so much about the warhead and its whereabouts.

He couldn't tell them about Bullfrog. He'd given his word to her. He would have to say Chandos told him everything. The man was dead and couldn't get into any trouble. But it didn't explain all of his actions. They would want to know why he hadn't reported what he'd learned.

The more he thought about it, the less he was looking forward to arriving in the US. He lay down across several seats and got himself comfortable. Perhaps he could come up with a plausible explanation, but his gut feeling told him he wasn't going to find one. He closed his eyes. The air was chilly and he pulled his fleece around him.

Within a few moments he had drifted off into an uneasy sleep.

20

Stratton opened his eyes. He'd slept in a state of semiconsciousness, always aware of the constant drone and vibrations of the engines, the cold air and the crew passing him every so often.

He checked his watch and was surprised to see he'd managed to remain comatose for several hours. He sat up, dropped his feet onto the metal floor and rubbed the sleep from his face. His mouth tasted bad. He needed a drink of water. Hetta wasn't in her seat. He looked down the hold but the only thing he could see was the pallet. Maybe she'd decided to lie down somewhere. The only other place she could be was the cockpit, or in the little kitchen. Perhaps she was making that communication she mentioned.

He got to his feet and glanced again towards the back of the cargo hold. He had to do a double take. Someone was lying on the floor behind the pallet. Two people were in fact — he could see two sets of feet. He made his way down the tail and saw both crewmen, tied up like the Sunday roast with tape around their mouths. The one called Jim was looking at him with a vexed expression. The crate containing the nuclear warhead lay undisturbed on the pallet.

Stratton looked back towards the cockpit, wondering what he'd find in there. This was undoubtedly Hetta's handiwork. But why?

Jim made a squeak, hoping Stratton might release him.

Stratton walked the length of the plane. As he approached the cockpit he saw the pilot, lying on the floor on the other side of the door, tied up like his crewmen. His eyes were open and he looked at Stratton with a frown, as if his predicament were every bit as much Stratton's fault. Stratton stepped over him into the cockpit.

Hetta was flying the plane.

'Didn't you like the service?' he asked.

'They were landing in Houston,' she said. 'My orders are to take the device to New York. It was a lot easier to take control of the aircraft myself than get them to change their flight plans.'

'New York?' he said, surprised. 'We're taking this into JFK?'

'No. A small airfield upstate.'

'Why?'

'Those were my orders.'

He wondered what military facility was near New York. 'I take it you've filed a new flight plan,' he said.

'Everything has been taken care of.'

She switched on the autopilot and released the controls.

He wanted to think on that for a moment. 'I'm going to get a coffee,' he said. 'You want one?'

'OK.'

As he passed Doug, Stratton looked down at the pilot lying on the floor and decided he couldn't leave the man there for the rest of the flight. He also didn't want to have a discussion with Hetta in front of him. He got behind him,

270

sat him up, lifted him to his feet and part-carried, part-dragged him into the hold and over to the seats. He laid him down across several seats and stood up to check the guy was OK. Doug stared up at him with a frown.

'It's all for a good cause,' Stratton said. 'You and your crew will be fine.'

That didn't appear to do anything to improve the pilot's mood. Stratton didn't like the thought of the pilot looking at him that way every time he walked past. He saw a CAMCO hat on the floor, so he picked it up and fitted it over Doug's face. Then he went to the galley outside the cockpit and set about making some coffee.

When he went back into the cockpit, Hetta was getting a message over her headphones, which she replied to briefly and made some adjustments to the controls. The plane changed direction a few degrees.

He thought he could detect a level of contentment in her manner. 'What are you so happy about?' he asked, handing her the coffee.

She shrugged, as if not entirely sure herself. 'I'll soon be going home, I suppose.'

He continued to be bothered about the warhead, as well as her. He couldn't give up all control over it, not yet.

'Who are you handing that thing over to?' he asked.

'The authorities.'

'What authorities?'

She gave him a look as if to suggest he was interfering. She put the cup of coffee to her lips.

'I asked you a question. And I want an answer.'

She flashed him a threatening look.

271

He wasn't in the least bit intimidated. He'd been impressed by her fighting skills since the nomad camp, and he respected the fact that she had more of a will to shoot him than he did her. At the time. But now the tide had shifted. The lack of answers from her up until then suited him because they were both headed in the same direction with similar ambitions for the bomb. Yet suddenly he no longer knew where he was going exactly.

He set down his coffee and put the end of the barrel of his handgun to her head. 'Tell me who you're delivering this bomb to or I'll put a bullet through your skull. I'm not a qualified pilot but I can fly this crate well enough to put it on the ground.'

Her expression went to ice. She didn't move.

'If you doubt I'll shoot, let me assure you there's too much at stake for me not to,' he said. He tilted the barrel down to aim into her torso. 'At this angle there's too much body mass for the bullet to damage the plane. I'll ask you one last time, which authorities are you handing this nuclear warhead over to?'

She turned to look at him and saw something in his unwavering green eyes that she hadn't been aware of before.

Suddenly, something appeared at the window. They both looked out at an F-22 Raptor jet fighter, clearly US Air Force. The pilot was looking over at them and waving. Another F-22 appeared on the other side of the cargo plane.

'Those are our escorts,' she said. 'I'm not entirely sure who will be taking control of the device, but they work for the same authority that owns those aircraft.'

Stratton looked at the jets and saw the pilot indicate for them to keep on their heading.

'That's fine then,' he said, putting the pistol back in his holster and giving her a little smile. 'Carry on.'

The USAF was good enough for him. They were difficult to argue with. It also made sense, a powerful escort to guide such a dangerous cargo into the country. He glanced at her. She was looking straight ahead and didn't look pleased. He didn't feel apologetic because she was far too arrogant and needed a wake-up call.

They broke through cloud at twenty-two thousand feet and he saw a patchwork of fields and woodland scarred by roads and dotted with towns. It was a nice day. She controlled the aircraft expertly as they continued to descend and an airfield eventually came into view on her side. It didn't look very big to Stratton. He wondered how far it was from New York City. He couldn't see any sign of skyscrapers on the horizon. Perhaps the city was behind them.

As they turned and approached the runway, Stratton could pick out the main buildings alongside the tower and several vehicles parked up around them. The place appeared to be deserted otherwise. The airfield buildings looked like they could have done with a refurbish. There were no other aircraft, save a couple of small Boeings parked beyond the buildings out to one side and looking like they hadn't flown in years.

Hetta raised the nose slightly and brought the

plane smoothly down onto the runway, reversing the thrust of the engines immediately. The runway seemed just long enough and she applied the brakes hard before they could run off the end onto the grass, then turned it around and headed back towards the buildings.

As they got closer, Stratton had a good look at the vehicles, large, shiny Suburban-type SUVs, much like the ones the spooks had used in Bagram. He saw a couple of suited men wearing sunglasses standing by them and several other men in black fatigues or jumpsuits climbing out as the cargo plane nosed past.

Hetta brought the craft to a stop and shut off the engines, whose whining rapidly decreased as if they were deflating. Stratton stayed in his seat while she opened the cabin's forward side door. He heard voices. They sounded cordial. He heard several people climb on board. As they entered the main cabin, they turned towards the hold, ignoring the cockpit. After a minute, Stratton heard the shrill electric whine of the rear ramp opening.

His reluctance to meet the authorities remained, but he couldn't put it off for ever. He sighed inwardly as he got out of his seat and stepped from the cockpit. Four of the men were unfastening the netting on the pallet. He went down the steps onto the asphalt. One of the suits had his back to Stratton, talking to several of the other men. There was something familiar about him. They all looked heavy set and a couple of them looked past the man they were talking to at Stratton. Their eyes were inexpressive.

The suit stopped talking and turned, and Stratton found himself looking at Jeff Wheeland. He was momentarily stunned. Wheeland had a long, fresh scar across one of his cheeks and an ugly matching bruise on his forehead.

'You look as surprised as I was when I heard you'd joined the team, Stratton,' Wheeland said. He had the air of a man who knew everything that had taken place and was in complete control of it all.

Two of his men moved either side of Stratton, who could only stare at the spook.

'We need to have a little talk, you and I,' Wheeland said. 'You can tell me all about what you were doing in Bagram and how you knew about the bomb.'

If there was one spook Stratton didn't want to speak to, it was Wheeland. But then, he never thought he would have to ever again. The men took hold of his arms and Wheeland stepped closer to him.

'I don't know what it is about you, Stratton,' Wheeland said. 'But you really do piss me off more than anyone I've ever known.'

Stratton had his arms twisted behind his back and secured with thick plasti-cuffs. One of the men removed his handgun and searched him for any other weaponry. Wheeland slammed a fist into Stratton's stomach, which knocked the wind out of him. He would have doubled over in pain if he wasn't being held so strongly.

'That's for muscling in on my game, again,' Wheeland said.

One of the men holding Stratton said

something to Wheeland in Russian.

'Oh, yeah. I almost forgot,' Wheeland said, as he hit Stratton in the body once again. 'That's for Ivan, who you killed and stripped off in Bagram. His friends want you to pay the full price for that one. And they can have you, as soon as I've finished with you.'

Stratton fought to deal with the searing pain in his kidneys and Wheeland walked away, up the steps into the hold where his men were opening the crate. One of them had raised the inner lid and was examining the contents. After a brief inspection he looked in Wheeland's direction and gave him a thumbs up, as the two escort jets screamed low overhead.

'On their way home,' Wheeland said, giving Stratton a wink.

Stratton glanced over at the SUVs to see Hetta standing beside one of them looking at him. There was something seriously wrong here. He might deserve a slapped wrist for interfering but not what Wheeland had threatened him with. And judging by the men's voices, they were a mixture of Americans and Russians. That was all very weird.

Stratton had mixed feelings as he looked at her. He didn't think she'd duped him. His instincts still told him she'd been straight with him, as far as she was concerned.

Wheeland stepped back onto the tarmac. 'You look confused, Stratton,' he said. 'So many questions. Sorry, but I'm not at liberty to give you any answers. Take him away,' he said to his men. 'And hood him.'

The hood went over his head and everything went dark. He was walked to one of the vehicles and he felt a hand on his head pushing it down as he was guided inside. Whoever it was got in the seat next to him. They remained there for several minutes in silence. Then he heard a loud bang, a familiar sound to him. Not a gunshot but close to it. A rushing sound followed, like a dull roar that grew louder. Then another sharp bang. He could smell fumes. Gasoline. A waft of extreme heat came in through a window.

'Let's go, people,' someone shouted. It was echoed in Russian.

The plane was on fire. Stratton was certain of it. Wheeland's men had set it alight. He could hear the roar of the flames getting louder.

Men climbed into the vehicle and it sank with the extra weight. The engine started and the doors were slammed shut and the vehicle lurched away. He wondered if the aircrew had been taken off or left to die on board the CAMCO plane. He couldn't fathom why the spooks had destroyed it. He couldn't understand any of it.

The first step had to be declassifying the spooks. They weren't spooks, not the Russians. As for the Americans, why destroy a commercial aircraft in their own country? There was too much he didn't know. He couldn't begin to even guess the answers.

One thing was for sure. Wheeland wanted to know how he knew about the warhead. And then he wanted to do something very bad to him once he found out. That wasn't the reaction he'd been expecting.

21

Stratton felt a twinge of regret sitting in the Suburban. He estimated the vehicle had driven for something like forty-five minutes through clear roads or less built-up areas before it hit the stop-go rhythm of a city. The sounds outside became those of heavy traffic, vehicles of all sizes. Horns blared, engines growled or whined, and he heard distant sirens, whistles and the occasional shout. At times they went at speed while at others they moved slowly, surrounded by vehicles.

The driver seemed anxious to get wherever they were going. Every opportunity he had to put his foot down or swerve into a gap, he appeared to do so. About two hours after leaving the airfield, Stratton felt the Suburban drop down a steep ramp and the light change, even though he was hooded. He guessed daylight had been exchanged for artificial lights and when he heard the tyres screech as they turned a corner he knew they were inside an underground car park or something like it.

They turned several corners and drove down more steep inclines before coming to a stop, and this time the engine was turned off. The doors opened and all the passengers climbed out except the one beside him.

There was a conversation outside. Men's voices echoed in the concrete structure. That odd mixture of English and Russian. Stratton couldn't get a precise bead on what they were saying. It sounded like they could be organising personnel and assigning people to different tasks. He heard a metallic clunk outside. Machinery. What sounded like a heavy door sliding open on rollers.

Someone called out something in Russian and Stratton was hauled out of the vehicle and held against the side of it. There was another metallic sound. Bearings that needed oiling were moving. He guessed a trolley, rolled across the concrete and onto a hollow-sounding floor.

Then he was grabbed away from the SUV and walked into the same hollow space. Metal doors closed and clunked together. There was a pause before a shunt and he felt sure they were going up. He listened to the sound of machinery and the men around him breathing. The elevator was slow. No one talked. After a minute the lift shunted to a halt and the doors opened. He was held still while the trolley was rolled out.

'He goes to the floor below,' said an American voice.

It seemed like everyone left the elevator except the man in charge of Stratton. The doors closed and it descended for a few seconds before stopping. When the doors opened again, Stratton was led out and turned a sharp left. After thirty or so paces he was stopped and brusquely turned about.

'Sit,' the man said. It was only one word but Stratton suspected he wasn't American.

He bent his knees to lower himself, expecting

his backside to come into contact with the seat of a chair. He kept going down until his behind rested on what felt like a rolled-up carpet. His hands behind him came into contact with a concrete wall.

'Don't move,' the man ordered as he stepped away.

Stratton leaned back until his shoulders touched the wall. He could hear voices across the room. Two men, one of them his minder, both Russian-sounding. He didn't know the language well, but enough to get by. The men were talking in low tones and he couldn't understand a word. The way their voices echoed, the room sounded large and empty.

One of them walked back towards him. 'Stand,' he said as he grabbed Stratton harshly by his clothing to assist him.

The man shuffled him a few metres to one side and pushed him down again, this time onto a metal chair. The Russian attached a restraining system, the type used for transporting high-risk criminals. He secured the apparatus to Stratton's feet and the legs of the chair, then he brought the ends of several cables together and connected them at a junction. He locked it with a key, which he removed, and gave the apparatus a firm yank to ensure it was locked.

Stratton felt like a turkey ready for the oven. The man walked away and the soft talking resumed. Stratton racked his brains for any clue he might have missed. The only Russian connection to all of this came from Bullfrog and the former KGB general Mikhail Gatovik.

How the hell could ex-intelligence officials like Betregard and Gatovik be working together in the business of bringing a nuclear weapon to the US, namely New York City? A combined operation? If they wanted the bomb to be secured, it would be in the hands of the military right now. But it wasn't. It couldn't be. Stratton thought it was pretty safe to assume the military knew nothing about a nuclear warhead being in the US.

Except that didn't explain the F-22 escorts.

But even if he ignored the fighters, he couldn't think of any possible explanation for Betregard concealing a Pakistani nuclear weapon from the administration. He felt something nagging at the back of his mind, something Bullfrog had said.

He needed to get away from these people.

The elevator doors opened and someone stepped out. Whoever it was joined in the conversation with the others. They walked over to him. Stratton's hood was pulled off none too politely.

Jeff Wheeland stood over him, smirking.

'I have to admit, Stratton, you get me nervous,' he said. 'You're the kind of guy who'll find a way out of a situation if there is one.' Wheeland began to pat him down and check his pockets. 'Just in case the boys missed anything,' he said, feeling inside Stratton's jacket pockets. 'You going to tell me how you knew where to find the bomb?'

'Tell me something first,' Stratton said.

''What's this all about?'' Wheeland guessed. 'No.'

'I was going to ask why you killed Berry Chandos.'

'Never heard of him.'

Stratton believed him. Wheeland felt something inside one of Stratton's trouser pockets and pulled out the coin on its chain that Chandos had given Stratton.

'This is an SBS stone, right?' he said. 'I've seen one of these before. 'Chandos,'' he said, reading it. 'Your dead buddy?'

Stratton could only stare at him.

Wheeland pocketed the stone. 'You going to answer my question now?' he said.

Stratton flicked a look past the spook, taking advantage of his removed hood. He was in what seemed a large storage area, one practically empty. The walls looked fairly old, sixties perhaps, and in need of repair. There were construction poles and planking in one corner. Two men were standing in a narrower space outside the elevators.

Wheeland tapped him on the side of the head aggressively. 'You're not going to answer me, are you? I expect you've figured out that you're only alive until you tell me what I want to know.'

Stratton looked back into Wheeland's eyes. The new scar almost reached the left one.

'You know the techniques we use to extract information,' Wheeland said. 'I don't expect pain will do it on its own. Not with you. I bet you enjoy pain, eh? I don't have any drugs with me at the moment. I wasn't expecting you. I'd dearly love to know how you knew how to find us. It strongly suggests others. I need to know who they are. I plan to send you to some specialists later on today. They'll get it out of you.'

'How did you survive the ambush?' Stratton said.

'Luck,' Wheeland said, opening his shirt to expose another ugly wound to accompany those on his face. 'Only two of us made it. Remember Spinter? He bought it. The bastards executed him. I was unconscious and taken for dead. Just goes to show, no matter how meticulously you plan anything, there's always Murphy's Law. Did you know that was the first ambush on that road for four months? And we walked right into it. And the assholes had no idea what they took. Always have a back-up plan.'

'Hetta,' Stratton said.

'Not my idea, but it turned out to be a good one. How'd you get on with her?'

'She's a bundle of fun.'

Wheeland smiled. 'Yeah. They don't come any colder than that one. Was Kandahar her idea or yours?'

'What did she say?'

'That one doesn't talk to me. She talks to God and no one else. Probably the only person I've ever met who truly scares the hell out of me, and it's a woman. I think. I can't even fantasise about screwing her and she's got a look I would otherwise kill for.'

Maybe she outranked Wheeland, Stratton thought. But then, why would she be doing the hard graft? Did she work for the Russians? If the rewards for this venture weren't about patriotism, it was for something else, most likely money. But she didn't seem the type to be driven by wealth.

'What's your cut of this?' Stratton said, hoping Wheeland might shed some light on it.

The American chuckled. 'What's the point in finding out the mystery, Stratton? I'm going to put you back under your little hood now. I've warned the men about you. That you have a reputation for causing problems. They're all professional and would love a chance to see how good you are. But even so, they won't want to take a single chance. That's why you're all tied up nice and secure. And if you even look like you're going to cause trouble, they'll kill you. But if you're a good boy someone will come and collect you later on and you'll be taken to our interrogation centre near the Potomac, where you'll eventually tell us anything we ask you. And then it's bye-bye.'

Wheeland placed the hood back over Stratton's head and walked away. Stratton gave the chains a firm yank again. They felt solid.

$$\star \quad \star \quad \star$$

He sat there for what felt like an age. He heard the elevator arrive several times and the doors open and close. It sounded like one of the men would leave for a while or perhaps they were exchanging duties. He heard no other sounds from inside or outside. He felt he had lost track of time. It could have been around four or five hours since the CAMCO cargo flight landed, but maybe it was less than that.

The opportunity to escape would have to come on his move to the interrogation centre. After that he doubted there'd be any other chances. CIA interrogation centres had a habit of being secure places. If he remained chained up the way he was, he didn't have any hope. From what he'd seen, these men weren't amateurs.

Stratton felt a niggle of despondency. It was only to be expected. He brought it under control. There was nothing to be gained by feeling that way. He'd been in tighter situations. Positive thinking was always the best approach. If nothing else, it put the mind in the frame to react correctly if an opportunity did arise.

The elevator doors opened again. This time he heard no voices. This time there was a muffled thud as if someone had dropped something. Then sounds of human exertion. Stratton strained to listen, but it all went completely silent. Then a gentle padding of feet. Coming towards him.

Whoever it was took hold of his hood and yanked it off.

Stratton looked up into a face he knew so well but had never expected to see again.

'Berry?' he muttered, unsure his eyes weren't deceiving him.

'How are you, my boy?' his old boss said softly, a tight smile on his face. 'Bet you never thought you'd see me again.'

Stratton could only look at him.

'Don't look so startled,' Chandos said.

He inspected the chains and cables securing Stratton and tugged on them. 'How are we going to get this off?'

Stratton put a myriad of thoughts to one side. 'There's a key,' he said.

They both looked towards the elevator at the figure lying on the floor. Chandos went over to the man and after a short search found something and returned to Stratton. The key fitted neatly into the slot. He turned it and the clip fell open.

'You're supposed to be dead,' Stratton said, shrugging off the restraints.

'Misinformation is such an effective tool.'

'How'd you get here?'

'Through Cuba, up to Miami and then to New York.'

'I meant, how'd you know I was here?'

'You still have my stone on you, don't you?'

Stratton was about to reach into his trouser pocket when he stopped, remembering Wheeland had taken it. 'No.'

'Bugger. I was looking forward to saying I told you I'd have it back one day.'

'So how did you find me?'

'The stone's a transponder. Just enough juice for one ping every six hours. Lasts two weeks. You can access the tracking manager on any internet connection. I knew you were here three hours ago.'

Stratton noticed the injuries on Chandos's face. 'What happened to you?'

'Ah. There was a price to pay to make my escape, fortunately not a big one. I couldn't just hide. I needed to convince the assassin that I was dead. Come on, we have to get going.'

They went to the elevator.

'Perhaps we should take the stairs,' Chandos said. 'We've been lucky so far. I think there are a lot more where he came from.'

'Wait,' Stratton said. 'What are your plans?'

'What do you mean?

'What are we doing now?'

'Getting out of here, of course.'

'Then where?'

'Home. Back to the UK.'

'Then what?'

'Get on with our lives. I came here for you, not just because I got you into this in the first place. You're my friend. You'd do the same for me.'

'You and Bullfrog had it all wrong.'

'And thankfully so,' Chandos said. 'But do we have to talk about it right now?'

'You were wrong, but something else is happening. Just not what you suspected.'

'Fine.' Chandos was sounding exasperated. 'I'm looking forward to discussing it on the plane home while we do our best to drink the bloody thing dry.'

He started to head for the emergency exit but Stratton held him. 'The bomb's here,' Stratton said.

A look of confusion crossed Chandos's face. 'What do you mean?'

'I mean it's here. In this building.'

'What are you talking about?'

'I got it here from Afghanistan. It was brought here by Betregard's people. I don't know why.'

Stratton went to the emergency exit door.

'Whatever it is you're thinking, I'm pretty sure it isn't a good idea,' Chandos said. 'Not on our own. We should go and get help.'

'And tell them what? We think there's an atomic bomb in the building. And how do I know? Why, because I just happened to be the one who smuggled it into the country from Afghanistan.'

Chandos thought about it a moment. 'Yes, I see. But neither can we just politely ask these people to explain whatever it is they're up to.'

Stratton tested the emergency door to see if it was unlocked. It wasn't. 'Let's go back to basics and start with a recce. Then take it from there.'

Chandos didn't like it at all but as he watched Stratton open the door, he knew he had little choice.

Stratton stepped inside a dark stairwell that zigzagged down for a dozen or more floors. He looked up but all he could see was a single stairway leading to the next and possibly top floor. The landing was blocked by a wall and a metal door. He went back through the door to the comatose man on the floor, grabbed him under the arms and dragged him through the door. Chandos stepped inside the stairwell and let the door close behind them. Stratton dumped the body in a corner and walked up the steps to take a look at the door. It looked solid, near enough impenetrable.

'How're we going to get upstairs?' Chandos said in a low voice behind him.

Stratton went back down the stairs, out the door and returned a moment later with one of the construction poles, an extendable one. Chandos watched as he went up the steps to the metal door and positioned the pole horizontally, one end facing the wall and the other against the door, just above the lock. He began to unscrew the support and the arm extended, jamming tightly between door and wall. He kept turning the joint around and around and the door and frame flexed slightly. Chandos lent a hand and finally the door frame started to crack. With each turn of the screw the pressure on the lock increased until, with a sudden bang, the lock broke and the door flew open. Stratton caught the scaffold as it fell.

They both stood still for a moment, listening, but there was nothing, so Stratton put the scaffold on the lower landing and the two men stepped through the doorway and up a half-flight of stairs into complete darkness. At the top, they came to another door and nothing else. The fire door was heavy and sealed around its edges. Stratton turned the handle slowly. As it reached the full extent of its turn, Stratton pulled it towards him ever so easily. When he did, they heard a distant, muffled voice.

Stratton opened the door enough to put his head through the gap, and found himself looking along a corridor, the elevator opposite. He stepped into the corridor and Chandos followed, easing the door shut behind them. The ceiling was twice the height or more of the floor below and a confusion of air-conditioning piping and conduits. Beyond the end of the short corridor he could see a large space, almost warehouse-sized. A large piece of machinery hummed on the far side of the room and what looked like a couple of generators were against a wall.

They stepped as quietly as they could in the near darkness to the end of the corridor and looked around the corner as the voices became clearer. Half a dozen men in one-piece black fatigues were gathered around a large table. A handful of others sat operating radios and other technical equipment.

Jeff Wheeland was holding court, and every word was being interpreted by another of the men into Russian. Chandos nudged Stratton and indicated a set of metal steps behind them leading up to a walled storage platform. He saw a slatted opening in the wall. Stratton nodded and they eased their way back to the steps and climbed up onto the platform to the opening and looked down onto the meeting through the slats.

A scale model of a built-up section of Manhattan covered most of the table. On a board nearby lay a vast map of the same section zoomed down onto Chinatown, south Manhattan.

'Team Alpha will assemble here on Chrystie,' Wheeland said, indicating a road on the model. He paused so that the translator could repeat what he'd said in Russian.

'Team Bravo, here on Canal. Team Charlie, opposite them here on Bowery. Air cav and the sky cranes will maintain positions here over the water west of the 9/11 rebuild site. We have a licence to provide air-crane construction support to the site all day, so nobody's going to question any of our air assets in that location.'

Wheeland turned to the large map. 'The

bullion trucks will have only two options,' he continued. 'Both routes have to converge here at the Manhattan Bridge approach. It's the bottleneck where we'll set up our impact point.'

One of the Russians said something.

'When will the general public hear about the nuclear device?' the translator said.

'Pretty soon. The New York City Radiation Detection Agency has already recorded traces from the bomb, aided by a small teaser we provided an hour ago. The agency has verified its findings and informed the White House and the Pentagon of a nuclear spike in the city.'

Another Russian asked a question that was translated. 'The plan depends on the public being told about the bomb,' the translator said. 'How can we be sure they'll be told?'

'This ain't Russia. If a bomb were to go off in this city and someone found out that the authorities knew about it, the President could end up in jail. The public will have to be told.'

'Why haven't they found the bomb already?' an American asked. He looked towards a corner of the room as he spoke.

Stratton followed the man's gaze to the now familiar black crate on its trolley. He nudged Chandos, who, despite the warning, was still surprised to see it.

'We didn't choose this tower block just because it's close to the impact point,' Wheeland said. 'The first wave of detection systems will be ground units. They outnumber air detection assets ten to one. They won't be able to find the device this high up and by the time the air assets are airborne, we'll be on the road and the bomb will be on its way uptown.

'By now the Treasury and the banks will have received a Protocol Notification Communication from the Pentagon and the Federal Gold Reserve will be moving out. The last thing any of them want is trillions of dollars' worth of gold they can't touch for fifty years because of contamination. There's only so much security available to protect those convoys. And even less when there are desperate terrorists like us at large with an atomic weapon. All resources will be directed at finding the bomb.'

He checked his watch. 'The media will be learning all about the bomb about now. When that news hits, it'll provide the panic exodus we need. That's not only going to absorb more security, it'll greatly reduce their ability to move across town.'

'The federal trucks will have a helluva lot more gold than HSBC,' an American said.

'More than we can carry too. The Federal Reserve can employ not only city police but home guard units. HSBC won't be able to provide the same level of security because they draw on the same resources and the Federal Reserve has priority. HSBC have used the covert technique before and it's worked for them. They'll rely on secrecy, as well as the expectation that everyone else, criminals included, will be too busy trying to escape from the city to notice them. We can only hit one of the convoys anyway, so we're going for the weakest. But don't worry, gentlemen. The value of the gold in that convoy, along with a couple bags of diamonds, is estimated to be in the region of 2.8 billion dollars. Let's not be greedy.'

Some of the men around the table laughed.

'Shortly after we depart, the bomb will be relocated to Central Park,' Wheeland said. 'Once the RDA gets a reading on it, it'll attract cops like the biggest doughnut this side of Brooklyn. More panic means less organised response when we make our move. If all goes to plan, gentlemen, we won't even see a cop. An atomic weapon is way too high a priority over a street robbery. That, my friends, is the whole beauty of the plan.

'But don't get complacent. On completion of removal, on my command, all teams dump any clothing, weapons and equipment and join the crowds escaping from the city. All of your equipment, including the helicopters, is untraceable. And if any one of you is caught, just remember the money will be waiting for you on release.'

'What about the gold?' one of them called out.

'The gold will be flown directly to a ship in the bay, and the rest, I'm afraid, is confidential, just in case one of you does decide to tell stories. No offence, I'm sure you understand.'

An encrypted voice boomed over a loudspeaker. A second later it was decrypted and audible. 'This is OP Jake at HSBC. We're observing heightened activity at the departure airlocks. Three bullion vehicles have rotated out of the loading bays and are in the departure port.'

An operator seated at a communications console looked to Wheeland for a reply.

'Does he have an estimated departure time?' Wheeland asked.

The operator asked the OP the same question.

'OP Jake estimates potential for departure in fifteen minutes. Will advise and update as and when.'

'We're ten minutes from the impact point,' Wheeland said, looking at the map. 'The HSBC convoy will take fifteen minutes minimum from their departure point. The media will make an announcement any time now. That'll add an estimated 20 to 40 per cent extra traffic density on Route Gold. Within twenty-five minutes this city will be in gridlock and no vehicle will be able to move anywhere. Everyone knows what they have to do. Let me reiterate one thing. Anyone who falls and is injured is lifted out. Anyone dead is left behind. Anyone seriously injured, I leave it to you to decide but termination is advised. We're playing for big stakes. We expect to pay them too.'

The men looked resolute.

'Be ready to move in five. And gentlemen, good luck to you all, not that it's a factor.'

The men dispersed to half a dozen large plastic containers along one wall. They pulled on weapons harnesses, ballistic helmets, gas masks, belt equipment and ammunition. Everything was black nylon, plastic or leather. Each man had an M4 assault rifle and a pistol in a holster. Webbing harnesses were stuffed with smoke and shrag grenades. Stratton now saw that the black one-piece battle suits they were all wearing each bore the same badge on arms and backs.

A badge declaring them to be members of the New York City Police SWAT team.

'Team commanders muster by the elevator,' a voice called out. It was shouted out with equal vigour in Russian. They all walked out of sight from Stratton and Chandos into the short corridor that led to the elevators.

Half a minute later, the room was suddenly quiet, except for radio messages coming over the speakers. Only three of the men remained, one at the communications console.

Stratton and Chandos looked at each other, both stupefied. Stratton mouthed a silent 'wow'. He eased his way down the steps and back into the corridor. He quickly went back through the emergency exit door and onto the fire escape landing. Chandos followed and Stratton carefully closed the door behind them.

'My god,' Chandos said. 'This whole thing is about robbing gold bullion reserves.'

'An atomic bomb threat against the city would be enough to get them to move it,' Stratton said.

'And quickly.'

'And without all the security they'd like in place.'

'And through a city in chaos,' Chandos added. 'It's bloody genius. And to have the balls to pull it off, now that's something else.'

'I underestimated Wheeland.'

'Wheeland?'

'The one doing all the talking. Betregard's number two.'

'Well. That's that,' Chandos said.

'What do you mean?'

'This has nothing to do with us any more,' Chandos said. 'I mean, we've no moral obligation to remain involved. It's a simple robbery. No one's going to detonate the bomb. It's no longer political. It's a handful of spooks turned rotten, that's all.'

Stratton frowned. 'No moral obligation?'

'All they're going to do is rob some gold. We can walk away. We'll inform the authorities later who was responsible.'

'That easy, huh?'

'Why not? We can go directly to our own people. They'll understand. They'll look after us.'

'For how long? Do you really believe you'll make it to a courtroom to testify against them? You of all people know how dangerous Betregard is.'

'What are you suggesting?'

'Our only option is to destroy the operation,' Stratton said. 'Expose them before they succeed.'

Chandos didn't look pleased to hear it. 'If we get out of the country, our problems will be about surviving weeks from now. If we stay, we might not get through today. You said yourself — there's no one we can talk to. No one who would believe us. And we can't stop them on our own.'

'No, we can't do it on our own,' Stratton muttered, forming an idea.

'So what's the point in us staying?'

'We can't do it without help from the New York police and the military. We have to work it so they just don't know they're helping us.'

'You've completely lost me,' Chandos said.

'Instead of us going to them, maybe we can lure them to us.'

'I'm still none the wiser.'

'Wheeland said the detection units will be all over the city, right?'

'Yes.'

'New York also has fixed nuclear radiation detection systems placed in key points, doesn't it?'

'At the ports and select bridges and intersections. But the precise locations are obviously secret.'

'OK. But the RDA is already aware of a device, so it'll be actively searching for it,' Stratton said. 'The bomb will be a magnet for the response teams. Part of Wheeland's plan is to use it to lure the response teams away from the heist.'

Chandos was thinking. 'Where the bomb goes, the response teams go.'

'That's right.'

'It sounds simple enough.'

'It's all about timing.'

'And one or two other things,' Chandos said.

'We could start by getting the bomb out of this building,' Stratton said, going for the door handle. 'You happy with that?'

'I'd be exaggerating if I said I was.'

They stepped carefully back through the doorway into the corridor and to the end of it. The radio operator was still seated at his desk, talking to the various call-signs. The others had their backs to Stratton.

Stratton eyed the line of boxes from which the soldiers had collected their equipment. The nearest one was a few metres away. He left the cover of the corridor and inched his way across the gap. He could see the butt of a handgun.

One of the men happened to turn and see him and went for the pistol in his holster as Stratton snatched up the one from the box. Stratton had him by a second, but the gun felt light. There was no magazine attached to it. He could only hope the man didn't know.

'Careful, now,' Stratton said.

The other men turned to look, both contemplating going for their own weapons.

'The easy way or the hard way,' Stratton said. 'The stakes are high and I'll shoot to kill.'

Evidently the men believed him because they slowly raised their hands.

Chandos hurried over and grabbed their weapons, tossing one to Stratton, who exchanged it with the unloaded one. The three men frowned at the bluff.

Chandos found several restraining harnesses like the one Stratton had been secured with. 'On the floor,' he said.

Within a minute he had them all firmly secured. For good measure he grabbed some tape off a table and bound their eyes and mouths. Stratton went to the bomb on the trolley and opened the lid of the box to find the device sitting neatly in its framework.

Chandos came over to have a look. 'Good god,' he muttered. 'It's a live one, isn't it?'

'Very much so.' Stratton shut the lid and wheeled the trolley in the direction of the corridor, pausing at the model and map Wheeland had used for the briefing.

'How well do you know New York?' Stratton asked.

'Not very well,' Chandos said.

There were several folded maps on the table by the radio. Stratton opened one up and compared it to the various markers on the model. He tore away the relevant section, folded it and stuffed it in his pocket.

'Let's go,' he said as he wheeled the trolley to the elevator.

Chandos made a quick diversion and rejoined Stratton holding a couple of coats. 'It's a bit chilly outside,' he said.

Stratton saw a shoulder holster hanging over a chair and quickly pulled it on, and then the jacket Chandos handed him over the top.

Chandos put his pistol into a pocket and Stratton hit the elevator call button.

22

They pushed the trolley out of the elevator and into the building's confined lobby. The marble floor was the only touch of opulence about the place. An empty reception desk lined one wall.

A television monitor on a wall was silently playing a local news station displaying breaking news. Real-time subtitles streamed across the bottom of the screen:

' . . . *despite the panic it could cause, the people of New York City had a right to know, the governor's spokesman said. Everything was being done to locate the device, but meanwhile the authorities had to do everything conceivably possible to facilitate the rapid exit from the city of all those who wanted to leave . . . '*

It felt surreal in the quiet lobby. They heaved the trolley to a set of glass doors.

'The panic's started,' Chandos said as he pushed the button to open the door. They pushed the trolley through and out onto the pavement, looking down the four-lane boulevard at people moving in all directions, some running, others ambling along, a mixture of awareness of the threat.

The street was tree-lined, high-sided by apartment blocks and offices, and busy. They heard the whine of a distant emergency siren. Stratton took a quick check of the map to get his bearings. 'Avenue of the Americas,' he said, reading a sign. 'We need to head south.'

'How far?' Chandos asked.

'Two, maybe three miles. If we keep up a good pace, we could be in the area in half an hour.'

'What if the detectors ping us before we get there?'

'That's only one of the what-ifs I'm worried about.'

Several police vehicles escorting a couple of large vans between them were preceded by sirens as they turned a corner into the street. The convoy muscled its way through the traffic and disappeared down a side street.

'This entire island is going to become a car park in a short space of time,' Stratton said, quickening the pace.

The trolley was easy to push considering the weight it was carrying, the pneumatic wheels helping to absorb the dips and bumps, particularly when they crossed roads.

'Stand aside!' Chandos called out to a group of people ahead with their backs to them. 'Please stand aside. Emergency.'

The process worked well and where there were hardly any pedestrians, they managed to break into a light jog. All the time, Stratton kept a wary eye on the passing cars, in particular any Suburbans like those at the airfield. Several people suddenly came running towards them, rudely pushing their way through people. One, a woman, stopped quickly to talk to a man. After a brief exchange the woman ran on, followed by the man. There was clearly a distinction between those who'd heard the news and those who hadn't. That also applied to vehicles, with some drivers trying to get going while others weren't.

'Make way! Coming through!' Chandos called out again to several people ahead.

The pair kept looking skywards as they hurried along the street, searching between the towering buildings for any sign of RDA aircraft.

'Shouldn't we find a vehicle of some sort?' Chandos said. 'We might get to the ambush RV before the traffic builds.'

'I'm working on it,' Stratton said.

'If they find us they'll shoot first, considering the circumstances. You know that, don't you?'

★   ★   ★

Wheeland sat in the front passenger seat of a black Suburban, its windows darkly tinted, as it left the underground car park of the building. Two large, windowless black vans followed it and behind those came two more Suburbans. Each of the vans contained twenty men, all dressed as their team commander in black one-piece suits, body armour, webbing, ballistic helmets and goggles. They were loaded for bear.

They headed up the street towards a main intersection, where they turned left and joined busy traffic. Communications between the vehicles and observation posts blared from the radios Wheeland and the team leaders were wearing. He was a little nervous about the upcoming attack. It wasn't his normal line of work. It was outside of his comfort zone. But he was doing this one for himself, his own personal profit. And if all went well, it would be his last ever job.

Two years before his visit to Afghanistan to get the codes, he had been assigned to Henry Betregard's office as a consultant analyst. Wheeland had never heard of Betregard prior to joining his personnel staff, but Betregard had heard of Wheeland, on paper at least. Betregard had done his homework when selecting personnel. During Wheeland's fifteen years in the service of the CIA, he'd proved himself to be intelligent and highly resourceful in the field, but there were also several question marks about his integrity. No substantial evidence suggested he might be corruptible, yet inferences had been made by more than one previous department head who thought they'd detected signs.

As for Wheeland, when Betregard asked him if he was interested in doing something of great personal profit that wasn't in the interest of the flag he'd served for so long, he wasn't entirely surprised. He'd formed his own suspicions about Betregard's out-of-office activities after only a couple of months in the man's employ. The same degree of questionable integrity could be applied to everyone else who worked for Betregard. They were all up for a little extracurricular activity.

Wheeland's cut of the day's heist, for the part he'd played in the planning and execution of the operation, was going to be a cool thirty million dollars. As soon as the gold was carried by the sky crane helicopters onto the vessel in the bay, his money would be dropped into his account. He didn't even have to wait until the ship sailed to Russia, where the gold would be melted down. Betregard had even given him a six-figure deposit for his work so far. The plan was perfect down to every detail. The shell company that had been set up to purchase the weapons and equipment and rent the small fleet of crane and support helicopters would disappear, its owners untraceable. Even if the FBI suspected any of those involved, proving it was going to be impossible. None of the men would talk if captured. There was a fortune waiting for any who were unlucky enough to be imprisoned. They had all been specially selected. Each would happily kill friend and foe to achieve his goals.

Betregard also had the unwitting support of the CIA, which trusted him completely. Langley had fully accepted that all the work Wheeland and his team had been doing in Afghanistan and elsewhere was in the interest of national security.

And if it looked a little deeper, it still would.

Wheeland would remain in the government's employ for another few months after the heist, for the sake of appearances. After that he would quietly slip away and begin a new life. He didn't have a single doubt that he deserved every penny of it for the services he'd rendered to his country. It was only just and fitting.

Looking back, he actually thought it had all been too easy to put together. The execution phase was going to be little more than a formality. Sound planning was the key to success. Accurate and detailed risk assessing and analysis, combined with the right personnel, the right procedures and the right equipment. The better the preparation, the less a plan relied on luck. Of course, there was always an element of good fortune required. A simple vehicle accident at this stage had the potential to impede the success of the operation, but even that had been planned for.

As he sat there, staring ahead, wondering if there was anything he'd overlooked, he saw two men pushing a trolley along the sidewalk. He saw a black plastic box on the trolley. And then he recognised one of the men pushing it.

It took a second to hit him.

'Stop the goddamned vehicle!' Wheeland shouted as he pushed a button on the console and the driver's blackened window slid down to let the daylight flood in.

*   *   *

In his peripheral vision, Stratton had seen the vehicles come to a stop and he knew they were in trouble. When the window began to open, he saw someone lean across the driver holding a black-barrelled tube.

'Down!' he yelled, grabbing Chandos and pushing him forward to put a car between them and the Suburban.

Wheeland opened up with the high-velocity weapon on fully automatic. The powerful bullets slammed through the relatively soft skin of the vehicle, shattering its windows, trashing the interior and upholstery, and peppering it with small, jagged holes.

Chandos hugged the front wheel while

305

Stratton lay down behind the rear, praying the wheel hubs would protect them. The windows of a shop behind them shattered and the display was ripped apart. He saw someone stood at the counter inside struck several times.

People in the street scattered, most of them dropping to the ground where they stood. And then the shooting stopped. Stratton knew well enough why. Wheeland had exhausted the magazine and was exchanging it for another. In the passenger seat of a vehicle that would be more cumbersome and time consuming than on one's feet. They had five or six seconds to move. 'Go!' he shouted as he got to his feet and shunted the trolley forward.

Chandos was quickly up and the pair ran as hard as they could behind the trolley while keeping low, threading between prone pedestrians like a two-man bobsleigh team trying to get their bob up to speed.

'Left!' Stratton shouted and they took a sharp turn into a one-way street of traffic at a standstill trying to head towards them into the main street.

'Follow them!' Wheeland shouted at the driver. 'That way! Cross the street!'

'It's a one-way street, boss,' the driver said.

'Parallel it! Go!'

The driver put his foot down and tried to muscle through the building traffic.

'Send the other vehicles to the RV,' Wheeland shouted to one of the men behind him. 'You take the next turn!' he said to the driver.

They passed the end of the one-way street and Wheeland caught a glimpse of the two men.

Stratton and Chandos ran for all they were worth, the trolley rattling along in front of them.

'Right!' Stratton yelled.

They turned in sync, crossed the road between a couple of parked cars and down an alley, emerging onto a street and, after a quick check to ensure the black 4×4 wasn't coming, tore across it, through a gap in a fence and into a small car park.

Stratton heaved the trolley over the pitted lot while Chandos did everything he could to keep the box from falling off.

Wheeland's driver turned the corner to leave the main road and accelerated hard, flying past the car park, but Wheeland caught a glimpse through his side window of Stratton and Chandos halfway across it. 'Stop! Back up!' he shouted.

★   ★   ★

Stratton and Chandos were already running to the car park exit when the Suburban appeared again. As the two Englishmen came into view, Wheeland took out his pistol and aimed, but he was too late. They ducked around a corner and were out of sight.

'Go!' Wheeland shouted. 'Next right!'

Stratton and Chandos had crossed the street and headed back towards Avenue of the Americas, which they went south on. Several sirens blared, followed seconds later by two police cars screaming past. Stratton glanced back as the squad cars came to a halt further down the street and officers leaped out, guns in hand, crouching behind their vehicles while they tried to figure out what had taken place.

He looked at Chandos, who was beginning to feel the strain of the physical effort. Stratton slowed a little in order for them to stick together. He realised they needed an alternative form of transport.

'This way,' he shouted, wanting to get off the major route. He turned down another side street, crossed the road and hurried through a piece of derelict ground between the apartment buildings.

As they reached the other end and another side street the trolley's front wheels snagged in a deep pothole. The impact turned it violently and the black box jumped off its platform. They watched in horror as it hit the ground, the lid snapped open and the bomb rolled out of it like a big black lead buoy.

The warhead bounced onto the road and started rolling across the street, right into the path of a slow-moving car. The thud of the impact sent a shudder through Stratton, but the bomb slid down the street, apparently undamaged.

'Dear god,' muttered Chandos, and they ran hard in full pursuit, as vehicles swerved to avoid the barrel. Finally, it hit a pile of trash cans, slowing down enough for Stratton to grab it.

'Is it OK?' Chandos asked, completely out of breath.

'If it wasn't, we wouldn't be here.'

Up ahead they saw a man easing several boxes

on a crate mover off a ramp attached to the back of a panel van. The man pushed the boxes into a building.

Stratton knew precisely what he wanted to do next.

23

Wheeland's Suburban drove at reduced speed along a street, the men inside looking in every direction for signs of Stratton and the bomb.

'There,' one of the men shouted as he pointed at the trolley in the wasteground. They saw the black box alongside it, lying on its side.

The driver stopped the SUV and Wheeland jumped out. He hurried along the street and the Suburban followed him.

★　★　★

Stratton and Chandos rolled the bomb up the ramp and inside the back of the van.

'Secure it,' Stratton said as he jumped back down onto the street to remove the ramp, but then he saw something that stopped him instantly.

It was Hetta, standing some thirty metres away and looking at him. She was wearing a black one-piece suit with a nylon weapons harness, an empty holster at her hip, her Magnum semi-automatic pistol in her hand down by her side. Her expression was as cold as ever.

Chandos looked up the street to see what Stratton was looking at.

'Who's that?' Chandos asked.

Stratton stood slowly upright. 'Don't do anything sudden.'

'She's holding a gun,' Chandos said.

'And she knows how to use it.'

Hetta walked towards Stratton, her eyes fixed on his. She stopped several metres away.

'I wondered what happened to you,' he said.

'That's still my responsibility,' she said, indicating the device. 'Don't get in the way of my mission.'

'I don't believe you know what's going on. I think if you did, you might reconsider your position.'

'I doubt that.'

'You act like you don't have a conscience. But I think you do.'

'I can't afford to have one,' she said, staring into his eyes.

★ ★ ★

Wheeland stepped off the sidewalk and out from behind a parked car, then stopped when he saw the integer down the street. He held his arms out to halt the two men by now with him.

★ ★ ★

Stratton looked past her. Noted Wheeland had halted. That was no doubt because he knew Hetta was going to take care of everything for him.

Stratton looked back at her. 'I can't let you have it,' he said.

'Then I'll kill you,' she said.

'At least tell me why you're doing this. I think you owe me an explanation.'

She seemed to consider his request.

'You work for Henry Betregard,' he said, helping her along.

'No. Betregard is only the messenger.'

'He gave you your orders?'

'He delivered them.'

'What if he was more than just the messenger? What if he was creating the orders himself?'

'He couldn't do that.'

'How would you know?'

'It's impossible.'

'You're not following a directive from the White House,' Stratton said. 'We were both tricked into bringing this nuclear bomb to Manhattan. Betregard is nothing more than a criminal. This is about a bullion robbery. It's about gold. And I'm trying to put things right.'

Her expression didn't change.

* * *

Wheeland couldn't hear what was being said but he was growing concerned with the lack of action by the integer. She should have killed Stratton by now. 'Be ready to kill them all when I say,' he said.

The man on his right moved a hand to grip his pistol.

'Nice and easy,' Wheeland said.

* * *

Stratton saw Wheeland's men take hold of their guns.

'You'll only be helping them,' he said. 'You have to trust me. You've learned how to do that, haven't you?'

'I can't let you take the device,' she said.

'Then we'll get it to the authorities together.'

There was another pause. This time longer. 'Do you have a plan?' she asked.

'Kind of.'

'Those usually work for you.'

'Wheeland's behind you with two of his men.'

'I know.'

'I don't think he's too pleased you haven't shot us yet.'

The delivery man exited the building and stopped dead on the sidewalk when he saw Hetta holding the handgun.

'Your keys, please,' Stratton said to him.

The man didn't move.

'Haven't you heard? The city's evacuating,' Stratton said.

'There's an atom bomb loose on the streets. You need to run,' Chandos added.

The man looked more worried about the gun at that moment and slowly handed Stratton the keys.

★   ★   ★

Wheeland decided enough was enough. 'Kill them.'

The two men pulled out their handguns.

'Wheeland!' Stratton warned.

Hetta swivelled on her heels as she brought her gun up. Her strength and speed were impressive as she angled her body to reduce her

313

profile and steadied the barrel of the Magnum for a fraction of a second before firing.

The boom was deafening. The delivery man threw himself to the ground and one of the soldiers took a high-velocity round in his chest with the force of a cannon ball. His body armour took the impact as he was lifted off his feet and thrown back several metres before he hit the ground.

As that first bullet struck, another exploded from Hetta's gun, aimed the other side of Wheeland. The target spun around onto the hood of a car, cracking the windscreen before he rolled to the ground. Both men lay unconscious. Hetta aimed the weapon at Wheeland, who dived back between the parked cars.

Stratton hurried through the van to the driver's seat. Within seconds the engine gunned to life and Hetta stepped into the back as he crunched it into gear. He drove them off down the street, the ramp disconnecting and rolling away. She held onto a rope hanging from the top as she looked out of the open back.

Chandos held onto the wooden slats fixed to the insides of the van and stared at her, uneasy in her presence.

'Was it you, in Lagos?' he asked.

She took her time answering. 'You were lucky to survive that explosion.'

'So were you.' He studied her face. She didn't have a mark on her, in stark contrast to the injuries on his face. 'But at least I lost you,' he said, a hint of victory in his eyes.

'You went to the port and boarded a Russian

bulker for Buenos Aires.'

His smirk melted. 'Why didn't you come after me?'

'I was reassigned.'

Chandos continued to stare at her as she watched the road.

In the cab, Stratton consulted his map and the way ahead. A crossroads loomed. He went through a red light to take a right towards Manhattan Bridge, causing several oncoming vehicles to swerve to avoid his wide turn.

He glanced in the mirrors and as he looked to his front a black Suburban shot out of a side street almost level with him. It swerved violently, leaning hard over so that it was almost on two wheels, and smashed into the van's flank.

Stratton fought to keep control as the panel van lurched over to the other side of the road, swiping the near side bumper of an oncoming car. The car was far lighter and, while it careened off at an angle into a parked car, the van was knocked back into its original lane.

The black Suburban seemed hardly affected by the collision. It was also much more powerful than the van and quickly drew level on the passenger side. Through the open driver's window Stratton saw Wheeland at the wheel, gun in hand, about to fire.

Stratton touched the brakes to put the SUV slightly ahead and Wheeland fired, hitting the windscreen. At the same time the operative whipped the nose of the van into the Suburban's rear quarter, sending it fish-tailing violently as Wheeland fought to keep control. The Suburban's nose side-swiped a parked truck, which completed Stratton's effort, and it spun around so that it was facing the other way.

Stratton swerved the van heavily over to avoid colliding with the Suburban and pushed the gas pedal to the floor as he looked in his wing mirror in time to see Wheeland's vehicle smash backwards into a line of parked cars. He had to brake hard as he caught slower traffic up ahead. He flashed a look to his rear at Wheeland climbing out of the Suburban, holding a rifle. There was no way he was going to drive the van through the traffic before the bullets began to fly.

'Get ready to debus!' he shouted.

★ ★ ★

In the skies above the city, a Bell helicopter swooped low over the streets. Stencilled on its side was the name of the organisation that owned it: 'Radiation Detection Agency — New York City'.

Projecting from a gantry under the nose was a large, white probe similar to the one on the spook detection vehicle in Bagram. Inside the helicopter, seated behind the pilot and co-pilot, were two engineers surrounded by a complex array of electronic hardware and monitors displaying data and analytical information. Several oscilloscope signals peaked, the analysed data automatically transmitted by a radio.

Twelve blocks away, inside the operations headquarters of the RDA, the diagnosed signals received from the helicopter were highlighted down the side of a large screen. A quadrant displayed a satellite map of New York City. Flashing indicators showed the locations of static and mobile radiation detection sensors. Half a dozen of them were airborne.

The room bustled with activity. Eyes were on the monitors as data alarms flashed. The operations director saw the new information and paused as he watched it develop.

'Strongest indicator is in the area of Wooster and Canal,' an analyst called out.

A US Army general in combat fatigues stepped beside the operations officer. A senior NYPD officer in uniform joined them.

'That reading's got high potential,' the agency operations officer said.

'I can't afford to commit my resources on a shadow,' the general said.

'Analysis will focus over the next few minutes,' the ops officer said. 'That's a helluva lot of the wrong kind of radiation someone's moving across the city. You want my advice, General, whoever that is I'd wipe them out as soon as possible and apologise later if we got it wrong.'

The general looked at the police officer. They agreed without words and went to their respective phones.

★　★　★

Stratton turned the vehicle hard to the side as he applied the brakes. Hetta threw herself to the deck of the van as a hail of bullets splattered through the skin. Chandos held the wooden framing along the walls while bullets spat through either side of him.

As the van wobbled to a stop Stratton leaped from his seat and grabbed the bomb as it slid across the floor. 'Let's get this out of here!' he shouted.

Wheeland stood in the street with vehicles swerving and screeching to get out of his line of fire as he dropped to a knee, aimed and let rip with another series of bursts. The bullets slammed into the van, one of them zinging off the side of the bomb as Stratton rolled it the length of the bed. Chandos hurried to help him and Hetta jumped to the ground and between the three of them they hauled it out and around the back of the van as more rounds hit the vehicle.

Stratton saw a yellow taxi cab the other side of several cars and ahead of the traffic jam. 'That way!' he shouted as he took the strain of one end of the bomb.

They shuffled the awkward, heavy device between the cars. The taxi driver was crouched beside his vehicle avoiding the bullets. To his surprise he saw the trunk open and the vehicle drop as something heavy went into it.

Stratton checked on Wheeland. He was still heading towards them.

'In!' he shouted.

Rounds hit the vehicles around them. Pedestrians screamed as they dived for more solid cover, some of them hit as they ran.

Wheeland changed magazines as he marched down the street and Stratton started the taxi's engine and they screeched away, leaving the terrified taxi driver huddled on the sidewalk.

When he saw the taxi drive off, Wheeland turned and stepped into the path of a motorbike that was headed towards him. He aimed the rifle at the rider who, filled with horror, dropped the bike and skidded along the road behind it. Wheeland simply walked over to the bike, shouldered his rifle and, with a great effort, lifted the machine back onto its wheels. He straddled it and started the engine, which fired up instantly.

He threaded his way through the stalled traffic, past the empty van in pursuit of the taxi.

★ ★ ★

Stratton divided his attention between his rear-view mirror, the road ahead and the skies above. He saw a helicopter making a wide turn across their front.

Chandos looked out through the rear window to see the helicopter turning tightly around the back of them. 'Has to be radiation detection,' he said.

'I hope so,' Stratton said.

'As long as the response teams don't get to us too soon. How much further?'

Stratton consulted the map. They were on Canal Street towards Manhattan Bridge. The ambush point wasn't far away, but the traffic had slowed to a crawl as it converged from every nearby street towards one of the major bridges that led off the island.

Stratton turned sharply over the road and along a narrow cross street.

Wheeland weaved the bike through the congested streets. Saw the helicopter and knew instantly what it was. There were dozens of yellow taxis in every direction. There wasn't time to check them all out. He dropped a gear, mounted the sidewalk and rode along it, scattering civilians hurrying for the bridge.

★ ★ ★

Stratton emerged from the cut-through and turned onto another busy avenue. Checked the map again.

'Four blocks to the ambush site,' he said.

They turned the corner into a mass of vehicles and came to stop. Stratton's frustration grew and he opened the door to look ahead, behind them and in the air. Hetta climbed out.

'I need to stop Wheeland,' he said to her.

Her expression didn't appear to change, but he knew her well enough to read the approval in her eyes. Chandos stepped out, looking in the air.

'You should just walk away,' Stratton said to them both. 'When the response teams get here, they'll be trigger happy.'

'Go,' Hetta said.

He needed no further encouragement and started to head out.

'Wait a moment,' she called out to him.

He stopped and she walked over to him, taking her Magnum from its holster and handing it to him, along with a couple of spare magazines. 'Better than that cap-gun you're carrying.'

He took the weapon, appreciating the offer.

'Take care,' she said. Her expression was as blank as ever, but Stratton detected something in her eyes. There was warmth.

He headed away. Hetta watched him reach a main road and disappear around the corner.

24

Wheeland rode the bike along the Canal Street sidewalk with the rifle slung across his shoulder. But there were so many people walking in the direction of Manhattan Bridge that he couldn't make headway fast enough. On the road, traffic had come to a near standstill. Horns blared, engines gunned. People shouted. Tempers were high. And so was their fear.

He gave up trying to threaten his way through, stopped the bike, climbed off it and walked onto the road, threading his way between vehicles. He wasn't the only pedestrian with that in mind, but his progress was quicker.

The broad street opened up as he approached the large intersection that was fed by four other main roads — Chrystie, Canal, Bowery and the Lower Roadway — and led directly onto the northern mouth of Manhattan Bridge. The intersection was a complete zoo of machinery and humanity, every inch of it taken up by vehicles, the gaps between filled by pedestrians, all heading for the bridge and over into Brooklyn. Precisely what Wheeland had planned for. He craned as he walked into it, looking for his men.

He looked where Chrystie Street entered the intersection and saw one of the black Suburbans. As he closed on it, he saw one of the large troop trucks immediately behind. The teams were climbing out amid the chaos, and pedestrians were pushing through them to get to the bridge. Two of the men were hauling an M60 machine gun onto the roof of the Suburban, where it was fitted into a robust tripod, its legs secured by clamps. They loaded it with belt ammunition. Anyone who noticed the hardware showed little interest in knowing why.

'Everything OK, boss?' one of the men asked Wheeland as he arrived.

'It will be,' Wheeland muttered, taking his rifle off his back. 'Are the others in position?'

'Yes, sir. The bullion's heading down Bowery right now.'

Wheeland stepped onto the side of the Suburban to get a look at the large intersection. He placed an earpiece over his ear that was connected to the radio in his pouch. 'This is Wheeland. Give me a sitrep.'

'Air cav and cranes are maintaining their position,' a voice chirped.

'HSBC convoy on Bowery towards Canal and Lower Broadway,' said another voice. 'Traffic is heavy but it's moving. Convoy should be at the intersection in less than a minute.'

Wheeland used a pair of high-powered compact binoculars to scan the bridge. He moved slowly across the entire intersection. Bowery was to his right and, although anxious to look for the convoy, he remained concerned about Stratton and the device.

'Sir, this is air cav,' another voice boomed over the radio. 'We're looking at six, maybe seven air serials towards Manhattan Bridge. Blackhawk troop carriers. They're taking the north side of the water. You should have them visual in three to four minutes.'

Wheeland adjusted his view to the skies. Much of the south-west side was blocked by skyscrapers and he couldn't see the described flotilla. However, he could see the lone white radiation detection bird hovering several blocks west of the intersection.

'All stations stand by,' Wheeland said into his radio. 'There's every possibility this place is going to get hot very soon. Understand this. It's nothing we can't handle. We own this intersection and no one's gonna take it from us until we're ready to leave.'

'I've got a visual on the bullion convoy, boss,' one of his machine-gunners called out from the roof of the Suburban. 'The lead vehicle's entering the junction now.'

Wheeland could make out the top of a plain white armoured bullion truck. 'Let's get this job done,' he said.

The twenty men in their black SWAT overalls, helmets and goggles divided up into four teams and spread out into the intersection, pushing their way through the vehicles and crowds. Every man, woman and child, in vehicle or on foot, was focused on the bridge and how soon they could get across it.

The twenty men from the other troop carrier parked on the south side of the intersection also spread to take up control positions. Two of the teams converged on Bowery Street where it met Canal. Four of the men were carrying a couple of hand-held rocket launchers on their backs.

Wheeland watched the lead bullion truck gradually move into the intersection, closely followed by another. 'Wait until they're all exposed within the intersection,' he said into his radio.

The distant thud of a helicopter reached him and he looked to the skies to see the white Bell turning in a curve from where he saw it seconds ago. He told himself that the bomb was now superfluous. It had done its job. The bullion had arrived. Stratton nevertheless remained an untidy loose end that niggled him.

He focused his attention back on the gold and watched the fourth and last truck turn the corner. 'Now,' he said.

The men carrying the rocket launchers climbed onto the roofs of the nearest vehicles while their colleagues ordered the drivers at gunpoint to keep stationary. The curiosity of some pedestrians grew as they noticed the men taking aim. Those who had figured out what was about to happen pushed to get away.

The first rocket shot from its launcher across the busy traffic above the heads of pedestrians and slammed into the cab of the lead bullion truck, exploding with a deafening crack and blast, sending flames and burning debris skyward and into the crowds. Several of those nearby were killed or seriously wounded. The men in the cab were killed instantly and fire spewed out of the front. The truck rolled on, its engine dead, and came to a crunching halt against a line of cars.

People nearby erupted in hysterical panic. Fire, death and destruction was what they were all fleeing from and, although it hadn't been an atomic blast, it was possibly an overture to what was to come. Those in the distance looked to see what had happened.

The other shooters loosed their rockets, each finding its own target. The remaining three bullion truck cabs exploded as the missiles hit. The hysteria only multiplied, as did the surge of humanity forcing its way towards the bridge.

Vehicles were abandoned as occupants joined the wave of stampeding pedestrians heading towards the bridge and traffic came to a complete standstill. Many of those who fell were trampled.

Wheeland's men climbed onto vehicles to avoid the rush of humanity. None had envisaged the kind of insane panic they were witnessing, and the intersection wasn't emptying. If anything, it was getting fuller. Despite the numbers fleeing for the bridge, many more were coming from the adjoining streets.

Smoke from the burning trucks spread across the intersection into the skies, adding to the confusion. The sound of machine-gun fire sent another shockwave through the intersection — the team on the roof of the Suburban had opened up with short aimed bursts at the bullion trucks, intended to keep up the noise and violence and clear as many people from the vicinity as possible, as well as dissuade any guards inside or out from trying to save the gold. Like a herd of wild bison, pedestrians changed direction in reaction to the new threat, running away from the loud staccato but all the time focused on getting to the bridge.

'Move in!' shouted Wheeland. 'Air cav and transport proceed to acquisition RV,' he said into his radio.

He stepped off the SUV at the head of his men, who were firing into the sky to scatter the pedestrians.

★　★　★

Stratton was a couple of blocks away when he heard the first salvo of rockets and broke into a run, pushing through people as best he could. The heavy sound of machine-gun fire joined in, echoing between the buildings.

He scrambled up onto the roof of a car and jumped from one to another to make better headway. When he arrived at the corner of a street that led directly into the intersection, he saw the bridge to his right and the flaming trucks with black smoke billowing from them straight ahead. The air was filled with screams as people pushed towards the bridge and the ground was littered with abandoned baggage, shoes, clothing. And occasionally those who had been trampled.

Stratton headed across the grain of the stampede. He jumped onto a car to avoid a mass of people but at the same time to look for Wheeland. He saw several men dressed in black, standing on vehicles, wearing helmets.

Wheeland's men.

The machine-gun fire opened up again and Stratton quickly found the source — the gun team on top of a black Suburban. He couldn't identify Wheeland but the man had to be in there somewhere. Even if he did find him, it was going to be difficult to engage him with his men around him. Stratton needed the response teams to arrive. The problem was, they'd be going for the bomb, which was several blocks away.

There was another short clatter of heavy machine gun and Stratton decided it was the greater threat and that it had to go.

* * *

Chandos was growing more frustrated as he listened to the distant sound of machine-gun fire. Once again the RDA helicopter zoomed low overhead. More and more people were abandoning their cars and heading for the bridge despite the gunfire coming from that direction. A family hurried past, the father shouting at two young children who did not seem to be taking their evacuation seriously.

'This is ridiculous,' Chandos said, partially to Hetta but mostly to himself. 'If the response teams land here, they're not going to be of any bloody use to Stratton four blocks away.'

She was looking into the distance, thinking.

Chandos looked as far along the line of traffic as he could to see if it was moving. It wasn't. He walked over and kicked the side of the taxi.

'What would Stratton do?' she asked.

He looked at her, still not at all comfortable talking to her in a casual manner. 'I don't know,' he said, thinking. 'He usually breaks all the rules.'

'What are the rules about driving on the sidewalk?'

He looked along the sidewalk to the end of the road. Other than pedestrians, there were no obstacles. He looked at her. She seemed to be waiting for him to make a decision.

A helicopter thundered overhead. It wasn't the white Bell but a military Blackhawk. He watched it disappear above a rooftop. Then he jumped into the driver's seat and started the car as Hetta climbed in. He crunched it into gear, turned the wheel hard over, powered up the kerb onto the sidewalk and tooted his horn continuously to warn the pedestrians ahead, who scattered to let him pass.

When Chandos reached the end, he remained on the sidewalk and turned the corner. It was clear ahead to the next junction. He wound down his window. The machine-gun fire sounded louder as it bounced between the tall buildings and echoed down the street. He spotted a gap in the traffic just large enough for the taxi to squeeze through and didn't hesitate, swerving the vehicle through the gap and up onto the sidewalk the other side.

★   ★   ★

The Bell helicopter turned sharply between tall buildings in an effort to fly closer to the streets. Inside it the technicians were working hard to recapture the readings they had minutes before.

'I think I have it,' one of them called out.

★ ★ ★

In the RDA operations room the director and his team were glued to the giant screen. Computer operators and analysts on the operations floor coordinated the readings to try to vector the Bell onto potential sources.

'Why are you having so much goddamned trouble?' the general asked the operations director, growing frustrated with the lack of accurate information.

'Locating a static radiation source is difficult enough from a ground vehicle,' the operations officer said. 'It's even tougher from a helicopter. Tracking a moving source is, well, not easy at all. By the time we've run the data through the algorithms and produced any kind of a result, the source has moved on and we can't reliably point to the original.'

'Reacquired!' a voice from the helicopter boomed over the speakers. 'There's a lot of traffic down there but not much of it's moving. Our source is.'

The NYPD's assistant at a computer console looked around at his boss. 'Sir? There's a major incident taking place at the Lower Roadway intersection and the north Manhattan interpass.'

'That's two blocks from the radiation source,' the operations director said.

'There are reports of heavy machine-gun fire,' the police assistant said. 'An officer at the scene has come under fire from what he described as a SWAT team. He believes they're robbing bullion trucks.'

330

A live feed from the intersection CCTV came up in a window on the big screen. Smoke and flames billowed among hundreds of abandoned vehicles. People were running across the screen.

'I don't give a damn if the Treasury is being robbed,' the senior NYPD officer shouted. 'This is my city. I want that bomb!'

'Readings have gone static at the intersection,' the helicopter technician's voice boomed.

'Put my men on the ground. Now,' the general said to his aide, who responded immediately by grabbing up a phone.

25

Stratton hurried between vehicles towards the north side of the intersection, where the machine gun continued to fire sporadic bursts. There were fewer civilians running towards the bridge than a few moments before but still enough to make his diagonal move across their path more difficult.

He jumped over a low concrete road boundary and headed into an open space where other bollards prevented vehicles from entering. Pedestrians were still in abundance, but none were in the adjoining space that led to a blocked archway before the bridge.

As Stratton made his way across the space a voice boomed out at him from behind. 'Stop! Right there!'

Stratton stopped and looked for the source of the command. Two of Wheeland's men stood by the archway covering the route to the bridge, M4s in their hands.

'How come you ain't going over the bridge like everyone else?' one of them said.

Their faces were covered completely, nylon hoods hiding what little flesh was exposed by their helmets and goggles.

'I need to find my family,' Stratton said, pointing.

He might have been convincing, except that the grip of the Magnum was poking out of his trousers. One of the men mumbled as much to his colleague in Russian.

Stratton understood the word for gun and dived over the line of concrete bollards as the men levelled their M4s. He rolled, got to his knees, the heavy pistol in his outstretched hand, and fired. The report was massive and hurt.

The man howled as the round struck his hip, shattering the bone, which wasn't where Stratton had aimed. But the size and power of the slug made up for the poor shot. The man crumpled to the ground, his gun clattering from his grip.

The other man, who was taken as much by surprise, fired but Stratton had ducked behind the bollard. He rolled a metre, came up on aim at the body mass and fired, hitting the man's knee, exploding it, sending pieces of bone and cartilage flying out the back of his trouser leg. He screamed as he went down, grabbing his shattered limb.

Stratton abandoned the fight and hurried on into a mass of vehicles.

★ ★ ★

Wheeland and his men closed on the bullion trucks. 'Let's move it!' he shouted.

The first men used fire extinguishers to put out the fires and others carried long spans of steel cable with shackles attached. They crawled beneath the vehicles and threaded the cables through the chassis, stretching out the ends to lie on the ground. More people hurried past, their single focus to get to the bridge and cross it.

'Where's the goddamned cranes?' Wheeland shouted into his radio as he looked skywards.

In the distance, to the north, was a flotilla of helicopters. As they closed in, four of the craft, the largest ones, became visible. They were massive flying cranes. They had large cockpits with narrow bodies and huge, powerful engines with rotor blades the length of a bus.

The little support helicopters were at the opposite end of the scale when it came to size and manoeuvrability. They were MH-6 Little Birds, acrobatic light choppers each carrying just a pilot and gunner. As the sky cranes lumbered over the intersection, the Little Birds dispersed to protect the scene from interference.

★   ★   ★

Stratton watched the air activity quickly develop. The operation was clearly well on its way. It was pretty obvious the part the sky cranes were to play. A smart way of avoiding the congested roads. The Little Birds were playing safety. Wheeland had everything covered.

Stratton then saw another group of aircraft flying over the water from the Upper Bay towards Manhattan Bridge. Half a dozen of them. Blackhawks. There was no way they belonged to Wheeland. He could rent a dozen Little Birds and sky cranes easily enough. Both were civilian and readily available on the commercial market if you had the money. Pilots were also two a penny. But a squadron of Blackhawks was something else. Not even Betregard could fool a squadron of military aircraft and their crews into taking part in a robbery.

A pair of Little Birds broke from the crane flotilla and headed towards the Blackhawks. Stratton wondered if his plan was actually working and that he'd succeeded in drawing the response forces to Wheeland's bullion heist. Either way, he had to do more to neutralise the assault. He looked for the machine gunners again and started towards them.

⋆   ⋆   ⋆

One of the Blackhawks that had broken away from the main flotilla came into a hover over the north end of Manhattan Bridge. A long rope dropped out of its side to the road and seconds later, soldiers began sliding down it.

⋆   ⋆   ⋆

Chandos and Hetta stopped the taxi at the end of Bayard Street, where they could overlook the intersection. Smoke was everywhere, people running past, an endless supply of humanity heading for Brooklyn.

There was a sudden and thunderous roar from somewhere above and behind them and the wind whipped up as if a hurricane had arrived out of nowhere, blowing trash and dust around them. Chandos looked back to see a dozen heavily armed men in fatigues one by one slide down a thick rope to the road and crouch in defensive postures.

'Time for us to go,' he said, opening the door.

Hetta climbed out, her attention focused ahead into the intersection.

The rope behind them ascended and the helicopter moved away, taking the windstorm with it. The platoon rushed a few metres past the taxi to a line of concrete barriers and formed a defensive position behind it.

'Stay where you are!' the platoon leader shouted to Chandos and Hetta as he hurried past. 'For your own safety remain in the vehicle.'

'They obviously don't know precisely where the device is,' Chandos said. He looked skywards at the buzzing Little Birds and Blackhawks. 'I expect the detection helicopter has pulled off to a safe distance.'

Another platoon roped down out of a Blackhawk on the other side of the intersection beyond the entrance to the bridge.

Bursts of gunfire were coming from everywhere. Bullets strafed the concrete barrier where the platoon was positioned in front of Chandos and Hetta, hitting one of the soldiers. The others wanted to return fire but couldn't identify targets and there were too many civilians running across their front.

Hetta walked to the front of the taxi to look into the intersection. The platoon leader noticed her standing in the open.

'Lady!' he shouted. 'Get down! Are you nuts?'

More bullets strafed the low wall, but she didn't move.

'Get down or I'll drag you down!' he yelled, running over to her.

She held an ID card out to him. It showed she was a member of the State Department's Intelligence Agency. He didn't know anything about that organisation, but he did understand she outranked him.

She pocketed the card and walked into the intersection.

'Lady!' the platoon commander shouted. 'Are you crazy?'

★ ★ ★

Wheeland's men were engaging all the platoons with enough fire to cause confusion and keep their heads down. Some people continued to run for the bridge but most lay on the ground.

Hetta ducked between cars as she made her way into the middle of the intersection, pausing to avoid several of Wheeland's men running past. One of them went right by the gap she was hiding in, so she reached out a foot and tripped him. He clattered to the ground, his weapon falling out of his hands.

He was athletic and sprang to his feet as he saw her move towards him. He gauged the distance to her and to his gun and chose to go for her. Not because she was closer. He was former Russian special forces, Spetsnaz. And she was smaller than him, and also a woman.

He lunged at her, not with all the force he could muster. Why would he? He reached out to grab her, but she slipped to one side, feathered her hand. With a flick of her arm, she whipped the leading edge of her knuckles at his throat,

337

striking just below the Adam's apple. His momentum added to the force of it and his body crumpled as the blow invoked his gag reflex. As she passed him her elbow slammed back into his neck vertebrae. The blow struck the nerve that controls the need to breathe and he went unconscious.

As the frightened civilians watched, Hetta took his gun, placed it in her empty holster, removed his magazine belt and picked up his M4. At that moment, the man's partner returned to see what had happened to him and saw Hetta holding the carbine. He brought his own up on aim, but she twisted her body behind the weapon and fired. A round struck his body armour, sending him back. Two more went through his head.

She turned, looking for other targets. There was nothing close. As she moved off, she saw what she'd been looking for and her expression softened.

★ ★ ★

Stratton walked between cars towards the Suburban, where Wheeland's machine-gun team were still creating havoc from its roof. Despite having to step over numerous frightened civilians huddled between abandoned vehicles, he didn't take his eyes off the pair as he approached from their flank.

The gunners were busy engaging the platoons that had occupied the perimeters of the intersection, specifically those on the bridge and behind the low concrete barrier that lined the south side of Upper Broadway. Stratton didn't think the platoons could afford to expose themselves without further support, and by the time that arrived, Wheeland would have completed his task. If the gun was neutralised, it might be of some help to the pinned-down units.

The number two of the gun team was preparing another length of link when he saw Stratton approaching, pistol in hand. The man grabbed up his M4, but Stratton had been ready for such a reaction and fired, already getting used to the heavy Magnum. The massive bullet struck the man in the torso and although the body armour plate prevented penetration, the force of the round threw him off the Suburban to land hard on the concrete sidewalk, knocking him senseless.

The gunner threw himself to one side in an effort to swivel the M60 and bring it to bear, but like his colleague, he was too slow and Stratton shot him in the chest. He rolled off the side of the vehicle and landed on his partner.

A round slammed into the building close to Stratton and he rolled forward to find limited cover behind the base of a narrow lamppost. Another round struck the post inches above his head and he rolled to one side, got to his feet and scrambled out of the kill zone. Yet another round ripped through his shirt, grazing his shoulder. Another creased his thigh. He threw himself behind a car but his attackers pressed their advantage and fired a hail of bullets at it.

He scrabbled behind a wheel hub as the rounds shredded the car, smashing windows, bursting tyres. Two people hiding behind a nearby car couldn't stand it any more and got up to run. The marksmen killed them almost instantly.

'Stay down!' Stratton shouted to others in case they had a similar idea.

He had to go on the offensive, and decisively so, or he was done for. He raised the Magnum over the hood, fired a round at the hint of a target and as he fired at a better one, all he got was a clunk. It was the worst sound in the world for a soldier in battle. The magazine was empty.

'Shit,' he exclaimed as he struggled to get a spare from his pocket. It was why he hated guns like this. The bullets were effective for sure, but there just weren't enough of them in a single magazine for a decent gun battle. His shoulder felt on fire where he'd been grazed.

He rolled to the other side of the car as he ejected the magazine and slammed another home. He cocked it as a figure hurried past the side of the vehicle. He dropped onto his back, the gun between his knees. The man began to appear — Stratton held his trigger finger in case it was a civvy — the figure wore black — a helmet. Stratton fired and the man was thrown back against the wall of a building.

Stratton had to forgive the Magnum temporarily, as it did have its qualities, but his senses suddenly warned him of footsteps along the other side of the car towards his back. The enemy had played the sure hand, dividing their attack, knowing one of them would nail him. He swung the gun over his head but he knew he would never get off the shot in time.

Wheeland's man came into view. The kill was an easy one for him. Unfortunately for him, someone else closing in was considerably more adept at combat than he was and had every intention of saving Stratton's life.

The round left the muzzle of her M4 and hit the man's cerebral cortex at the base of his skull, instantly cutting all the motor functions between his brain and muscles. He crumpled to the ground like a broken puppet and skidded to a halt, eyes open but no light in them.

Stratton had watched the man fall, his gun almost there, but not quite. Hetta stepped into view and sauntered over to him. He sat up and leaned back against the car, feeling the bloody wound on his thigh. She squatted near him and checked the rounds left in the magazine of her M4 before pushing it back home. 'How do you like the Magnum?' she asked.

'Takes a little getting used to,' he said, straightening his leg painfully. 'Less of a pull than I've experienced before, though. Nice balance.'

'It's a clever design.'

'Not enough bullets though.'

'You said that before.'

He offered the butt of it to her. She took it.

'That's a new magazine minus one,' he said, handing her the other full spare and the empty.

'You kept ahold of the empty mag.'

'It wasn't mine to throw away.'

When she looked into his eyes, Stratton thought he could see a smile. The battle raged around them, though most of it further away. 'I came to say goodbye,' she said. 'The device will be in the right hands now.'

He nodded, unable to think of anything else to say. She'd grown on him despite his misgivings.

'Wheeland's beneath that helicopter,' she said, indicating a sky crane coming into the hover a block away.

Stratton eased himself painfully onto a knee in preparation to go. She leaned the M4 on the car beside him.

'I enjoyed our time together, in the end,' he said.

She looked like she was thinking about something. 'My name's Lara,' she said finally.

'I'm relieved to hear that. You never quite looked like a Hetta to me.'

Every shred of coldness had gone from her eyes.

He leaned his head towards hers and she didn't move away, but kept her eyes on his mouth. He put his lips against hers. She closed her eyes as they kissed.

Stratton eased himself back, got to his feet and looked for the helicopter. The sky crane was rising up, a taut cable hanging from it, a bullion truck on the end. As it moved away, another came in to take its place.

He picked up the M4. 'Take care of yourself.'

He started walking towards the helicopter, doing his best to loosen up a slight limp.

'You too,' she said, though it was too soft for him to have heard. She watched him disappear around the corner of a building, then she turned around and walked down Chrystie Street and away from the intersection.

26

Wheeland and half a dozen of his men stood beneath the heavy downdraft of the massive sky crane. The noise of the engines combined with the chopping rotors was intense. A cable attached to the crane's spine directly beneath the rotor hub dangled to the ground. The men were connecting it to several heavy duty cable strops attached to the chassis of the armoured truck.

'Take it away!' Wheeland shouted into a radio.

The noise from the helicopter increased as the pilot altered the pitch on the rotors and the massive beast began to climb. The steel cables went taut and the truck creaked as the strain was taken. The rear of the vehicle began to rise off the ground as the helicopter gradually increased height.

A Blackhawk headed into the intersection from the bridge. It turned over the battlefield and straightened up towards the sky crane. A couple of Little Birds waiting nearby swooped on it. The gunners sitting half outside the open cabs fired streams of shots at the Blackhawk, which immediately turned away, its crew clearly still unsure as to what exactly was going on and why the Little Birds were firing on them.

As the sky crane moved away, the noise around Wheeland reduced. They had one more bullion truck, its cables already prepared. The last sky crane lumbered in to pick it up. Its cable bumped into the side of the bullion truck and the men rushed to it with the ends of the strops.

'Move to your evacuation RVs!' Wheeland shouted to the men as they connected the final strops. 'Let's go,' he shouted. 'We're done here.'

The message was translated for the Russians among them and the men headed away. Wheeland looked up at the sky crane as the wind whipped around him once again.

* * *

Stratton watched the flying crane move in, the cable stretching from its slender middle down to the ground. He looked elsewhere in the sky, at the sporadic air battles. A Blackhawk was spewing smoke as it flew over the intersection. A Little Bird disintegrated as a missile struck it and exploded it into pieces. The other Little Birds, like persistent wasps, were harassing the other Blackhawks, desperate to maintain air superiority to protect the cranes. Stratton could only believe they were being paid a fortune.

As he closed on the sky crane, several of the team headed his way, so he ducked behind a coach. They didn't see him as they ran past and Stratton wondered if Wheeland was one of them. He decided to keep going and check the bullion truck first.

People were still coming into the intersection from adjoining streets. Stratton continued on against the flow of human traffic. He saw a lone figure in black beside the remaining bullion truck, a radio to his mouth as he looked up at the sky crane.

Wheeland.

As the spook signalled the helicopter to start lifting the load, it was as if he sensed he was being watched by one set of eyes in particular. He looked in Stratton's direction.

Stratton aimed his M4 as he walked towards him.

The American didn't move. 'I don't suppose you're up for any kind of a deal?' he shouted above the swirling wind and noise from above.

Stratton wondered what to do with the man. The wisest course would be to shoot him there and then. The spook still had too much support in the area. If any of his men returned, the situation could quickly reverse. He doubted Wheeland would have any second thoughts about killing him. The man had everything to lose.

But Stratton wasn't into cold-blooded killing. Neither did he hate Wheeland enough to end his life there and then, despite what the spook would do to him if their situations had been reversed.

Something in Stratton's eyes made it clear he wasn't into any kind of deal. 'I'm only a tool in this whole thing,' Wheeland said.

'They forced you, did they?'

'Betregard's the one you want. He's the boss. This was all his idea. Him and Gatovik.'

'Why is it people like you are so pathetic once you've lost your power?'

'I never really had any,' Wheeland said, trying to wriggle some sympathy out of the operative.

345

'What are you going do with me? People like us can't do time.'

'I would've said it was the best place for people like us when we even think about crossing the line. That or dead. If you'd rather I killed you, let me know. Otherwise jail is where you're headed. I understand the CIA can't bear the thought of traitors seeing the light of day ever again.'

Wheeland grimaced, like he'd never given a great deal of thought to being captured. The idea appeared to fill him with dread. More so than death. He took his hand out of his pocket, gripping a grenade. He pulled the pin. All he had to do was release his grip and the lever would spring, initiating the fuse.

Stratton felt confident that if Wheeland dropped it, he could get clear in the four seconds before it detonated. His only consideration was whether to shoot him first. He was beginning to lean heavily in that direction.

Wheeland let go of the grenade and it bounced on the tarmac between the two men. He remained still.

Stratton hadn't expected that. If Wheeland had run, he might have shot him before taking off himself. Wheeland didn't seem the suicidal type, but because he hadn't moved, Stratton couldn't shoot.

With two seconds to go, Stratton ran. Wheeland went with him. They reached the corner of the bullion truck as the grenade exploded. The force caught their backs and Wheeland grabbed Stratton as they were lifted up and Stratton's M4 clattered away. The armoured truck shielded them from the worst, so both suffered fragment wounds but nothing serious.

Wheeland ripped a combat knife from a sheath and it became the focus of the fight. As they rolled around, jostling for position, the back of the bullion truck began to rise off the ground. The sky crane pilot increased power as the aircraft took the strain. The nose of the truck scraped the ground before rising up above it. Stratton and Wheeland rolled under it as they fought desperately for control of the knife, exchanging blows.

★ ★ ★

As the pilot continued his ascent something came into view directly ahead, something Stratton instantly knew would change the dynamics of the entire battle.

A pair of Apache gunships came flying low over the rooftops towards the intersection. One of them loosed a missile that slapped into a Little Bird. The explosion, above the middle of the intersection, seemed to announce the beginning of the end as the flaming remains of the small helicopter dropped, its mangled engine slamming through the roof of a car. The cavalry had arrived. The Little Birds were no match for Apache gunships and neither were Wheeland's men.

The ground fire intensified as Wheeland's men fired all that they had as they disengaged, running back in the direction of the city, into the endless wave of people still coming out of the streets, secure in the knowledge that the soldiers wouldn't open fire on them for fear of hitting the innocent. It had been the original plan anyway, to make their way to prearranged hiding places in Manhattan and lie low for days. Only a couple of the men were picked off as they escaped.

As Stratton struggled with Wheeland, he saw the M4 lying a few metres away. It was time to change tack. He kneed the spook in the crotch, released his grip on the knife with one hand and used it to push his fingers into Wheeland's throat. The American released a hand to remove the interference to his breathing and as he did so, Stratton pushed away completely and rolled across the ground to the M4.

Directly above, one of the gunships came into the hover in front of the sky crane. The pilot did the only thing he thought prudent to indicate he was surrendering: he reached for the emergency cable eject button and pushed it. There was a bang outside as the cable was severed by a small charge. The helicopter shuddered violently as it released the 25,000kg weight from its crane.

Stratton, still on his back, brought the gun up on aim towards Wheeland. The spook, also outstretched on the ground, the knife in his hand, realised he had been outmanoeuvred. He could do nothing but wait for the shot. And Stratton felt happy at that point to oblige. The CIA man had used up all of his chances. It was time to call the game to an end.

But as Stratton squeezed the trigger several tonnes of metal dropped in front of him, burying the end of the assault rifle into the road. He could only lie there in shock as bits of the armoured truck fell about him. When it all went still he looked at the huge piece of smoking wreckage, the butt of the M4 sticking up at an angle above him.

He got to his feet and walked around the side of the truck in search of Wheeland, expecting to find his flattened remains. The man had been barely a couple of metres away. But there was no sign of him. No squished body or blood oozing from under the wreckage. There was no evidence Wheeland had even been touched.

Stratton looked up the street in every direction. The spook had gone. He looked skyward and, other than the sky crane still hovering, the airspace was all military. The shooting around the intersection had also come to an end. It would seem the robbery had been thwarted.

'Stratton!' he heard a voice call out. He looked around to see Chandos making his way to him between cars. Civilians were still heading past them, those who had just arrived from side streets totally unaware of what had been going on.

'Stratton, my boy,' Chandos said as he got closer, a smile on his face. 'Are you OK?'

'I'm fine. Where's the bomb?'

'Over there.' Chandos pointed at the taxi. 'Where's Wheeland?'

'Gone.'

'Bugger. Well, we won and that's the most important thing.'

'Not quite. Not while Betregard and Wheeland are still out there.'

'There's nothing we can do about that now, is there?' Chandos said decisively. 'You have to know when to let go and allow others to take over. They're gone, and that's that. And I suggest we do the same.'

Stratton couldn't let it go. There had to be a way of getting to Wheeland. The trail had hardly gone cold. His eyes fell on a briefcase lying in the road outside the open door of an abandoned car. Beside it was an iPad. He walked over to it, picked it up and turned it on. It booted to life. He opened the browser.

'What was the tracking program you used to find your stone?' he asked Chandos.

'Monarch. Why?'

Stratton handed him the iPad. 'Wheeland has it.'

Chandos logged into the program. Within a minute a satellite image of the city of New York came to life on the screen. On it they saw a lone marker in Little Italy.

'I have him,' Chandos said, and Stratton was already marching away towards the taxi. 'It's only a matter of time before they find us,' Chandos said as he followed, looking skyward.

'Then we'd better hurry.'

* * *

Wheeland drove an abandoned car into West 28th Street in Midtown, weaving between several trucks that had been left in the middle of the street. There was no one around. The place was empty. An abandoned city in the middle of the afternoon.

He turned into the entrance of a car park

350

nestled between a pair of towering buildings and smashed through a flimsy wooden barrier to enter the lot. Empty parking bays ran along one side of a low, windowless, concrete building. He pulled the car into one of them and killed the engine. He climbed out and looked around. A gentle wind blew trash along the ground. The only sound was a distant police siren.

Wheeland walked to the only door into the building, a metal one without handles, locks or any clues that it actually opened at all. There was a clunk and the door moved. He looked up to see a CCTV camera aimed down on him. He pulled open the door and stepped inside. He was faced with a long, narrow corridor with a door at the far end. He had never been inside the building before and was unsure of himself.

He walked to the door, which was similar to the first one: metal, no handles, locks or hinges. Another clunk and it moved slightly inwards. Wheeland pushed it open. There was yet another door immediately to his front but it was already open. He pushed through it and stepped into a large room lined with maps, charts and half a dozen flatscreen monitors showing parts of the city and harbour, most of them aerial shots and city-link CCTV.

He saw two men seated in comfortable chairs, turned so they could look at him as he walked in. They didn't appear to be pleased at all.

'How did you find out about this place?' Henry Betregard asked. He wore a dark suit and in the dim light it was hard to see his eyes, which were like well-holes in his face. Mikhail Gatovik leaned back in his chair, his portly stomach fighting against the buttons of his shirt.

Wheeland became nervous now that he was in front of them. He was in uncharted territory. He had the realisation that essentially he was a civilian now. A privateer. A criminal, and an unsuccessful one at that. And he had no future other than with Betregard. With Stratton still out there, he would go to jail if caught.

But now that he was there, Wheeland didn't feel much safer in front of Betregard and his Russian buddy. Gatovik was looking at him in a dangerous way. He knew his choices were limited, and he was prepared to take his chances.

'I dropped you off here once, six months ago,' Wheeland said by way of explanation. 'I was curious about the place and found out you were building an ops room.'

'You snooped,' Betregard said.

'You sound like you don't trust me any more.'

'Why should I? You just destroyed my operation.'

The screens showed the mopping up of the intersection by police and military. A sky crane was being escorted somewhere by an Apache gunship.

'I did everything we planned,' Wheeland said.

'Then why did it fail?'

'Stratton.'

'What the hell is a Stratton?'

'A Brit. SBS. SIS. He brought the bomb out of Afghanistan with the integer.'

'You were supposed to kill him,' Gatovik said.

'Then you did screw up,' Betregard said. 'You

352

expect me to believe one man wrecked this operation?'

'She helped him,' Wheeland said. 'The integer was the one who betrayed us.'

'Integers don't betray,' Betregard said. 'They have no opinion. They just do.'

'He got to her.'

Betregard and Gatovik watched him coldly.

★   ★   ★

Stratton and Chandos turned the taxi into a corner of a broad street void of life. Abandoned vehicles were everywhere.

'He's two blocks on the right,' Chandos said.

Stratton looked skywards to see several helicopters cut across the street half a mile ahead. 'Here they come.'

Chandos wound down his window. 'Hear that?'

A distant sound of sirens appeared to be getting closer.

★   ★   ★

A gentle alarm beeped on the ops console and Betregard and Gatovik turned to look at one of the screens. The view was of the parking lot outside. A yellow taxi cab was driving in through the broken barrier.

Wheeland watched as the taxi came to a stop and the doors opened. He saw Stratton climb out, followed by Chandos.

'That's him,' Wheeland said. 'That's Stratton.'

Stratton tossed the iPad onto the seat. 'They're in this building,' he said. He noted a couple of CCTV cameras. 'Come on.'

He went to the back of the taxi, opened the trunk and took hold of the atomic bomb. Chandos grabbed the other side and together they struggled to heave it out. It thumped heavily onto the ground and the pair of them rolled it around the vehicle and placed it on its end in the open.

'Now what?' Chandos asked.

'I think this is it.'

'Do we stay here?'

'Might as well.'

★ ★ ★

Betregard sat forward in his seat with a look of disbelief. 'Is that what I think it is?'

'It's the bomb,' the Russian said, shocked.

'You led them here.'

Wheeland could only watch, just as stunned as they were.

'You're a damned fool, Wheeland,' Betregard said as he raised a pistol and shot Wheeland. The bullet struck the spook in the forehead and he fell back to the floor with a heavy crash.

Betregard got up out of his chair and went to a cabinet, which he unlocked. 'My instincts tell me that if we get rid of those two, we'll have a lot less explaining to do,' he said, handing Gatovik an assault rifle and taking another. Together they marched out of the room.

As they headed down the corridor towards the door at the end, Betregard said, 'I'm going to give you a quick lesson in Wild West diplomacy, Gatovik.' He cocked his weapon and brought it up into his shoulder. 'We're going to settle this the old-fashioned way. Open the door and come out shooting.'

Gatovik loaded and cocked his weapon. 'I always liked the Wild West way of doing things,' he said.

Betregard kicked open the door and brought the barrel of the weapon up as he marched outside. Gatovik moved out behind him and to his side.

The first thing Betregard noticed was Stratton and Chandos standing with their arms high in the air. Half a second later he realised why.

Several hundred police and soldiers surrounded the entire place. A couple of squad cars screeched to a halt in the street. An Apache gunship thundered low overhead.

Gatovik turned around to see soldiers roping down onto the roof of the building from a helicopter, a line of them already in position and aiming their guns at him.

'Put your weapons down and hold your hands in the air,' a voice boomed over a loudspeaker. 'You have three seconds to comply or you'll be killed.'

Betregard lowered his weapon to the ground. When he straightened up, he stuck his hands in the air and looked at Stratton coldly.

The operative stared back and gave him a wink.

Epilogue

Chandos and Stratton walked through the departure hall of JFK International airport towards their gate. Stratton had a slight limp. One of his arms was bandaged and in a sling. They were cleaned up and wearing new casual clothes, care of the Central Intelligence Agency. And two suited men from said organisation were escorting them along the hallway.

They reached their gate, a BA flight to London Heathrow.

'We'll leave you to it,' one of the agents said with a friendly smile.

'Thanks very much for your hospitality,' Chandos said.

'Thank *you*,' the agent said. 'You have a good flight.'

They all shook hands and the suits departed. Chandos sighed heavily and sat down. He wore a look of immense satisfaction.

Stratton sat beside him, looking troubled by something.

'So, we return conquering heroes after all,' Chandos said. 'When we get onto the plane I strongly suggest we have champagne right away. One must always grab any opportunity to celebrate.'

Stratton forced a smile but his thoughts were elsewhere.

'What is it?' Chandos asked. 'If you're still

bothered about the interrogation from our chaps when we get home, don't worry about it. I'll take full responsibility.'

That wasn't what Stratton was thinking about.

'By the way. Lydia asked me to tell you thank you very much for everything.'

'Lydia?'

'Bullfrog. She's unable to take any credit for her side of things, of course. After a pat on the back, her people would more than likely fire her for the way she got the information out of the meeting room in the first place. There's also no way of knowing how many senior Russians were involved. So mum's still the word as far as she's concerned.'

Stratton saw someone across the hall who suddenly consumed his entire focus. She was wearing a colourful, summery skirt and looking fresh and quite beautiful. Her expression was blank, to the uninitiated that is. But Stratton was one of the few people in the world who had learned to see the smile in her eyes.

He smiled back.

Lara walked towards him. He pushed himself out of his seat.

'What are your plans?' Chandos asked him, unaware of Lara. 'Are you going to take that vacation you're owed?'

'Possibly.'

Chandos realised Stratton was distracted and followed his gaze.

The operative walked over to meet her and they stopped in front of each other. She didn't take her eyes off his.

'Hi,' he said. 'I was hoping I'd see you.'

'I find myself with time on my hands,' she said.

'You have a break from work?'

'More like work has broken from me. I've been released.'

'You did the right thing.'

'I don't have any regrets. But I expect the organisation will be disbanded. We were compromised.'

'What will your father say?'

She smiled at the thought of him. 'He would've done the same thing.' She looked into Stratton's eyes. 'I'm going to be in Geneva tomorrow evening.'

'I'm envious.'

'A Swiss International Air Lines flight leaves for Geneva three hours after you land in Heathrow. There's a first-class reservation waiting for you at the check-in desk.'

Stratton did his best to control his surprise. 'Right.'

'I'll see you at Geneva arrivals.'

He was suddenly unsure about something. 'Is this business or pleasure?'

'I'm going to take you to a log cabin in the mountains where there's a fire, a cauldron of hot water and a small bed on the floor,' she said. 'I want to start some things over again.'

She leaned close to him and her lips met his. They kissed gently, the sparkle mutual.

She stepped back, her eyes lingering on his for a moment. Then she walked away.

Stratton watched her go until she was out of

sight and went back to sit beside Chandos. He was a changed man. Relaxed and now as content with life as Chandos.

'You have a date with an integer,' Chandos said, unsure if he could believe it.

Stratton shrugged, acting indifferent. But the smile on his lips would have been impossible to erase at that point.

Chandos smiled along with him. 'I think that just about sums you up, Stratton . . . Yes, that just about sums you up.'